The Crystal Dragon

The Crystal Dragon

a young adult fantasy

S A McDonald

Dedication

To my family for their never-ending support

In memory of my mother

Roll over and wipe the night's dreams away. In the space in between sleep and awake, turn over and see the face crystalize. Be brave and hold the full view within your mind. Two golden eyes, bright and burning, stare unblinkingly. Look, look back and ignore the strain. The eyes trap you in place and time. Radiant orange fur ripples around a massive head. Hot air huffs through a fierce snout. See the shiny, black stripes? Feel the silent invitation? Do you? Shift and stretch when you can hold its gaze no longer. The morning light creeps in to pull you into the room. You flutter your eyes open and try to focus in the bright light. What was that creature? What did it want? And without thinking too much, you turn and heave a long sigh. Challenge accepted.

Chapter One

Theodora Yates needed to make the biggest decision of her young life. The man in front of her was bristling with impatience. His face, long with age, dipped closer to hers. The rind of his skull showed beneath his papery skin.

"So? What's it going to be? I haven't got all day to wait for you. I have a train to catch and important people to meet."

Theo shifted her weight from foot to foot. She looked longingly at the two tickets the old man held in front of her. Tickets to the event of the year. Tickets that had sold out months ago when it was announced the Equinox Festival would be held outside of Greenstone for the first time in decades. Tickets for an event people rarely got to see in person. And it was showing in *her* home town.

Theo wanted to go so badly she could think of little else. She had begged her Aunt Georgia every day for a month, and so many times, she was close to getting a 'yes'. Aunt Georgia loved her niece and would have happily taken her, but then Uncle Ken would hear about it and fly into a rage. He hated the festival with a passion that no one understood. Despite Theo's disappointment, Aunt Georgia thought it was better to keep the peace by dropping the matter.

But now Theo was being offered the opportunity of a life time. Theo stared at the tickets. The edging around them was golden. She could see the tickets not only offered a way into the event but also gave her the best seats in the house. These were VIP tickets. The man had some authority because he wore the uniform of the high rank within Central Government. Theo didn't dare ask why he couldn't go.

"Come on, girlie. I haven't got all day."

Theo thought of her aunt and how she could convince her. She deliberately didn't consider Uncle Ken and his bad temper. She would worry about that later.

"Okay, if you don't want them..."

The old man turned to go but Theo stretched out her hand and touched his sleeve. "Yes, please." Her voice was soft but determined.

The man's lips pulled back from his teeth but it wasn't any kind of smile Theo had seen before.

"Here then!" He practically threw them at her.

The man didn't wait for her reaction and hustled off in an instant. When Theo looked up from the bounty in her hands, she saw the tail of his coat flicker around the corner of a building before disappearing completely.

Theo couldn't help but smile. What she had wanted so badly she now had. She was delighted and excited, but there was another feeling too. On the edge of it all, she felt nervous, fearful. It was faint but it was definitely there. She decided to ignore it and rushed home to beg her aunt's permission.

Theo's attention was drawn back into the room by the sound of plates clattering loudly onto shelves. She had been too excited to sleep the night before and had let her eyes close briefly. This wasn't her first night of troubled sleep.

An apple-shaped woman slammed the cupboard and bellowed, "Theo! We need to be out of the house now if we are going to be in time for the Festival. Come on, you don't want to be late!"

No sooner had she finished calling when Theo stumbled to her feet and threw her jacket carelessly over her skinny shoulders. "I'm ready, Aunt Georgia," she said.

Theo went to a bench near the door and pushed her feet into her boots. Looking over her shoulder, she caught sight of the sunset through the transparent pane on the outside door. The deep oranges and pinks smeared the evening sky. Striking as it was, she looked past it to see any sign of her uncle's car, due home at any moment.

Theo jumped to her feet and stood beside the older woman. Theo was a good deal taller and more angular. She had a massive crop of dark hair that overwhelmed her face, as her features were small. Only her grey eyes stood out because they were so much bigger than everything else.

"Good, Theo," said Aunt Georgia, brushing grey hairs off her forehead. "Let's get out before we get jammed up here."

The two of them stepped outdoors into the early fall evening. The snow would not be coming for weeks, and the ground was covered with a thick layer of red and golden leaves. The house itself was a two-story, wooden cottage built long before the Great Shift. Except for a few modifications, it retained its

2

original structure and look. Perhaps the builders had some prescience of the future to come or were just lucky. They had made the right house for the changing environment. It had access to deep wells for water, a biodegradable waste disposal system for refuse and a heat extraction furnace for warmth. Solar panels and wind turbines provided electricity. Only one vehicle on the property needed gasoline to fuel an engine that was constructed with an indulgent fascination with speed. And this car and driver were due back from town at any moment.

Theo and her aunt scurried across the yard to the small, bubble vehicle plugged into an electrical post. Theo disconnected the thick cable from the plug within the grill while Aunt Georgia climbed into the driver's seat and engaged the engine. Theo jumped into the car and barely had time to close her door before Aunt Georgia shifted into gear.

The car slowed as it approached the end of the lane. Both Aunt Georgia and Theo scoured the main road, craning their necks to see any sign of the Uncle Ken's car. Aunt Georgia pulled out just as an engine roared around a bend and raced toward them. Their backs stiffened but Aunt Georgia kept her course and waved with feigned cheerfulness to the thunder-faced driver as they passed.

Theo stared at the muscle car and felt her stomach sink. "He is going to blame me for making you go to this thing."

"Ah, let him," said Aunt Georgia. "He can't have his way all the time." She tried her best to sound light-hearted but couldn't quite manage it. Theo looked out the back window and watched her uncle's car disappear down the lane.

Finding parking was difficult but it was to be expected as people had come from all over to see the ceremony. It wasn't common for the Equinox Festival to be held outside of Greenstone, where the main Oracle temple was located. The unusual location added a layer of mystery to the grandeur of the night. The Autumnal Prediction was the key forecast for the next year's harvest. The current year had been poor and many people needed to hear good news. No doubt, this was the biggest event this small town had ever seen.

It remained unclear why the town of Kitchie had been selected for the honour in the first place. It was announced some months ago, much to the chagrin of larger cities who resented the slight. Even after hearing the vigorous complaints, the Oracles still insisted upon the modest town. Eventually, all grumbles faded. It didn't matter that the Great Shift happened decades ago, resisting the recommendation of the Temple just wasn't done.

Theo and Aunt Georgia finally found parking in a soccer field that had been repurposed to hold the overflow of cars. Theo looked at the lush grass that surrounded them. She remembered being told as a child about a time long before the Great Shift when grass never grew in these parts. For centuries, there had only been rocks and acres of evergreen trees. However, the climate change following the Great Shift made this area more suitable for farming after the South dried up from the heat. For years the area had echoed with the sound of explosions as the great boulders were blasted away to make way for the fields. Theo couldn't even begin to imagine what it looked like before. She only knew the green.

Theo looked toward the town. The dusky sky glowed above the newly constructed showgrounds. Theo felt fluttering in her stomach, but she believed she was just excited for what was about to come.

"Well, we better get a move on if we hope to be on time. Looks like everybody and their brother is here tonight." Aunt Georgia locked the car and began walking toward the lights.

Theo pressed in close to her aunt as she craned her neck to catch sight of it all. Stalls of merchandise and games lined the side streets to tempt every passer-by. Small stages with loud bands and performers squeezed into any alcove they could find. Theo, fascinated by the new and curious, would have stood glued to the spot if her aunt hadn't kept pulling her along.

Theo and Aunt Georgia followed the flow of people toward the main event. The closer they got to the show grounds, the denser the crowds became. Theo loved seeing the flocks of young women in their traditional white dresses and garlanded hair. She couldn't believe how pretty and glamorous they all looked. As well, there were young men in their crisp Greenline Corp uniforms who looked equally handsome and dashing. Unable to contain their exuberance, the soldiers shouted and banged into each other. Theo blushed when any one of them chanced to look her way, but she was pulled forward by her aunt before she had to deal with the attention. But the festival wasn't just for the young. Groups of multi-generational families pushed into the crowds as well. Theo and Aunt Georgia watched out for them and patiently stepped aside to make room for strollers and wheelchairs. Everyone who could get a ticket was here tonight.

"I've never seen so many people!" Theo said. But Aunt Georgia didn't hear her as her voice was lost among the din.

Soon the two of them were being ushered to their seats in the third row. People glanced their way but no one challenged their presence. Theo turned around to look at the crowd and marvelled at the sea of people that stretched as far as she could see.

The Crystal Dragon

It had rained off and on for most of the week but within the last few hours the sky had cleared completely, leaving a few maroon streaks on the horizon. The orange tip of the harvest moon was just starting to creep upward and would be high in the sky at the right time during the ceremony. People in town had worried all week about the rain; however, the word from the Temple was that all would be clear. Why people still doubted the Oracles' ability to predict weather was cause for amusement. In nearly a hundred years they had never been wrong.

The crowd hummed with excitement. Some had started a chant for the ceremony to begin; others were singing popular songs. The audience was alive with nervous energy and expectation - many had never before witnessed an Equinox Celebration, certainly not Theo at her young age.

Suddenly Theo's stomach was churning. Her charming, flitting butterflies had morphed into something bigger. The sensation was now more fear than excitement. She didn't know why she should feel this way but she knew she didn't like it. She looked to her left and a lady with shocking pink hair returned her glance without humour. When she looked behind her, a man with a checked suit boldly stared back. Their acknowledgment only amplified her nervousness, not that she understood at all why she was feeling this way. Her anxiety was growing at such an alarming rate that she began to look for a way to the nearest exit. She was already feeling the pressure of being visible to the prominent people around her and could not bear the idea of being seen by the high ranking Oracles on stage should she have to leave.

Theo leaned forward to stand up but it was too late. The orchestra began to blast out a tumultuous fanfare, the cue that the ceremony was about to start.

The crowd went wild, clapping and shouting. Theo grimaced and sank back into her seat, heavy with the sense that something great and awful was about to take place.

Chapter Two

People cheered through the entire overture. It continued until a man appeared in front of the curtain and walked to the centre of the stage. He stopped behind a microphone stand and looked out into the crowd. Only then did everyone settle down to listen to him.

"Derrick Mullens!!" exclaimed a woman to Theo's left. Theo wanted to ask Aunt Georgia to explain who he was but was too busy quelling her nerves to speak.

Derrick Mullens was a tall man with a slim build. He was handsome, perhaps even pretty, with ice-blue eyes and a full mouth. His dark hair was combed sleekly over his head, giving him the look of a smug cat.

Derrick drew a devilish smile and said, "Hello, my name is Derrick Mullens."

The crowd cheered. People shouted back at him, "We know who you are!" "We love you Derrick!"

He laughed and gestured for the crowd to settle down again. "As I was saying, I am Derrick Mullens and I am thrilled to introduce tonight's festival." He unhooked the microphone from the stand and started to walk around.

"This is a great honour for me. It's the first time I've been asked to do this. Goodness knows, I've made myself available so many times before..." He let the sentence hang long enough for the crowd to react. The audience rumbled with amusement.

"I'll make myself available to you!" someone shouted.

He smiled at the comment but it quickly faded. His voice deepened.

"We celebrate the Autumnal Equinox every year. We revere the cycle of the Earth around the sun because we have become only too aware of how fragile the whole system is. We are standing here today because we have survived a great catastrophe some hundred years ago. We all have experienced first-hand the effect of the system falling apart, bringing us to near extinction, bringing us to the edge of losing our world."

He paused. The crowd mumbled as they remembered. For a second his eyes came to rest on Theo's face, and when they did, Theo's stomach fell hard. Fortunately, he didn't linger on her and quickly moved over to the next the person. The nervous pangs increased when she understood how visible she was to the person on stage.

"The survival of mankind has come about from so many things. But what was most important? What was essential to the guidance of people at a time when our technology failed us and we were left blind in the face of a storm? We were as blind and helpless as kittens in the night and at the mercy of the elements that had no sympathy for our plight, no feeling for our suffering." The crowd murmured with recognition of the past hardship.

"Blind and helpless," he went on. "until the visions and sight of the Oracles allowed us to see, helped us find our way. They guided us when our technology failed us and led us like beacons through the murky mist. When all else failed, they came to our salvation. And they continue to save us, to navigate us through the pitfalls of an indifferent universe!"

The crowd went wild.

Before the audience could settle down, Derrick shouted over the clamour, "Ladies and gentlemen, boys and girls, it is with the greatest honour that I introduce to you the Autumnal Equinox Festival!" On cue a spotlight landed on the curtain behind him and it began to part.

The orchestra played a majestic overture. Colourful spotlights and explosions dazzled the stage. Dancers, some in white goddess dresses, some in feathered costumes, swirled and leaped across the stage in a mad rush. They swished into impressive lifts and dizzying turns, then stopped and posed with chests heaving, in anticipation of the Parade of Oracles.

With another explosion of light and surge of music, a large globe began lowering from the rafters. The audience immediately understood what was in the ball and started to scream with excitement. Theo, who had never seen a spectacle like this before, was so enrapt she forgot her discomfort. Once the sphere landed on the stage and was secured to the floor, a door slowly dropped forward to reveal what was inside. A pride of Oracles, standing gloriously in their colourful ceremonial robes, was there for all to see.

One by one, the Oracles exited from the ball and walked grandly onto the stage where they could be better admired by the crowd.

The Oracles, all women in this case, were unlike any people Theo had ever seen before. To call them beautiful was not enough. They carried an aura so powerful that all she could do was stare.

7

Aunt Georgia said she didn't recognize any of them. She guessed most were juniors within the Order. But it didn't matter as they all possessed an unearthly quality that made them seem less like a human and more like beings from another plane of existence. Most of the senior Oracles had remained on the Hill in Greenstone; however, the Head Oracle, the Great Oracle, Ceres Theroux, was to be in the ceremony tonight. Without a doubt, everyone was here to see her. She was the eldest of the Oracles and the most famous. More importantly, she was the last of the original vanguard to survive from the early days following the Great Shift and was rumoured to be almost one hundred years old. She rarely left the Temple and only addressed issues of great significance. And she had expressly insisted on attending tonight's ceremony in Kitchie. Like the location selection, her presence outside of the Greenstone was odd and cause for curiosity, and it added greater excitement to the already impressive event.

Once the Oracles were in place on stage, the music halted abruptly. The crowd hushed and waited. Finally, a blast of trumpets broke the silence. Ceres Theroux was about to come on stage. She did not come down from the ceiling as had the other Oracles. Instead, she was raised from below on a small hydraulic platform amid apoplectic applause and heroic music. She smiled graciously, allowing the moment to unfold theatrically. Although visibly older than the other women, she was still vibrant with a slim figure under her diaphanous robe. Her white hair was stylish and her red lips and eye makeup were dramatic. Although trying to appear pleasant for the adoring public, her dark eyes remained strange and faraway.

Aunt Georgia leaned in to whisper to Theo, "I last saw her when I was a young woman and, bless me, she hasn't changed much at all!" Theo understood but could only nod as she had lost her ability to speak.

Ceres Theroux smiled then looked to her left to cue the Maestro. Suddenly the scene shifted. The Oracles glided away from centre stage to chairs that were set up for them at the sides. Ceres Theroux took her place in a large wooden high-back chair adorned with carved vines. Once she was seated, the music stopped and the stage went black.

"They are going to tell the story of the Great Shift," whispered Aunt Georgia. "Just watch."

Quietly the orchestra introduced the next theme as everyone sat in the dark. Slowly the lights came up to reveal the stage full of dancers in old-fashioned clothes, bustling about with the old technology in their hands. The music increased in volume. Dissonant chords were emphasized to illustrate the hurried nature of the world at that time.

Then, without warning, the music crested and crashed. All the dancers careened and threw themselves about the stage. Some went up in a puff of smoke. Some grabbed the sides of their heads in agony.

The music continued to blast harsh tones. The surviving dancers thrashed and grasped each other, lost and dismayed, throwing their machines away. Screens secured to the stage flashed with projected images of fires, floods, mudslides and earthquakes. Elaborate bird puppets swooped across the top of the stage and fell to earth, struck down by invisible winds. Dark clouds were shown overhead and the dancers fell to their knees feigning signs of hunger and thirst. Some fell in mock death and were dragged off stage by the living.

The music turned grim and hopeless. Only a few dancers remained huddled together in the middle of the stage. The lights lowered and the orchestra went quiet. The audience waited.

A single spotlight pierced the darkness and illuminated the figure of a lone girl. Slowly she looked upward with a gesture of understanding. She wore the same colour robe as Ceres Theroux.

Without any accompanying music, she ran around the stage looking for something. Gradually others appeared. They started to join her, rushing about.

The music returned with a theme that introduced hope. The group circled about and halted at centre stage to find the remaining dancers, now lit from above, still clinging together.

The group swung their arms in wide circles to beckon the dancers to follow them. The children pointed to things and the dancers pretended to eat or drink them.

As they continued to move about the stage, transparent sets of trees and fields were dropped from above. The dancers started to sway with slow, deliberate movements: swinging their arms as if chopping wood, or pulling heavy loads, as if ploughing fields. Soon all the dancers returned to centre stage and the music became determined and purposeful.

At this point a principal dancer, dressed in black, arrived on stage. He beckoned all the dancers to him. As they followed him about, the crowd started to react with shock.

Aware of something going on, Theo turned to Aunt Georgia for an explanation. Aunt Georgia pursed her lips and whispered, "They've included Orfeo Cotswold in the story. That won't be a popular decision." Aunt Georgia looked at Theo's confused face and shook her head as she continued, "Never mind. Just keep watching."

All danced with Orfeo for a while. The sets were transformed into houses, then into towns and finally into cities. More and more dancers began to arrive. All the performers circled Orfeo and followed him off stage. He returned with dancers wearing red Oracle robes. Orfeo, now garbed in a golden one, stood majestically centre stage. And around him, the stage became a temple.

All the performers turned to the audience, and their movements were unified as they swept and twirled with buoyant steps. As the music built to a crescendo, the troupe stopped dancing and formed a chorus line. The line opened to direct the audience's attention to a full, neon moon that was lowering from the ceiling. An altar was raised from the stage floor to meet it.

The music shifted again and the notes of a familiar song were played. The performers stood at attention and began singing the "Song of Sight", and the audience joined in.

> From the World that strains
> To the World that bends
> We stand here undeterred
> Because of Clarity
> We have view of the future
> We have released the past
> We are undeterred in change
> Freed sight forever.

Once finished, the crowd erupted in frenzied, patriotic applause. As people hooted, the performers and Oracles slowly exited, leaving the stage bare except for the glowing moon and altar.

In the pause between scenes, Theo shifted in her seat. Coughs echoed throughout the outdoor amphitheatre. The lights muted to a soft red to help change the mood for the next segment. Soon shuffling shoes and creaking floorboards drew her attention back to the stage. Men in black hoods carried long torches with flickering flames. They placed the torches in tall, silver holders on either side of the altar then quickly left the stage. Whatever was troubling Theo was almost here - she felt this instinctively. All she could do, however, was hold tight and wait.

Finally, it began.

A bell chimed from behind the curtain. The sound started softly at first then grew slowly. It grew much louder as an Oracle dressed in purple vestments came into view holding a single silver bell. Behind her came another Oracle, also wearing purple, swinging a decanter holding smoking incense. Behind her was another with a snake, and behind her, one with a raven. Following in procession were the remaining Oracles, dressed in various colours, all pacing with pomp and solemnity.

They began to sing a low and eerie chant. Its monophonic tones were both beautiful and stirring. They circled along the lip of the stage so Theo was able to see them clearly. Most of them had their eyes closed entirely, which surprised her, as they were near enough to the edge to fall to the ground below. The Oracles continued to march around until they stopped in a line just behind the altar. Once in place, the chant ceased. And they stood there, waiting.

They stood there so long that the crowd started to grow restless and rustled impatiently. Theo's stomach bounced about once again, but she ignored it and held her breath, anxious to see what was coming.

An Oracle in a sky-blue robe held up a brass gong and struck it with a small mallet. She did this seven times. As the seventh chime finished ringing, all the Oracles suddenly opened their eyes and lifted their heads upwards.

The full moon was now high enough in the sky to be visible to the stage. All the women raised their arms to the moon, in homage to the lonely satellite. The gong was struck again and the Oracles stepped back, bowed their heads and were silent.

They stayed like this for an unbearably long time. Just as Theo believed that it would end still the silence endured. No one in the audience moved or spoke. The crowd held focus until, finally, the gong was struck again. With the final ring, the Oracle released the raven. The bird jumped into flight and flapped its long wings to gain lift into the night sky. As if trained to do so, it flew from the woman's arm in a straight line to the moon. It squawked overhead until it was out of sight.

The Oracles shuffled to form a circle around the altar. Suddenly there was a low rumbling sound. Theo couldn't make out what it was or where it was coming from. As it grew louder, she realized that the sound was coming from the Oracles themselves. It was unlike anything she had ever heard before. The strange chant was guttural and throbbing, and Theo's body tensed in response to it. It made everything feel so much worse.

The women began to sway from side to side, then backwards and forwards, undulating with the same pulse. Soon they began to move a little faster and their drone grew louder. Theo could see people around her edge forward in their seats with anticipation. However, Theo grew more fearful with each beat. She desperately wanted to cover her ears with her hands.

Just when Theo thought she couldn't stand it any longer, she saw faint lights appearing from within the centre of the Oracles. Like fireflies, the small floating, blue lights spiraled upward. This was enough to distract her from her physical discomfort, if only for the moment.

Theo said, "Are these special effects, Aunt Georgia?"

Aunt Georgia shook her head. "No, they are not. Keep watching – it will get stranger still."

More blue lights drifted upward until there was a giant swirl of them spinning over the heads of the women like blue mist. The Oracles continued droning their curious, atonal mantra, amid the cloud of spectral lights.

The chant started to change ever so slightly, and the blue haze began to respond to the shift of tempo. Like smoke in a glass bottle, the blue lights began to curl and form shapes in time to the song. When the voices went higher, the glow morphed into a ghostly bird, a raven, flying to a full moon. As the raven's wings flapped, the women incorporated the bird's call into their chant, "Caw Caw Caw". When the raven reached the phantom moon, it parted and drank the animal in. Then the moon grew and grew until it exploded into hazy shapes of people, moving and spinning. And in an instant, the image was smeared away, like a hand wiping sand from a table.

The Oracles changed their rhythm. The blue lights swirled into the shape of a man's face, sad then angry, and from this, transformed into a young woman's face, wide-eyed and innocent. The blue lights twisted into a funnel and spun as the Oracles chanted even louder and swayed with greater abandon.

Finally, from the centre of the storming whirlpool the dark figure of a raven emerged again, flying and fierce. It burst out of the circle and screeched with a tremendous blast. Everyone in the audience jumped back in their seats, shocked by the power of the image. But then they laughed with relief when the animal dissolved into thin air.

And just like that, the Oracles stopped chanting. They opened up the circle and formed a line facing the crowd and, once again, stood there waiting, silently.

From behind the Oracles, Ceres Theroux walked past the women to stand at the front of the stage. She looked serious but then lifted her features with a small smile.

Without the aid of a microphone, she began to speak to the audience with a voice that was both silken and firm, and carried without any effort, "So have the spirits spoken. So have they said."

Ceres paused briefly before she continued, "They wish us a happy Equinox! And have promised a bountiful next season!"

The crowd erupted with applause, cheering for the spectacle they had just witnessed and for the good news about the year ahead. Theo looked around to see the reaction of the people near her and she was amazed by their delight. The thrill of the ceremony would last for hours, and the revellers would take the party with them into the night.

Suddenly Theo heard a voice call to her. She snapped her head around to see who it was. But when she turned, no one nearby was speaking. Aunt Georgia was busy organizing her things, and the lady on the other side was stretching for her bag in the aisle. Theo looked about in confusion for a bit longer until the voice said, "Look up, my dear."

So she did. To her surprise, Theo found herself looking into the face of Ceres Theroux. The grand lady had moved to the edge of the stage and her eyes were focused on her.

Without moving her mouth, Ceres said, "How nice to meet you."

Theo was stunned and could do nothing but stare. Suddenly the swells of anxiety made sense.

Ceres smiled. Then, without any explanation, she turned and walked back to the group of Oracles. At that moment an explosion of fireworks filled the grounds with colour. Under the flicker of the blues, greens and yellows, Theo watched Ceres Theroux glide off stage, calm and inscrutable, and Theo could not utter a word.

Chapter Three

A bright light glowed from the core of an obscured object and an unknown voice called out, "Now I'll finally know!"

Hands covered the light and within the gaps between the fingers a sparkling shape could be seen. Before it could come into focus, a rumble blasted through the air and everything began to fall.

Theo bolted upright in a panic. She soon breathed a sigh of relief, however, once she realized she was at home, safe in her bed. She looked around her wood-panelled room; it was lit from outside by the soft light of the bright moon. Although her chair heaped with her just-worn clothes looked otherworldly in the dim light, everything was as it should be.

"Just another dream," she sighed bringing her hand to her head.

Theo swung her legs over the side of her bed and glanced at the clock. She was disappointed to see the time. It had already taken her hours to drift off to sleep and she knew she was going to be exhausted again tomorrow. Troubled sleep was a common thing for her.

Now fully awake, she began to recall the strangeness of last night's event. Did Ceres Theroux really speak to her? Did she really hear her? How was that possible? Did she just get swept away with the excitement of her first Oracle ceremony? She didn't believe it herself, really. Away from the festival, home in her bed, she was beginning to think she had imagined it all. But try as she might to dismiss it, Theo couldn't remove Ceres' penetrating gaze from her mind's eye. She had decided not to mention it to Aunt Georgia. It was already enough that she had asked her to the ceremony in the first place. Why cause her aunt more concern?

After the ceremony she and her aunt had stayed a little longer for the fireworks display but left just as the popular bands took the stage. Aunt Georgia thought it best not to make a bad situation worse by staying out too late. But when they got home they were lucky enough to find Uncle Ken gone. Relieved, they hurried to bed to avoid him and his impending foul mood.

Theo's thoughts were all jumbled, making it impossible to go back to sleep. There were too many Oracle things invading her head. So to help relax, she decided to go downstairs and get a drink of water. She was too old to go to her aunt's bedroom these days, as she used to do as a little girl whenever she had a bad dream. Not that Aunt Georgia would mind but she knew that Uncle Ken would have something to say about it.

Theo crept down the staircase and winced with every creak in the old, wooden boards. It wasn't until she landed in the foyer that she noticed the light coming up from the basement through the open door. She stopped in her tracks, cold with alarm. She started to turn to go back to her room, but it was too late. Uncle Ken saw her as he arrived at the top of the basement stairs.

He scowled at her and slurred, "Don't let me stop you, Missy. You get whatever you want around here. Go right ahead and help yourself to everything."

He swung his arm wide with a mock invitation into the kitchen. He had only a few years on Aunt Georgia, but with his grey skin and the dark circles under his eyes, he appeared to be much older. He was sweaty and out of breath from climbing the stairs, and he tried to smooth the stringy hair off his forehead to cover the bald patch. Despite having never been sick, he never looked healthy.

Theo recognized the sloppy speech. Something in the process of distilling the fuel for his car caused him to behave this way. If she had known what he was doing, she would have stayed in her bedroom. Theo braced herself for the worst.

"So you saw the Oracles did you? You went anyway even though I told you not to waste your time on this nonsense. You went anyway."

"I had the tickets. They were free. It didn't cost us anything…"

"Everything costs something, Missy," sneered Uncle Ken. "And keeping you around has cost me plenty."

He lumbered toward the sink and poured himself a glass of water from the tap. "Even this water costs something, you know. Just because you don't pay the bills, doesn't mean you understand what it takes."

"I'm sorry, Uncle Ken," Theo said in a small voice. She never understood why he hated her so much. At this moment he was upset about the expense of raising her; another time it would be about her daydreaming.

"Ah, what do 'sorries' do? Nothing, that's what."

As he moved away from the sink, he lost his balance and had to move quickly to keep from falling over. Theo, too shocked to react, stood and watched him fumble over his feet. When he caught her looking at him, his watery, brown eyes clouded over with fury.

"You think I'm funny?"

Theo shook her head but didn't know what to say. She had encountered his temper before, but Aunt Georgia was always around to run interference on her behalf. This was the first time she was alone with him. And now, with him fully free to vent his anger, Theo was really scared.

"You think that I'm a joke, don't you?" He continued, "Just because I have to work for a living? Just because I don't believe in that hocus pocus? What utter rubbish that stuff is! And what is worse, people gobble it up like it's candy."

"I don't think you are a joke," Theo said feebly. But Uncle Ken pressed on as if she had said nothing, as if she wasn't even in the room.

"You think I'm just a slob with no class and no brain. I told you not to go to this stupid festival, but did you listen to me? Did you listen? No!! And what's worse is that you dragged my wife to it as well." He stepped forward and raised his forearm to clench his fist.

"She wanted to go…" Theo started to say but stopped mid-speech as soon as she realized this was making Uncle Ken angrier. She had tried defending herself over the years but it was always a losing battle. Uncle Ken never wanted to see her side of things.

"She wouldn't want to go to the ceremony if it wasn't for you! If it wasn't for you and your ways! Who gets free tickets to the most popular event in years? I mean, do you really think I'm so stupid to believe that free tickets just fell from the sky? I don't know how you did it, but I know you got them on purpose. I'm so sick of you lying and thinking you are so much better than me."

He stepped forward to close the gap between them. He put his face right up to hers. Uncle Ken's breath was hot and stale, making Theo cringe from the stench of it. She stepped back into the hallway but Uncle Ken followed her, intent on finishing what he wanted to say.

"You think you are so much better than me, don't you? That you are so special. Well, I don't think you are. I think you are trouble, that's what. And if it weren't for me, you would have starved a long time ago. Your mother and that fool husband of hers couldn't do it. Got themselves killed, didn't they? Even with their special gifts. I've managed to stick around and look after you. Good enough to pay the bills but is anyone grateful for this? No. No one appreciates what I do. What's worse, you are turning my wife against me."

16

Theo had never seen him so angry. He had often belittled her mother and especially her father over the years. But it came as little digs and snarky comments dropped into conversations from time to time. She never understood why he was so angry with her parents.

As he inched closer and closer, Theo scanned the hallway for a quick exit as she feared the worst.

"You are trouble, Missy, and I can't stand to look at you - you weird, useless girl. I wish we had left you where we found you and let nature have its way with you."

Uncle Ken had said many cruel things to Theo over the years but it didn't make this any less hurtful. Despite her best effort, Theo couldn't stop the tears that were brimming in her eyes.

"Crocodile tears, they are," he scoffed. "I would never believe anything coming from you. You see, I've figured you out a long time ago. Georgia is fooled by your manipulative ways but I know better. I can see through you."

Could he? Did he really see her as she was? Was she really that awful? She racked her brain for some information that would make sense of his hatred but she could find none. She began to shake her head involuntarily.

"Oh yes, I can. And I know what you are even if you don't. You are trouble, and I'm tired of shutting up about it just to make Georgia happy. I can't stand having you in this house, making me look like the bad guy because I'm the only one who can see you for what you are." And with the last phrase, he poked Theo in the chest to punctuate his point.

"You aren't special at all. You are just trouble. And the sooner we see the back end of you, the better off we will be." And with that, he pushed Theo hard on the shoulder to force her away from him, and she stumbled backward and fell to the floor.

Just then Aunt Georgia shouted from the top of the stairs. "Ken! Stop it!! Stop it! What are you doing?"

Aunt Georgia stood on the top stairs with her arms wrapped around her body to keep her robe closed. Her face was pained and her eyes were wide with alarm. "Ken, leave Theo alone! Stop it!"

Theo lifted her head up to see Aunt Georgia rushing down towards her. Although she knew Aunt Georgia would put an end to the fight, Theo was too wounded by what Uncle Ken said to think straight. Some part of her believed it. Maybe she was trouble after all. Maybe she was hurting the people she loved. Maybe she was to blame for everything, and it would be better if she left. It was all too confusing and too much, and Theo just wanted to run away from it all.

17

S A McDonald

Theo turned away from her aunt and jumped to her feet to go to the front door. She grabbed her shoes and coat and slipped out in a flash. Racing blindly into the cold night, she ran from the sound of her aunt's voice calling out, "Theo! Come back! Theo! THEO!!!!"

Theo ran until she couldn't breathe anymore, until it felt as if her chest would explode if she didn't stop. Even with her coat on Theo shivered in the crisp, autumn air. The sky was dotted with elongated clouds and the full moon was smaller and higher in the sky, illuminating the fields with its silvery light. There was a strange hush in the air as the trees stood silently, not bothered by wind nor animal. And despite being by herself, she felt safer there than being back at the house.

She wandered off the main road to avoid running into cars. She didn't want to explain to strangers why she was out alone in the middle of the night. Criss-crossing over properties and parks, she finally came to the edge of the housing development. She climbed over a fence into a freshly mowed field that was covered with large, round bales of hay, squeezed into protective plastic covers. She carried on until she arrived at an old logging trail and followed it to the top. The end of the path opened up to reveal the top of an ancient quarry, mined long before the Great Shift. The moon welcomed her there, like an old friend waiting for her to arrive.

She knew the quarry well and often came up here to think. Usually she went during the day when it was bright and familiar, but in the moonlight everything seemed unearthly and dreamlike. Theo climbed to the top of a rocky perch to give her a better view of the gorge, and once there, she paused to take everything in. Below, the vast expanse of the pit was filled with icy, black water and it reflected back the moonlight, giving the place an enchanted shimmer. She was mesmerized with the strange, muted colours of the rocks and trees she knew so well. Theo felt safe, whether it was warranted or not, and for the moment, all her troubles disappeared.

Theo sat down in her usual place, a flat bit of rock, smooth and contoured, and rested her head against the side of a mossy bank beneath a large oak tree. She felt around and found some of the things she had left before: a jar full of pretty, white stones, a spyglass, a pen, and some pieces of paper, damp and curled into waves. She could feel the exhaustion expand in her body and her head felt heavy. Without giving it much thought, she rolled herself into a tight ball and let her eyelids fall.

18

Suddenly Theo's eyes sprang open. She was aware of something approaching. If she had fallen asleep, she couldn't say for how long. It was still dark but the moon had moved farther across the sky. Theo jumped to her feet to look around as her instincts were now on high alert. She scanned the quarry for anything out of the ordinary but she couldn't see a thing. And yet the feeling persisted. She continued to strain her neck, looking in every direction for whatever it was that was alarming her. It took awhile to spot as the dim light made it hard to see, hard to make out.

When she finally saw it, she believed it to be a trick of the eye. At first, she thought something wasn't quite right with the sky. But as she stared at it, a faint, blue line grew into focus as it approached from above the treeline across the quarry. It was long and shaky, and made a soft hum which grew louder as it came nearer. Theo looked for the machine to which it must be attached but could find nothing mechanical, nothing that made sense to her. She stood in awe as the line grew in depth. It had points and gaps and glowed from within. A mist smeared the air around it as it hovered in the sky.

It hung there for a time. Then it suddenly dropped into the belly of the gorge. Theo waited for it to strike the water but the glowing thing continued to fall lower and lower, with no sound of splashing water or cracking rocks. Then it lifted up and shifted to Theo's right, past the edge of the quarry and into the wall of rock, undeterred as if there was nothing there.

Theo blinked her eyes to make sure she wasn't seeing things. She had to look hard to really absorb what was happening. The icy, blue line was dissolving the quarry, rubbing out million-year-old rock as if it were an eraser on the end of a pencil!

Frozen with disbelief, Theo stood and watched the glowing crevice shift across the landscape as it expunged, without strain, the world before her. Despite what it was doing, it moved quickly. Even if Theo had thought to run from it, there was no way to outmanoeuvre this thing. She was in its path and there was no way to escape it. The realization of that fact caused adrenaline to flood through her body and she began to cry out with fear.

The glowing band shifted its shape as it moved. Long, icy tentacles vined into the ground around it. Soon the terrible thing was close enough to cast its glow onto Theo's face. She sank to her knees, closed her eyes and waited for its ghastly touch.

Suddenly a loud, ferocious roar echoed from behind her. She looked up to see a massive ball of fire shoot over her head toward the radiating crevice. The fireball hurled into the centre of the thing, swallowing up every last bit of it, burning it away.

Within the centre of the fireball, Theo could make out the shape of an animal. Obscured at first within the dazzling inferno, it was now visible as the fire subsided and calmed. It was a tiger. It was larger than a house, and every part of it was alight with multiple shades of gold and amber. It too hung in mid-air, disregarding the rules of nature.

The Fire Tiger turned its head to look at Theo. Unable to turn away, she found herself staring into hot, fierce eyes. Terrified, she thought she might melt from the heat of its gaze. As if reading her mind, the Fire Tiger reduced its intensity and dimmed to a less daunting orange glow. But despite this, Theo remained rooted to the spot. She could neither move nor think. Only when the Fire Tiger let out another great roar was she released from her petrified state. She threw her hands over her ears and craned her neck to watch the firestorm race out of sight.

Theo was left alone in the moonlight once again but now everything had changed. She jumped to her feet and ran blindly, headlong into the night. Looking back over her shoulder to see if anything else was coming, she rammed full–on into a man who had just crested the corner of the logging trail.

Dressed in a police uniform, he grabbed hold of Theo and tried to steady her. "Whoa there, young lady! Take it easy. I bet you are the girl we have been looking for. You've had your Aunt in quite a state, worrying about where you've been. She said we might find you up here…"

The officer couldn't finish his sentence. He looked past Theo and was dumbstruck by what he saw. The quarry that had stood for hundreds of years, for as long as anyone could remember, was gone. And a crater three times its size, smooth and yawning, had taken its place.

Chapter Four

Theo sank into the plain, wooden chair and let her knapsack slide from her hand to the floor. She slowly looked around her to take in the details of her new surroundings. Gone were the wood panels of her aunt's house, and in their place were the empty plaster walls of her new room. There was a small wooden desk positioned under a high window, and a matching dresser, tall and thin, leaned against the corner for her clothes and personal possessions. There was a single bed on a metal frame against the longest wall, and above the bed was a shelf that held a small lamp and a wind-up alarm clock. An irregular shaped closet was tucked under a supporting beam, which was tall enough to hold a few garments and deep enough for cases and boxes. The small room was immaculate and bright, but its lack of warmth made Theo feel even more adrift and alone.

A lot had changed in the past few weeks. Too much had happened, and too many strange things couldn't be explained. Uncle Ken was determined to get rid of her, and nothing that Aunt Georgia said made any difference.

And there were all the questions. Theo was subject to an inquiry by the police regarding what happened at the quarry. She could not explain to anyone's satisfaction what she saw, and worse, she couldn't shake the stench of her involvement. Gossip around town was becoming unbearable.

It was decided that it would be in everyone's best interest for Theo to leave town and stay with a distant relative who lived near Greenstone. Gloriana Stokes and her family were far enough away to suit Uncle Ken.

Theo had just arrived at the Stokes' house a short while ago and was shown to her new room right away. The long journey from her aunt's house had begun at the crack of dawn. Theo slumped forward and brought her hand to her head. She was so tired. Still, she couldn't stop thinking about her last moments with Aunt Georgia.

****

Aunt Georgia had walked Theo down the front steps and helped put her things into the car. The driver, sent by the Stokes, opened the rear door and waited patiently.

Aunt Georgia's sad face masked nothing; she was broken but held her composure. Theo was too frightened to cry and mechanically walked to the car door. Before climbing in, her aunt grabbed her and hugged her hard.

"I am going to miss you so much, Theo," she said. "Please write to me. I can't bear the thought of you not being here."

"I'll try and write often." Theo squeezed her eyes shut tight as she hugged her aunt back.

"It's for the best, Theo," she barely managed to say. Theo clung onto the woman and tried to draw out the moment for as long as possible. Leaving Aunt Georgia was unbearably hard. She was the only family Theo had ever known.

Eventually, Aunt Georgia had to step back and let her go. Theo climbed into the car and the driver softly closed the door. Then he quickly took his position behind the wheel, and without ceremony, the car rolled away. Gripped with emotion, Theo twisted around to look through the rear window and watched her aunt follow behind waving goodbye. It took all of Theo's willpower to stop from jumping out and running back to her.

****

Suddenly there was a knock on the door. Theo was brought back to the immediacy of where she was and she jumped to her feet. She took a deep breath and waited to see who was there.

The door opened to reveal a boy with golden-brown hair and large, brown eyes. He wore jeans and a blue t-shirt, and his solid, round arms poked out of the faded sleeves. His skin was tanned and covered with small nicks and bruises, the kind you get from spending a lot of time outdoors. He stepped into the room and gave Theo a broad, friendly smile.

"Hello," he said. "Are you Theo?"

Theo wasn't sure what to make of the boy and merely shrugged.

The boy was unfazed and continued. "My name is Talim. I'm twelve years old. You don't look very old either – I'm almost as big as you!"

He went over to her and put his hand on her head and then to his. She was barely taller despite having two years on him.

"See? We are almost the same height. They said you were a little older than me but looks like we are about the same age. But I get that a lot –I'm pretty big."

22

He brought his gaze to her face and gave her a good looking over. "You have the biggest eyes I"ve ever seen though. Wow, what colour do you call them?"

Theo was utterly surprised by his question. She stammered a little before replying, "G-Grey. They call it grey."

"Oh. I didn't know eyes could be grey. Cool. They sure make you look different though."

Theo didn't know what to make of his comment.

He continued, "Yeah, you have a different look about you. Not the usual girly look I've seen so far – like with Kiryana Stokes or her friends. But it's interesting and so that's good."

"Um, thank you?" she replied hesitantly.

"Hey, no problem. Dad said I should try and be nice to you as you would probably be a little scared. Are you scared?"

Theo was taken aback by his directness. She just stared at the boy.

"Yeah, you look a little scared to me but that would make sense, you moving in with strangers and all."

"Would it?" Theo managed to say.

"Yeah, it would. I would be cut up if I had to leave my Dad."

Theo couldn't decide if Talim was trying to provoke her or not, but she knew if he continued asking these questions she would break down and cry. Fortunately, Talim turned away as he lost interest in the conversation and began looking through her things.

"You don't have a lot of stuff, do you?" he said as he opened one of her bags and pulled out a book.

Theo shook her head. Aunt Georgia made sure she had what she needed but Uncle Ken made sure she didn't have anything more.

"Mrs Stokes is loaded. I'm sure you'll get lots from her if you are related. Dad told me that we are to treat you like one of her family."

In all the conversations about moving in with the Stokes, no one mentioned that she would be considered family. Having just left Aunt Georgia this morning, she wasn't sure if she wanted a new one.

"Anyway, I've been sent to tell you that dinner is ready." He paused for a second. "Are you hungry?"

Theo felt overwhelmed and tired and not much else.

"I don't know," she replied.

"Don't know if you are hungry?" laughed Talim. "Boy! I don't have that problem. I'm starving. I could eat a horse." Bored of sifting through her stuff, he began nosing around the room and pulling open empty drawers.

"You should come downstairs and have dinner with me and my dad. The Stokes are out tonight doing something fancy so we don't have to do the whole dinner thing with them. Anyway, I like it when they go out because my dad makes me what I want. We are having sausages and fries tonight. They are good. You should try them."

He finished snooping around the room and went over to Theo. "So are you coming or not?" His soft eyes were open and encouraging.

It that moment Theo decided Talim was being straight with her. To her surprise she found herself saying, "Yeah, sure. That would be nice."

Talim's grin stretched across his face, and he motioned for her to follow him.

Talim took Theo down the hallway to a narrow staircase that led to the large kitchen on the ground floor. The house was built only a few decades before but it was constructed in a style that was reminiscent of an old-fashioned manor from before the Great Shift. Theo did know the Stokes family had a lot of money and that Mrs Stokes was a member of the Greenstone City Council. The house reflected the aspirations of the family. Theo had been amazed but not surprised by the size of it when she first drove up the long driveway.

Theo followed Talim into an open, square room and was greeted by the fragrant smell of food. It was then she realized she might be hungrier than she thought. A small, wood-burning stove was in the far corner and its smell made the air inviting and cozy. A large, wooden table with thick legs stood in the centre of the room, and chairs of all sizes and shapes were placed around it. Against the wall was a large oven with pots bubbling on top of it. Larger brass pans hung above it from a rack. An expansive bay window dominated the outside wall, and through it Theo could see the large lawn and gardens that stretched out behind it.

Talim walked straight up to the counter, picked up a carrot and started to munch on it. He offered one to Theo, who had not eaten since early morning, and not too much even then. She considered it but refused. Talim shrugged and stuffed the unwanted vegetable into his mouth.

From around the corner came the sound of whistling. Then a round man in his late forties came into view holding a bottle of milk. He smiled when he caught sight of Theo.

"Well, hello m' ducky," he said brightly, "I'm so glad you decided to eat with Talim and me. I guess the driver took care of showing you to your room? And if I know the man, he didn't take too much effort in getting you settled. Ah, you can't blame him though. Now he's off to get the Stokes, so it's been a long day for him too."

He went over to the table and pulled out a chair. "Come, make yourself comfortable, my dear. Dinner will be ready in a jiff. I hope you like sausages. I promised Talim I'd make them. I'm Talim's father, by the way. You can call me Chester."

Theo smiled weakly and sidled over to the chair. She curled one leg under her as she huddled in her seat.

"Believe it or not," Chester laughed as he rubbed his round belly. "I am not the cook here. Mrs Henderson is but she is off for the night so it's just me and the boy. I'm not the best in the kitchen but I do okay. Talim doesn't seem to mind, do you son?"

Talim, who was in the middle of stuffing another carrot in his mouth, nodded in agreement. Chester opened the oven door to check on the food and was pleased by the sound of sputtering sausages. He pulled out the trays and placed them on the range top to let them cool as he rummaged about in a lower cupboard.

"I look after the grounds," Chester continued as he stood up with plates in his hands. "I see to the gardens and the lawns and even have a plot for the vegetables and herbs. Me and the boy have been living here ever since Mabel, his mother, God rest her soul, passed away a few years ago. So it's been good for us, really, to stay here. The Stokes have been generous."

Chester drained the water from the bubbling pots while he was talking and put sliced carrots and peas, along with fries and sausages on the plates. Talim followed him to the table and sat down while Chester placed the plates in front of the two of them. The smell of the food was so enticing that Theo finally succumbed to the possibility that eating was a good idea afterall. She picked up her fork and started to nibble on a warm and crunchy fry. With each bite her anxiety started to ease, and she began to eat with gusto. Chester took another chair and lowered himself down with a great huff of air, and scraped the legs along the floor as he pulled himself to the table.

"Ah, I'm looking forward to this. Not to knock Mrs Henderson's fancy fare but sometimes it's the simple food that does the trick." He then winked at Theo as if to let her in on some secret, which made her smile a little.

Theo surprised herself by finishing everything on her plate. In no time, both Chester and Talim went for second helpings as big as their first. Chester poured Theo a large glass of milk and encouraged her to drain the cup.

"From our own cow, Lily," he said proudly, "milked her this morning. I know we don't need to keep her anymore because it's not like the old days when you didn't know where your next meal was coming from. But I like to keep her around as an insurance policy. You know what I mean?"

Theo looked blankly at Chester. After a moment, he started to laugh. "Of course you don't. You are only a young girl, for heaven's sake. Sometimes I forget how things have changed. Well, it's a good thing that neither of you had experienced the lean times, and I hope to heaven that you never will. I, however, will never trust another for food again, so I will keep gardening until my back won't bend."

Chester, obviously a successful gardener, groaned as he hoisted himself up from the table and shuffled over to an oversized, wooden cabinet. He began rummaging through the back of one of its drawers.

"I know where Mrs Henderson stashes her chocolates," he said conspiratorially. And, as sure as his word, he pulled out a box of chocolate-covered cherries. "Aha, here are the little dickens!"

He opened the box and offered the cherries to Theo first. Chocolate wasn't as rare as it used to be but Theo didn't see a lot of it at her aunt's house. She studied the darkly, draped confections and settled on one with swirls looping around the top. She placed the chocolate in her mouth and let the rich, sweet flavour seep onto her tongue. It was the nicest thing she had ever tasted. She could not help but smile with the pleasure of it. Chester beamed knowingly at her.

"Good?" he asked.

"Yes, very good."

"Won't you get in trouble for taking Mrs Henderson's chocolates?" asked Talim as he stuffed two in at a time.

"Probably," laughed his father as he gobbled up his portion, "but she has a sweet spot for me so I'll smooth it over later." He turned and grinned at Theo. "I'm always smoothing things over with Mrs Henderson. You'll see."

"Yeah, my dad winds her up pretty good, so he had to learn to get on her good side if he wants anything to eat." Theo barely understood him through his mouthful of chocolate.

Chester rubbed his belly as he said, "And proof is in the pudding! I've earned this belly from hard work!" Theo couldn't help but laugh a little. It felt strange and foreign, and she couldn't remember the last time she did it.

Chester was quick to notice her laugh and carried on to encourage more. "You think I'm kidding? Oh, the things I have to say to that woman: ah Mrs Henderson, my chicken, won't you spare me a drumstick? Or Mrs Henderson, my pretty pigeon, won't you share a wing? Or Mrs Henderson, my savoury tart,

26

how about a piece of pie? Oh, that woman loves a bit of buttering up but don't mind her when she complains about it. Secretly, she loves it!"

"She might mind the missing chocolate, though, Dad."

"She might. But I'll make her my tasty bonbon so she can't fuss.

"Or your caramel candy," grinned Talim.

"Or my cocoa confection."

"Or your sugar sweets."

"Or your beautiful brownie," interjected Theo, shyly. Both Chester and Talim looked at her and smiled.

"Yes," nodded Chester. "That's a good one, Theo. Mrs Henderson, my beautiful brownie, can you spare us your chocolate? That's the ticket, my girl, that's that one! How could she possible resist that?"

Theo realized that Chester was being kind to her but it didn't make the inclusion any less pleasing. She relaxed a little more and laughed at Chester's silly game.

Talim swallowed the last of his chocolate as he studied Theo. And without much consideration, he let his thoughts fall out of his mouth, "So how come you had to leave Kitchie then?"

"Talim!" Chester shot his son a look to shut him up but Talim just ignored it.

"I mean, what happened that you had to come live here?"

Of course, Theo dreaded this question. She didn't want to explain that she was kicked out by her uncle who hated her, or somehow she was blamed for a bizarre occurence over which she had no control. She cast her eyes down and fidgeted in her chair, unable to find the words to explain why she had been sent away.

Chester quickly jumped in and said gently, "Ah, don't mind Talim, honey. He is not old enough to realize that not everybody gets along. It doesn't mean anything really, he'll see. And it looks like we're destined to be the best of friends, so your uncle's loss anyway."

Theo jerked her head up to look at Chester and wondered how much he already knew. But whatever it was, he decided to keep it to himself. Instead, he glanced up at the clock on the wall and noticed the time.

"Okay, my little chickadees, it's going to be an early morning tomorrow for us all so up to bed. And no complaining about it, Talim, please!"

"Aw Dad, I wanted to work on my model after dinner," he whined.

"Now what did I just say, Talim?" replied his father with mild annoyance.

Chester continued with a softer tone, "Besides Talim, my son, I need you to show Theo where everything is. She must be exhausted."

27

He then turned to Theo and said pointedly, "Mrs Stokes made it very clear she wants to see you first thing in the morning before she heads back to the city. Is that all right with you, my dear?"

All right or not, did she have a choice? She nodded.

Chester clapped his hands and continued, "Okay, the two of you, up to bed then. I'll wake you in the morning." He motioned for Talim to come to him, and Chester gently kissed the boy on the top of his forehead. Then, after studying Theo for a moment, he approached her and kissed her as well.

"Good night and sweet dreams," he said benevolently. Theo couldn't look at him for fear of bursting into tears.

Chapter Five

Theo rolled over in bed as she drifted from sleep into consciousness. Something in the room was tapping erratically on something hard. Theo, in her semi-awake state, could not even begin to recognize what it was.

Slowly she opened her eyes and scanned her little room in the dim, morning light. At first glance, she couldn't make out what was making the funny noise. Then she allowed the sound to draw her gaze to the window. There she saw a little bird pecking on the window pane.

She swung her legs over the side of the bed and stepped onto the cold floor. She wrapped her arms around her shoulders to stave off the chill and scampered over to the window to see what the bird wanted.

The bird stopped tapping at once. It stared boldly at her as she looked through the glass. It was round and brown with little specks of black and charcoal grey dotted over the tips of the wings and tail. Theo didn't know the species. But more and more birds were starting to come back in recent years, and she was seeing new ones all the time. On the outside ledge, there was a plate with a few tiny crumbs scattered about it.

"Hmmm," said Theo. "Looks like someone forgot to feed you." In response, the bird chirped noisily and flew away.

Theo pulled the large handle and pushed the window open. She shivered as cold air blasted into the room. Quickly, she pulled in the plate and slammed the window shut. She then hotfooted it over to her desk and sank into the chair.

It had been a hard few weeks for her but last night she mercifully had a long, uninterrupted sleep. She felt a lot better for it but she still felt unsettled, as each day held a new uncertainty for her. As she sat there, she began to hear unfamiliar footfalls and urgent calls from the floor below. She was to meet Gloriana Stokes today, and she was more than a little nervous.

She sat upright when she heard heavy steps coming down the hall. They approached quickly and stopped outside her room.

"Theo, my lovely, are you awake?"

Thankfully, she recognized the rolling baritone. She cleared her throat before replying, "Yes, Chester, I am."

"Good," he replied, "you better shake a leg, my dear. Mrs Stokes wants to see you in fifteen minutes, and we don't want to keep her waiting."

Theo washed and dressed as quickly as she could. She entered the kitchen with the plate in her hand.

A middle-aged woman with shocking white hair was at the range stirring a large pot. She turned and widened her eyes when she saw Theo standing there.

She said bluntly, "So you are the distant relative?" Her attention then moved to a bowl from which she spooned some blueberries into the pot. She wiped her hands on a stained apron and approached Theo to get a better look at her.

She studied Theo. She came so close that Theo could see the pinkness of her skin and the twinkle in her dark eyes. No doubt this was Mrs Henderson.

Mrs Henderson said, "If you are related, I can't see it. You are not the looker in the family, are you? But you do have something about you. What colour do you call your eyes?"

Again with the eyes! "Um, I think they are grey," Theo replied politely.

"Grey, huh? Well, they are the biggest eyes I've ever seen. Be careful not to stare though. It could put people off."

Theo wasn't sure what to say to this and let her mouth hang open a little. Fortunately, Talim ran into the room and demanded their attention.

"I'm starving, Mrs Henderson," Talim announced as he slid into his chair. "What's for breakfast?"

Before she could answer, Chester came in and walked up to Theo and Mrs Henderson.

"Good morning, Mrs Henderson," he said as he surveyed the two of them. "I hope you are not giving Theo a hard time already."

"Good morning Chester," Mrs Henderson replied tersely. "I've got too much to do to give anyone a hard time. By the way, the girl won't have the chance to eat before seeing Mrs Stokes so I'll keep her breakfast warm until after." She returned to the stove and began dishing out portions of oatmeal.

"That's very thoughtful of you, Mrs Henderson," said Chester as he winked at Theo. He looked down and noticed the plate in her hand.

"What's that?" he asked.

"Oh, I found this outside of my window this morning. A little bird was tapping on the glass and it woke me up."

Talim saw the plate and quickly piped in, "Oh that's mine! I've been feeding the birds. Did you know that sparrows were once so common that you could find them all over this area? I read that in a book. But I've only managed to see ten this summer. Still, that's more than last year."

He jumped up from the table and rushed over to Theo. "Here. I'll take that." He pulled the plate out of her hand and bounded back to his waiting breakfast.

"Okay then," Chester smiled at Theo, "let's go and see what the great Mrs Stokes will make of you."

Despite her best efforts to look at ease, Theo felt more scared than she did when she first arrived the day before.

Theo followed Chester out of the kitchen and up the stairs to the main floor. As soon as she stepped off the staircase into the hall, her mouth fell open as she took in the grandeur of the foyer. A large, curved, oak staircase swept up from the marble floor to a balcony landing, and two-storeyed windows opened the front of the house to the bright morning sun. Rows of doors, some wooden, some glass, surrounded the large hall, making the main entrance the focus of the spectacular house. It was here that the Stokes hosted the cocktail parties and balls that they were famous for. Theo was awed by the size and luxuriousness of it all. She craned her head around to try and take it all in.

Chester, noticing Theo's reaction, pursed his lips for a silent whistle and said, "Yes, they do like to dress to impress."

He continued to lead her across the lobby, past the statues and antique urns, to the French doors nearest the front of the house.

"Here we are - the Morning Room," he announced before turning to Theo and taking her gently by the shoulders. "Now just answer her questions and you'll do fine." He gave Theo a little squeeze before he stepped forward and swung the doors open. Theo followed him in and held her breath.

As soon as she walked into the room, Theo was dazzled by the light, making it hard to see at first. Floor to ceiling windows and patio doors ran along the front and side of the room illuminating the space with the early morning sun. The interior walls were wall-papered with canary-yellow stripes and golden furniture was positioned in front of a striking, white marble mantelpiece. So overwhelmed by the brightness of it all, Theo didn't notice the small table at the rear of the room with the two figures sitting there. At least not until one of them spoke.

"Good morning, Chester. I trust you are well," said the polished, clear voice of the woman. Theo turned to look at her and understood immediately that this must be Mrs Stokes.

"Good morning, Theo," she continued, as she rose from the table to come and greet them. Mrs Stokes was a tall, pale woman with platinum blonde hair swept high into an elegant chignon. She smoothly crossed the room and gave Theo a stiff embrace. The strong, sweet fragrance of Mrs Stokes' perfume hovered about them like a cloud of bees. It made Theo feel a little dizzy.

Mrs Stokes stood back to take a look at Theo and continued. "My goodness, I haven't seen you since you were a baby. Why you are almost a woman now." Mrs Stokes had the metered, well-enuciated speech of someone who spoke for a living.

"Kiryana, come and say hello to your..., what are you, my dear, cousin? No, I was a cousin to your mother's mother so what would that make you and Kiryana, I wonder?" She paused long enough for Theo to feel uncomfortable. "Ah, no matter, our family is far and few between, are we not? So, cousin, it is. Kiryana, come and say hello to your cousin, Theo." Mrs Stokes finished with a calculated smile.

Tall like her mother but with long, chestnut hair and tawny skin, Kiryana Stokes was a beautiful girl. Being a few years older than Theo she had already developed her graceful adult figure. Her skin was perfectly clear and reflected the light in a way that made her luminous. Theo had never seen a girl like Kiryana before, and she suddenly became very aware of her own off-beat looks.

"Hello," Kiryana said politely. "It's very nice to meet you." She put her hand out to Theo in a well-practiced gesture, however, her bright, amber eyes narrowed as she studied her cousin.

Theo took the hand and shook it. She replied faintly, "It's nice to meet you too."

Mrs Stokes clasped her hands together with satisfaction and said, "Well, that's that then. Let's finish our breakfast. Chester? Has the girl eaten yet?"

Chester answered with his usual buoyancy, "No ma'am, not yet. And I'm sure Mrs Henderson would be thrilled to bring up another plate. I'll let her know right away."

"Very good and thank you, Chester," she said, not looking at him. "Come on, Theo, my dear, let's start to get to know each other." She put her arm around Theo as she walked her over to the table. Kiryana followed meekly and said nothing while Chester turned on his heels and left the room.

Mrs Stokes carried another cushioned chair from the wall and brought it over for Theo to sit on. "Here, my dear," she cooed. "Please, make yourself comfortable."

The last thing Theo was at this moment was comfortable but she sat down in her place without a fuss and remained very still.

Both Mrs Stokes and Kiryana took their seats again and began to pick at the food in front of them. After eating a berry or two, Mrs Stokes turned to Theo and asked, "How was your journey? I trust that you are settled in your room?"

Theo nodded and replied quickly, "Yes, I'm settled in my room. The journey was fine, thank you."

"Which room are you in? Are you in the front of the house, my dear?" she queried, taking a sip from a china cup.

"I think I look over the back," Theo replied. "I believe I'm near Chester and Talim."

"Ah," responded Mrs Stokes, "you are in the back where the rooms are smaller. Of course, you can move to a larger one in the front if you prefer but I think Chester was thinking he could look out for you better if you were nearer to him. I'm afraid my work keeps me away quite a bit, and Kiryana is busy with her studies."

Upon hearing this, Kiryana lifted her head up and said hopefully, "I could always move to the back too while you and Daddy are away."

To which Mrs Stokes responded curtly, "Don't be silly, dear. You have the best room in the house. Why would you want to give that up?" Aware of how harsh she sounded, Mrs Stokes softened her voice before continuing, "Besides, soon you will be a postulate on the Hill and won't be here at all." Defeated, Kiryana dropped the subject and went back to pushing food around her plate.

They continued in silence while Mrs Stokes read some documents. When she was done, she looked over at Theo who was having trouble figuring out what to do with her hands. Mrs Stokes tilted her head as she studied the girl.

"Do you know about Kiryana, Theo?" she asked. Theo shook her head. Kiryana looked up and scowled unhappily.

"Well, when Kiryana was a baby, I was invited by the great Oracle Lilith Crowe to see her. Do you know about Lilith Crowe?" Again, Theo shook her head.

"My goodness, Theo, we shall have to do something about your education, shan't we? No matter. Lilith Crowe was one of the first Oracles that came out of the Great Shift, part of the original vanguard. She was the High Seer on the Hill for ages and became a friend of the family."

She paused to let this impressive fact sink in before continuing, "So, as soon as Kiryana was born, I wanted Lilith to see her right away because we just knew there was something special about this girl." She reached over to squeeze her daughter's hand which made Kiryana squirm a little.

"She was such a beautiful baby with such a sweet temperament. My goodness, she was like a little angel from heaven. Lilith Crowe, who was very old at the time, agreed to see her even though her health was failing. So we brought Kiryana to the Oracle Temple right away and placed her into Lilith's hands." Mrs Stokes paused again while she picked up her cup and took another sip of coffee. She took her time in settling the cup back onto the saucer before continuing.

"We placed our dearest child into Lilith's hands. Right away she said with a voice as clear as a bell that Kiryana would have Clarity and that her vision would show a great truth. More importantly, that was the very last thing she said before she died later that day."

She stopped mid-speech when there was a knock on the door. Mrs Henderson came in holding a tray, and her grim face indicated she was not too pleased to be there.

"Ah, thank you, Mrs Henderson. Just put it in front of Theo, please. And can you clear the empty plates as well."

Mrs Henderson approached the table and put a bowl of warm oatmeal and berries in front of Theo. She then went about clearing the empty plates, making no effort to hide her annoyance.

Mrs Stokes took a deep breath and continued, "So where was I? Yes, so she said that Kiryana would have Clarity and she would see a great truth. And this prediction from the mouth of the great Lilith Crowe! So the news spread everywhere, and everybody wanted to see our beloved little girl. Everyone wanted to meet this special child." Mrs Stokes smiled proudly but Kiryana shrank more into her seat.

"So everyone who mattered came and saw her, and everyone agreed that she was destined for great things. For this reason, she has been groomed her entire life to become an Oracle, to fulfill the prophecy, the last prediction of the great Lilith Crowe. Kiryana is the pride and glory of our little family." Mrs Stokes finished her story with a self-satisfied sigh and took another sip of coffee.

"So when will she go to the Hill?" asked Theo, who felt obliged to say something at this point.

Mrs Henderson, who was still clearing the table, lost grip of a dish and it clattered noisily to the floor.

Mrs Stokes winced for a moment then expertly reframed her face to look pleasant and calm. "We are still waiting for her gift to develop, Theo. But it should be any day now. Wilhelmina Van Dorne, her tutor, says she has been making good progress."

Kiryana cringed with what her mother was saying. She looked up miserably and said, "Mother, I'm almost eighteen. Most Oracles have their gift long before now…"

"Nonsense," Mrs Stokes interjected, cutting her off. "Lilith Crowe would never make a mistake. She has given us a great treasure, and everyone is waiting to see it. Everyone is expecting it. Everyone!"

Unable to sit any longer, Mrs Stokes got up from her chair and wiped her mouth with her linen napkin. "Kiryana, I just need you to remember what it would mean to your father and me. Keep to your studies and follow Wilhelmina's advice, and everything will work out fine."

Mrs Stokes then closed the subject and turned to Mrs Henderson, who was picking up the pieces of the broken dish. "Is everything ready for my departure?" Mrs Henderson nodded to say that it was.

Upon hearing this, Kiryana jumped up and ran to her mother's side, "You are not leaving already, are you?! I thought you were going to finish the week here."

Mrs Stokes took both of Kiryana's hands into hers, "My darling girl, I have so much to attend to this week in Greenstone. And you have so many lessons yourself. You'll be so busy you won't even notice I'm gone. I'll be back before you know it."

"You always say that but I never get to see you," lamented Kiryana and pulled her hands away.

"Please, Kiryana, don't be like that. You know I miss you when I'm not here. I know it's hard work but it will be worth it, I promise." Mrs Stokes moved in closer and ran her hand over her daughter's thick hair. But Kiryana was unmoved.

"Ah, be a good girl and give me a kiss before I go. I'll be back soon enough."

Mrs Stokes offered one of her powdered cheeks to Kiryana, and unable to resist, Kiryana gave her mother a quick peck and a weak smile.

"That's the spirit, darling. Be good and study hard!"

Mrs Stokes then turned away from her daughter and hurried to the French doors. Over her shoulder, she called back, "Love you darling!" before she disappeared out of the room, letting the door shut behind her.

"Love you too, Mother," Kiryana muttered under her breath, looking down at the carpeted floor.

Theo didn't dare say a word, and they sat in silence for awhile. Eventually, Kiryana glanced up and caught Theo watching her. In a fit of pique she yelled, "What are you looking at?" She then turned and ran out of the room.

Mrs Henderson shook her head slowly as she continued to tidy the dishes. Finally, she said to Theo, "Pick up your bowl and come with me. You might as well finish your breakfast in the kitchen. No point you eating alone too."

Theo did as she was told and followed Mrs Henderson out of the glorious morning room back downstairs into the kitchen.

Chapter Six

Theo finished drying the last bowl and put it in the cupboard as directed by Mrs Henderson. When done, she stood there watching the older woman wipe down the counter and wring the water out of the cloth before hanging it to dry.

"Okay," huffed Mrs Henderson, wiping her moist hands on her cotton apron, "that's done. Thank you for the help, my dear. Now I need to get started on today's meals."

She hurried around the corner to the pantry and began rummaging through the large, white refrigerator. Theo followed and stood quietly in the doorway. It wasn't until Mrs Henderson spun around with arms full of vegetables and almost ran headlong into the girl that she noticed she was there.

"Good heavens, Theo!" exclaimed Mrs Henderson, reeling backward and losing hold of a vegetable or two. "Why are you standing there? Why don't you go do somthing else?"

Theo shrugged her shoulders and said, "I don't know what to do, Mrs Henderson."

Mrs Henderson thought for a moment and said, "Well, why don't you go and see what Talim is up to? He should be in the garden. What am I saying? He is always in the garden. As it is Saturday, class starts later in the morning. Chester will come and get you when it's time to go to the schoolhouse."

"Schoolhouse! No one mentioned school. I didn't know I would be going to school today!"

"Yes," sighed Mrs Henderson, "Kiryana must study hard, and therefore you and Talim must go with her too. No point complaining about it as it's the only rule Mrs Stokes insists upon. She does push her daughter awfully hard. It's a shame, really."

Theo was told she would go to school with her cousin but no one said where or when. Indeed, no one bothered to tell her that she would have class on Saturday morning. She cringed inwardly at the thought of it.

Mrs Henderson softened her face a little as she said, "Ah, it won't be so bad. Most of the attention is paid to Kiryana anyway, as it is very important for her to develop her Clarity. If you do the work asked of you, you'll do fine."

Theo smiled a little but she didn't feel any less worried about going to a new school.

"Okay Theo, off you go. Just follow the path until you come to a large garden wall." And having dismissed her, Mrs Henderson continued to make her way into the kitchen.

Theo pulled her jacket off the hook and slipped her arms into the blue padded material. She pushed through the back door and stepped gingerly into the cool morning. Red and yellow leaves were still on the trees but in a few weeks the branches would be completely bare and snow would cover the ground. At this moment, however, that was far enough away not to be a concern. She took a deep breath and savoured the cold air that filled her lungs.

A long, stone pathway stretched out before her. She began to follow it back farther into the grounds. Soon it turned at a right angle and followed a row of hedges. Once it passed the border, it turned again and ran down a gentle slope. There, Theo could see a high brick wall running along a flat expanse. The wall marked out a space that ran a good length, and as she approached, she could see other walls forming a massive square. She noticed that there was another wall within the first, with an alley between the two.

The path took her through an archway and into a garden resplendent with flowers and vegetable plots and small trees. The sun was high enough to shine over the garden walls and the air within the quad was noticeably warmer. Fruit trees and vines flourished against the warm bricks. Bees and butterflies still flew about. Theo felt as if she had walked back into summer and was amazed by the lushness of it all.

Talim was in the centre of the garden sitting on the rim of a water fountain fiddling with some reeds and balsam wood. Birds of all sorts were twittering and fluttering about, eating the seeds and suet that he had left out for them. Upon hearing her approach, he looked up and grinned his usual smile.

"Hi Theo! Just making a bird feeder. I thought I could hang it outside your window." His hands were weaving the flexible wood together to make a little basket. He was in the same faded, blue t-shirt as before. He didn't bother with a jacket in the warm air. Theo sat beside him on the cool stone ledge.

She craned her head around to take it all in. She couldn't help but say, "My goodness Talim! I've never seen a place like this before."

Talim looked up as well but quickly returned his gaze back to what he was doing. "Yeah, it's a special place, that's for sure. My dad built it years ago when he first came to work for the Stokes. It is called a walled garden. It faces south so the sun shines on the brick walls. It's warm in here so we can grow plants all year round. He read in a book that the English Victorians used to do this too. Anyway, it's where we get all our vegetables and fruit. And I'm always helping Dad with the gardening. I'm going to be a gardener too when I grow up. Well, after I join the Greenline Corp."

"You are going to join the Corp?" queried Theo, intrigued by the certainty of his decision.

"Yep, as soon as I turn eighteen, I'm signing up. I already have the forms. It's not so bad these days as most of the fighting has been sorted out. I'm mostly interested in the landscaping and farming of the reclaimed areas. That's what they call it anyway. I hear they keep pushing the farming borders farther and farther south as things are getting fixed. But there are still a lot of the Outlands that need work. I can't wait until I'm old enough."

Theo nodded politely. She had heard stories she wasn't supposed to hear, all about the trouble in the outlying areas. But things had settled down over the years and the Outlands weren't as dangerous as they once were. At least that was the official story. But no one was ever sure what they would find once they crossed the Greenline border.

Talim put the feeder down and rose to his feet. "Here, let me show you what we grow."

Theo followed Talim down one of the diagonal paths to a corner of the wall that faced the sun. Arched trellises stood against the south wall, and vines with bunches of grapes looped around them. Little trees, groomed as neat as a pin, were heavy with peaches, lemons, nectarines and oranges. In front of them were flower beds full of roses, geraniums, snapdragons and begonias. They continued down another path along the east wall past a few palm trees and coconut trees to a plot divided into rows of peas, tomatoes, lettuces and corn.

"The root vegetables are on the north side," informed Talim. "Anyway, we are pretty much at the end of the season so we'll be planting the winter garden soon."

He reached out and pulled a tomato off the stalk and gave it to Theo. "Here," he said, "if that's not the best thing you've ever tasted then I don't know what is."

Theo pressed her teeth into the smooth, red skin and after a good deal of pressure, it burst. Tangy, sweet juice filled her mouth and spilled down her chin.

39

Talim was right. It was delicious. She smiled and, to Talim's delight, said, "It's so good."

Talim then took her to his own garden, of which he was very proud. Interwoven between the green leaves were the warm orange and yellow vegetables of his autumn harvest. He pointed out his squash, pumpkin and marrow, and then reached into the midst of a green tangle to cut an unknown purple vegetable from the vine. He beamed as he showed it to Theo.

"This is our first year with eggplants. The seeds were hard to find. Thought we never would. But then one day Dad met a traveller and he had all kinds of things - eggplant and a special apple variety that we had never heard of before. This is the first crop and it's great. Here, have a feel."

Talim plopped the vegetable into Theo's hands, and she slid her fingers over its round, smooth shape. She loved the waxiness of its skin.

"What is this called again? Eggplant? I've never seen one before."

"Not surprised to hear that. Not everything survived the Great Shift. I still read about things I have yet to find. People don't travel like they used to. Anyway, we were lucky to get these seeds. Oh, for your information, it is also called an aubergine."

Theo had heard of the colour aubergine; it appeared in one of the rare crayon boxes she had as a child. She studied the vegetable's sleek, purple skin and realized this is where the crayon's name originated. She smiled at having made the connection.

But before she could say anything about it, she heard Chester's voice call out from across the garden, "Talim! Theo! Come on, get a move on! I have to take you to school with Kiryana."

Chester came across the quad carrying a khaki jacket which he promptly gave to his son.

Talim whined, "Ah geez, dad! I don't want to go! I have a lot to do today." But Chester cut him off before he could say any more.

"Talim, you are being given the chance of a first-rate education. Don't be so foolish as to pass it up. After that, you can spend the rest of your life doing what you want." To soften the delivery, Chester playfully mussed up Talim's honey-brown hair.

"I still don't want to go. They are all so stuck up and full of themselves," he moaned.

"I know, I know, but just know it won't be forever," Chester smiled patiently. He placed his hands on Talim's shoulder to guide him toward the garden gate. Theo followed, quietly preparing for what was to happen next.

The round, yellow car approached a white coach house which was situated not too far down the lane from the mansion. Chester turned the wheel and took the car up the short drive and stopped in front of a walkway leading to the main door. As soon as the vehicle stopped, Kiryana jumped out and sprang up the steps into the building. She had sat stonily throughout the short drive and ignored all attempts to draw her into the conversation.

"Oh dear," said Chester, "I hope her mood picks up once she is in the classroom. Okay you two, up and at 'em. I'll be back in a few hours to collect you after you're done. Talim, my son, make sure you help Theo get settled. I'm sure she is going to find this arrangement a bit different than what she is accustomed to."

"Okay Dad," replied Talim cheerfully. "I'll do my best. But I'm not sure I understand it either."

Chester chuckled at his comment and said, "I bet that's true. It's a strange arrangement, indeed. Do your best, regardless."

Talim opened his door, and both he and Theo climbed out onto the pavement. Theo stayed close to Talim and waited for his lead. They watched the car pull away, and when it was a good way down the lane, Talim sighed as he turned to go up the steps.

As it was explained to Theo in the car on the way down, Mrs Stokes had employed the great Wilhelmina Van Dorne to help develop Kiryana's gift. Wilhelmina Van Dorne, herself an Oracle, had managed the training program for the postulants at the Temple for decades until she left suddenly a few years back. It was then Mrs Stokes had convinced her to come to the mansion to teach. It was a well-known fact that Mrs Stokes was paying Wilhelmina a fortune for her services. It was also rumoured that Mrs Stokes had given her the coach house to help sweeten the deal. Regardless, she was a very talented educator and guide for the candidates. As a gesture of generosity, Mrs Stokes invited a small group of other hopefuls from the area to train with Kiryana. As well as being an act of generosity, the other students also provided her daughter with an incentive to develop her gift. Talim, and now Theo, were invited along as well to study the non-psychical curriculum as it was just easier to keep all the children in one place. As much as Talim complained about going to school, he knew he was the beneficiary of a great privilege.

Talim and Theo hung their jackets on a coat rack and walked into the classroom. Long tables with wooden chairs faced a podium and whiteboard. Heads of students already seated turned to look at Theo as she came in. She felt a warm heat rush to her face as they studied her.

"I normally sit by myself," said Talim, ignoring the others. "So it will be nice to have someone to keep me company."

Theo nodded in agreement but felt unsettled by all the watchful eyes and private comments flying about. Fortunately, she didn't have much time to worry about them as her attention was drawn to the classroom door.

A woman with dark hair streaked with dense patches of grey rushed into the room in a mad flurry. Wilhelmina Van Dorne had made her entrance. Her straight, solid frame held a deliberate stance and every movement was executed with precision. Her face was sharp and angular, and her dark eyes looked everywhere at once, missing no detail. She was not the type of woman to be ignored and she carried herself with the expectation of being taken seriously.

"Good morning class," she began after arriving at the podium and grasping the edges with her long fingers. "I trust everyone is well?" She briefly looked around the room and opened a ledger and began scanning its pages. "As it is a Saturday, I prefer to keep the lesson light as I don't want to get into anything too deeply today. Does this suit everyone?"

The students mumbled an affirmative which she ignored and continued, "Mr Trask, we have a new student today, yes? Who is with you?"

"Miss, this is Theodora Yates who is Kiryana's cousin. She is staying at the house now," Talim said.

"Ah Miss Yates, yes, yes, we have been expecting you. Some trouble in Kitchie, was it?" Wilhelmina's focused her penetrating gaze on Theo. Suddenly Theo had trouble finding her voice.

"Yes," interjected Kiryana with a tone of disdain, "there was trouble in Kitchie and she couldn't stay there anymore. So now she is our *problem*."

Theo felt bowled over by Kiryana's comment. She had moved to avoid the issue with whatever had happened that night in the quarry and her uncle. It had not occurred to her that she might need to confront the fallout here. Theo felt a sense of panic rise within her and she didn't know what to say.

"Oh dear," said Wilhelmina with a tone of mock concern, "a problem is it? Well, we shall see, shan't we? I am, of course, most interested in what happened that night that caused you to up and leave in such a rush. Do you care to share this with us, Miss Yates?"

All eyes turned to her, but Theo could only shake her head.

"Very well," conceded Wilhelmina, "another time then? My only question is whether or not the same problem will happen here. Is this going to be a concern for us, Miss Yates?"

Finally, Theo found enough wind to speak. "N,n,no, no, no. No, it won't happen here." Again, Theo was baffled by why people held her responsible for something that she had nothing to do with. She couldn't have stopped any of it even if she had tried.

"Good. I'm glad to hear that."

Wilhelmina then smiled in a deliberate way that confused Theo. And without any further fuss, she turned back to the podium and asked the class to pull out their textbook *The Rudimentary Elements of Transmundane Communication*.

"Mr Trask doesn't normally participate in these sessions, Miss Yates. However, you are welcomed to partake if you choose." Again, Wilhelmina's laser-like eyes were boring a hole into Theo.

No one was more surprised by the invitation than Theo. She looked around and saw the astonished faces of the others – Kiryana's, especially. Her eyes first opened wide with surprise but then narrowed with hostility. Theo felt immediately intimidated and shrank back. "No, thank you, Miss. I am to study the non-psychical curriculum like Talim," she replied meekly, sinking into her chair.

Kiryana smiled with satisfaction and flipped her warm-coloured hair over her shoulder as she turned to her own textbook.

"What a pity", said Wilhelmina. "I'm sure there is plenty in this that would hold some interest for you." Wilhelmina had a way of placing extra meaning into every one of her words that suggested more than was said.

"In that case, you may read *To Kill a Mockingbird* with Mr Trask, and we will start there. I will have questions for you on Monday so please read the first ten chapters by then."

Wilhelmina turned her attention back to the rest of the class. She asked a girl called Lauren, a round-faced girl with a slight overbite, to begin reading aloud a passage from their textbook.

Theo went up to the bookcase and found a copy of the novel, dog-eared and faded with use. She returned to the table and opened it to the first page. Talim made a silly face and rolled his eyes from behind his copy. His ability to joke at this moment made her relax a little. Soon enough, the class settled into what they were doing, and Theo started to absorb the words she was reading.

She loved the characters Scout and her brother Jem. She loved how honest and brave they were. She loved the freedom they had to run all over town. But when she started to read about Atticus Finch, and how he was such a good man, talking about how you never really understand a person until you consider things from his point of view-"until you climb into his skin and walk around in it" -that she started to feel a little sad for her loss of parents, her own father, and now her aunt too. She put down the book to escape the world long enough to recover her equilibrium. While doing so, her attention drifted over to the other side of the room and to the lesson there.

"So?" asked Wilhelmina as she moved to the whiteboard, uncapping a black marker. "What is the known hierarchy of transmundane transmissions? Mr Fossen?"

"Animal revelations," said Cory Fossen in a gentle, clear voice, "also plant links." He had a fragile frame with soft, blonde hair that hung over his eyes.

"Yes, that's right. But even more basic than that is the ability to read the vibrational energy of solid objects, rocks and such, as well as the fluid vibrations, from water and rain, and the magnetic currents and ley lines that circulate around the planet. You see, everything possesses energy and all transmundane communication is based on this fact. And so, to simplify things, we shall separate everything into the two categories of animate and inanimate. Let's focus on the animate today."

Wilhelmina wrote the word "Animate" on her whiteboard and wrote "Plant" and "Animal" under the heading.

"Miss Zhu, anything you would like to contribute?"

Elle Zhu was a short girl with a square face and bluntly-cut black hair. She replied quickly and mechanically, "Bio-energists: the ability to diagnose illness and heal the body. Psychic linkers: the ability to read another's thoughts. Signature locators: the ability to find anyone anywhere."

"Yes, very good Miss Zhu, very good," nodded Wilhelmina as she wrote each of the types on the board. To the class she asked, "Is this a complete list of all types of communions? Miss Rossi?"

"No, it's not," replied Caroline Rossi with a tilt of the head. She was a curly-haired brunette with dark, almond-shaped eyes.

"And why not?"

Caroline had to think for a moment and then lit up with a thought, "Well, we haven't mentioned the preeminent class- precognitive seers: the ability to see into the future and transmorgrafiers: the ability to shape any energy into another object."

"Very good, very good," smiled Wilhelmina. "Would we consider them part of the animate class? Miss Bolon?

Lola Bolon grimaced at the question and looked uncertain, "I'm not sure where they fit in the structure." She was a sturdy blonde with prominent cheekbones and a welcoming smile.

"Well, it seems to me you need to do more reading on the subject, Miss Bolan. Anyone else able to answer?" But when no one volunteered, Wilhelmina raised an eyebrow and continued, "They overarch both the animate and inanimate and are very powerful.

And why do we rank them in this way? Why is there a hierarchy to this list? Miss Stokes?"

Kiryana shuffled in her seat before replying with some hesitation, "They are ordered from the common occurrence to the rare."

"Indeed they are, Miss Stokes. The Temple on the Hill fully acknowledges the ability of most people to participate in some type of energetic communication; however, to be able to see into the future, for example, is considered a rare talent. Is this something that can be taught, Miss Stokes?"

Kiryana's shoulders dropped as she quietly replied, "No, it cannot be taught."

Without missing a beat, Wilhelmina carried on, "No, the higher-order transmissions cannot be taught. Either a postulant is receptive or is not. However, there is room for the development of the lower order as students can be trained with time and practice to be effective bio-energists, for example. Anyway, we are learning all the time, are we not?"

And finishing her statement, she turned and focused her crow-like eyes on Theo, who was embarrassed to be caught eavesdropping on the lesson. Then, to Theo's surprise, she said *Please bring me the eraser on the shelf behind you.*

Theo, uncertain of how to respond, hesitated for a moment. But then looking straight into Wilhelmina's fierce eyes knew she couldn't refuse. She jumped to her feet and grabbed the brush and hurried with it to the front of the room. When she arrived, she noticed that everyone was staring strangely at her. When she glanced back at Talim, he too looked surprised.

"What are you doing?!" shouted Kiryana.

Theo looked about in confusion. Then she finally stammered, "You, you asked me to bring you the eraser, Madame Van Dorne."

Wilhelmina put her index finger over her mouth as she studied Theo. Finally, she said with a strange, calm tone. "Did I now?"

Theo stared at her until the penny dropped. She hadn't asked her at all, yet somehow, Theo heard her, like the way she had heard Ceres Theroux the night of the Equinox ceremony. Overwhelmed by what just had happened, she stood frozen, too scared to speak or move.

Finally, Wilhelmina shattered the moment by saying, "Well, well, I think that's more than enough for one day, don't you?" She looked back and forth between Theo and Kiryana. Then she let out a slow sigh.

"Class may end early today." Then without any further ado, she turned away from the podium and sailed out of the room with her long hair fluttering behind her.

Kiryana was the first to jump to her feet. Her body was shaking and her face was red with rage. Theo recognized that look: it was the same as Uncle Ken's from that horrible night.

"What are you doing!" she shrieked. "What game are you playing at!"

Theo was too shocked to reply. She didn't understand what was happening herself.

Kiryana moved in closer and through her clenched jaw said, "Stay away from me, do you hear! I don't want anything to do with you. Why do you have to be here at all!"

She then turned and ran out of the room. The rest of the students gave Theo a dirty look and filed out of the class to find their friend.

Talim bounded up to Theo with a bigger grin than she had ever seen before. He gushed with unabashed joy, "Wow! That was the best day ever!"

Theo just gaped at him and wondered what on earth had just happened.

Chapter Seven

Theo and Talim stepped out of the dim hall of the schoolhouse into the bright light of the midday sun. The rest of the small class were littered about the front-drive waiting for their rides. Since Wilhelmina dismissed the class much earlier than usual, the students had settled in for the wait.

Kiryana was deep in conversation with Cory and Lauren, while Elle, Lola and Caroline were looking at pages in Lola's notebook. No one noticed Theo or Talim as they approached the low wall beside the driveway. Happy to be ignored, the two of them sat down and stretched their heads out with the hope of seeing the familiar bubble car.

Suddenly, the sound of an old-fashioned motor filled the air. From around the bend, a motorbike zoomed into view and skidded to a stop in front of Kiryana and her crew. The driver flipped down the bike stand with his heavy, black boot and turned off the engine. Theo could see that everyone was delighted to see him.

The long frame of the rider, dressed in jeans and a slim-fitting black jacket, stepped off the bike and pulled his helmet off his head. A young man, no more than twenty, shook out his jaw-length hair. He stepped forward and pulled Kiryana to him to kiss her. She smiled warmly and threw her arms around his neck. Theo wondered if this was the first time she had ever seen Kiryana smile.

"Eddie MacAvoy," Talim informed Theo, "yeah, that's the guy she is stuck on. Mrs Stokes hates him. Dad is pretty good about it, as long as it doesn't interfere with her school work. He's okay, really."

Theo couldn't stop staring at Eddie. Like meeting Kiryana for the first time, she was in awe of how good looking he was. And the two of them together, entwined and gooey-eyed, struck her as an overwhelming image of beauty and glamour. She had never seen a couple like them before. Again, Theo felt small and ordinary. She dropped her chin to let her dark hair fall over her eyes as she watched them.

Eddie said a few inaudible words to the group and they all laughed. He then gave the helmet to Kiryana and climbed back onto his bike. Before Kiryana could put the helmet on, Talim called to her, "Dad is expecting you to be here when he gets here!"

"I don't care what he is expecting," she replied tersely as she climbed on the bike behind Eddie. But then she relaxed her voice and added, "Tell Chester I will be home for dinner. Tell him not to worry." She ended the conversation by putting the helmet over her head.

Eddie turned the bike around and slowly rolled down the driveway. Eddie looked over and smiled at Theo, but she was overcome with shyness and couldn't meet his gaze.

"Later Talim," Eddie crooned as he waved goodbye.

"Yeah, see ya, Eddie," replied Talim with his usual unaffected manner, oblivious to how star-struck Theo had become.

"Hey Kiryana, don't forget to let the light show you the way!" shouted Cory.

Kiryana stuck out her tongue and everyone laughed. When Theo looked blankly, Talim quickly explained, "It's the motto for the Oracles. For some reason, these guys think it's funny."

"It's kinda dorky, if you ask me," said Lauren. "But hey, if it helps me with my grades, I'm happy to use it."

When Eddie reached the bottom of the driveway, he hit the gas and let the motorcycle jump forward and sped away.

Theo kicked her legs against the wall as she watched the motorcycle disappear. When she turned her head back to look at Talim, she noticed that the rest of the group had gathered around them.

Cory stepped forward and spoke first, "What was that about in the classroom? What were you doing in there?" Although the questions seemed demanding, his brows were raised with sincere curiosity.

"Um," stammered Theo, "I'm not sure what you mean." She knew very well what he meant but felt strongly it was in her best interest to say nothing.

Cory tilted his head and narrowed his eyes. "Of course you do. When you brought the eraser up to the front - why did you do that?"

But Theo was not going to give in so easily. A part of her understood something was going on but she couldn't trust anyone right now. She shrugged her shoulders and shook her head.

"Come on, Theo," piped in Lauren, "Wilhelmina is always pulling stunts like that. Testing us out of the blue to see what we really can do."

Again Theo shook her head but couldn't meet her eyes. "I don't know what you mean."

Elle shuffled her papers in her notebook which drew Theo's attention. She looked over at the girl, and without knowing why particularly, Theo immediately understood that Elle had heard Wilhelmina's request too. But for reasons unknown to her, Elle said nothing and dropped her eyes back to her books.

At this point Talim decided to pipe up. "Okay guys, back off. If Theo said she didn't do anything, just leave it alone." He paused for a moment then added. "So if Wilhelmina spoke in that way, why didn't any of you hear it?"

Caroline quickly retorted, "Talim, you know why. None of us can hear her voice. And besides, if any of us were to develop it before Kiryana, she would have a fit."

"More importantly," continued Lola, "Mrs Stokes would be furious. I mean, it's great that we can study with Wilhelmina and all that, but we all know once Kiryana is accepted at the Hill, it's all over for us here."

Finally, Elle spoke up, "Yes, I think Mrs Stokes would look very unkindly on anyone doing better than her daughter." She looked meaningfully at Theo. "She has been generous to let us study here, but we all know that it's really about helping Kiryana fulfill the prophecy. Remember what happened to Marley Stark?"

"Oh yeah, Marley Stark, I forgot about her," said Lola, with a hush of the conspiratorial.

"Yeah, Marley Stark," continued Elle, "she was very gifted, outdoing everyone, especially Kiryana. Kiryana hated her and believed she was making her look bad on purpose. And then one day she wasn't there. Gone. Just like that."

"That's right," said Cory. "Kiry hated her and had her mother kick her out." He gave Theo a meaningful look. But whether he was trying to warn her or toy with her, Theo couldn't tell.

"She was a nice girl," said Lola sadly. "It was a bit unfair, really."

"Yeah, it was unfair," said Cory, brushing his hair from his forehead. "Lots of stuff is unfair about the craft. And if Kiryana doesn't develop into an Oracle, I'm sure she will feel that is unfair too."

Caroline continued, "Kiryana is going to be eighteen in a month. There has never been an Oracle who has developed after eighteen. Well, except the Originals. So she and Mrs Stokes must be really worried."

"We all should be worried," interrupted Lauren, "Whether she develops or not." She paused and let the idea hang before continuing. "Whether she develops or not, it will be the end of the schoolhouse by the end of this term. Either she moves on or drops out. The Entrance Exam in a few months will be the last. And after that, I'm sure Mrs Stokes won't feel so charitable anymore."

They all stood in uncomfortable silence until Talim blurted out, "Well, that will suit me just fine! I'm going to be a gardener anyway, and I'll be happy to be rid of all this hocus pocus."

"Ha!" smirked Lauren, "we always knew you didn't belong here, Talim. But for the rest of us, there was hope of doing something with our lives."

"That's why I'm studying hard this term," said Elle. "I plan to pass the Entrance Exam this year."

"Me too," chimed in Lola. "Well, at least I'm going to give it my best effort." And the rest of them all nodded in agreement. Theo noticed they were a few years younger than Kiryana, probably closer to her age, and yet they felt the same pressure.

"I don't know what your plan is," said Cory as he studied Theo carefully, "but I don't think you'll have time to make it work."

Theo, who wasn't sure of what was happening from one day to the next, was certain that she didn't have a plan at all.

Chester picked them up on time and grumbled a little when he discovered that Kiryana had scarpered off with Eddie. After a quick lunch, Talim and Theo were free to do what they wanted until dinner. Of course, Talim wanted to take Theo back to the walled garden. He took great pleasure in showing Theo every nook and cranny. Then he put her to work. They dug out the summer plots and prepared them for the next planting. Theo never gardened before, but she did like the feel of the earth in her hands and the warm sunshine on her back. When the sun lowered beneath the high brick wall, she felt a sense of accomplishment and satisfaction.

Mrs Henderson rang the captain's bell outside of the back door to call everyone in for dinner. By the time Theo and Talim arrived in the kitchen, Chester was already seated, heaping mashed potatoes onto his plate.

"Hurry up and wash your hands or there will be nothing left," he teased. "I'm hungry enough to eat it all!"

"Pshah," scoffed Mrs Henderson as she brought a pan of roast chicken to the table, "why should today be any different than any other day?"

Both of the children ran to the toilet in the adjoining hall and did a quick rinse of their hands. The smell of Mrs Henderson's roast chicken was stirring their appetites and they couldn't get back to the table soon enough. She hovered about them until she had room to stretch in and load a good amount of chicken on their plates.

"Potatoes, dressing, sprouts, carrots and gravy are already on the table. So don't be shy. So you know, Theo, I don't like leftovers." She placed the pan on the island counter and took her place at the head of the table and laid a napkin on her lap. The children hadn't wasted any time and were shovelling food into their mouths as if someone was going to take it away from them. Mrs Henderson leaned back in her chair and surveyed the group with their heads down into their food and tutted with disapproval. "It's like eating with a pack of wolves." She rolled her eyes upwards and started serving herself.

As their bellies filled, everyone started to slow down and look up from their plates. Catching Chester's eye, Mrs Henderson asked about Kiryanna. Chester gave her an exasperated look, and she clamped her lips together to stop from speaking her mind. However, she did ask, "Will she be getting something to eat at least?"

Chester, with his fork still in his mouth, shrugged his shoulders. After swallowing, he replied, "Talim said she'd be home for dinner. She is usually good about saying when she'll be home but it seems as if things are getting worse. It can't be easy for her, though, not with the kind of pressure her mother puts on her. I feel sorry for the girl. But having said that, we can't have her running wild either."

Mrs Henderson turned to face Talim and Theo. "Was Wilhelmina harsher than usual? Did something happen at school today?"

Theo's hand froze in mid-lift. But before she could signal to Talim not to say anything, he blurted, "Wilhelmina was as usual as she can be. But Kiry did get really mad when Theo brought the eraser to the front of class."

"Brought the eraser?" questioned Mrs Henderson as she wrinkled her brow. "Why would Kiryana get upset about that?"

Theo was staring at Talim the whole time willing him to be quiet, but he wasn't paying attention to her cues. Desperate to shut him up, she kicked him under the table.

"Ow!" he yelled, glaring at her. "Why did you do that?"

"What's going on here?" demanded Chester. "Theo, what is it you don't want us to know?" Theo shook her head and stared at her plate.

"Okay then," Chester said with grim authority, "Talim, why did Kiry get upset when Theo brought up the eraser?"

Feeling no loyalty to Theo as he rubbed his shin, he said, "Theo brought up the eraser even though Wilhelmina didn't ask her to. It was all really weird, though, and Wilhelmina dismissed us right afterward. Kiry had a fit."

"Didn't ask her to…" Chester's words tapered off as he absorbed what Talim said. He looked over at Mrs Henderson as she too understood the implication of what was just revealed. She pursed her lips and looked away.

Chester softened his tone considerably and continued, "Theo, honey, did you hear Wilhelmina?"

Theo began to fidget in her seat. She only had been here for two days and she didin't want to give anyone a reason to ask her to leave. She knew she couldn't return to Aunt Georgia's, not how things were with Uncle Ken, and she didn't have any other family. The Stokes were her only chance. She really liked Chester and Mrs Henderson but it was too soon to tell if she could trust them with anything that might upset Mrs Stokes. Goodness knows Kiryana's reaction was worrying enough.

She stammered, unable to look Chester in the eye, "I, I, I must have guessed she wanted it. I didn't mean to upset Kiryana."

Chester studied the girl as she squirmed beneath his gaze. Just as he was about to challenge her, taking in a breath as he opened his mouth, the back door opened and slammed shut. Kiryana rushed in and looked about the room. She seemed genuinely sorry when she realized she had missed dinner.

Mindful of his role as her chaperon, Chester twisted around to fully face her. He said firmly, "Now where have you been, young lady? Am I going to have to let your mother know what you've been up to?"

Kiryana's regret quickly vanished from her face as she looked genuinely wounded. "You wouldn't tell Mother, would you?" she asked. "Chester, I'm sorry I'm late, really I am- just lost track of time. Please don't tell on me, Chester. It won't happen again."

"It better not happen again, Kiry, my love, else I will be forced to talk to your mother. I mean, I can only do so much on my own. Ultimately it's up to your mother to address these things with you."

Kiryana grimaced and shook her head to show she understood. "That's right, that's right. I'm not really your concern, am I? Just another thing you have to take care of here. Well, why don't you save yourself the trouble and go ahead and tell Mother right now and be done with it." She then ran out of the kitchen and slammed the hall door behind her. Everyone, too shocked to say anything, just stared at the closed door.

Mrs Henderson slapped her hands on the table and groaned as she lifted herself to her feet. "Chester, I'll make her a plate of food to take with you so you can smooth things over with her."

Chester sighed as he rose from the table and followed Mrs Henderson to the counter, muttering about teenage girls under his breath. Taking the heaping plate of chicken and potatoes from her, he crossed the kitchen to follow Kiryana to her room.

He turned before leaving and said to Theo and Talim, "No doubt I'll be awhile. Off to bed, you two, and I'll see you in the morning." Then he looked deliberately at Theo and said, "I guess you are off the hook tonight, my dear."

He winked at her as he pushed through the gap in the door. Theo let out a slow sigh of relief as she dug into the piece of apple pie Mrs Henderson had just placed in front of her.

Chapter Eight

Theo yawned as she tried to keep her focus on the math textbook. She was attempting to solve a trigonometry problem but the symbols jumbled around in her head. She glanced over at Talim who was happily scribbling in his notebook. Likely he found some useful information that would further his gardening. Theo marvelled at his single-mindedness and envied his certainty of purpose. She tried to apply the same attitude to her own work but soon had to give in to the fact that today wasn't going to be the day she solved it.

Normally she enjoyed these logical distractions as everything else in her life was so strange and unpredictable. She had settled in quickly enough at school during the past month and applied herself to her lessons. Other than the first day, nothing strange happened again. Theo had developed the habit of making sure Wilhelmina was speaking aloud before responding, but this was unnecessary. Wilhelmina never tried again. Instead, she went along with Theo's wishes to ignore her extrasensory abilities and structured an appropriate non-transmundane curriculum. Every so often Theo's attention would drift across the aisle to the lesson of the day. In it she would find something fascinating and familiar. But every time she looked over, she was caught by Wilhelmina's penetrating eyes and was rattled back to her own work.

Theo knew something was happening to her. She knew that she was developing Oracle traits. Everything she was hearing about in class proved this to her.

Theo's bad dreams were getting worse. They were unlike any she ever had before. They felt less like they belonged to her and her own perception of the world. Instead, she was stepping into someone else's experience, someone else's life. In the dreams, she would see a vague image of someone holding an object. Then a voice would mumble something about knowing everything. Sometimes the words would change; sometimes she could see more of where he was. But every dream she had always ended the same way. The person always died. She couldn't make out his face but she felt instinctively this would be revealed to her in time. Theo wasn't sure why she was having these dreams, or more importantly, what she was supposed to do with this information. She felt uncomfortable about it all and began to dread going to sleep.

Wilhelmina was the person to speak to about all of this. Theo knew it. But for some reason, something was holding her back. Somehow having Clarity seemed wrong. She held a fear inside that everything would fall apart should she admit it. So far, nothing good had come from it. She was afraid of what Kiryana would do once she found out. What would happen to Theo? Where would she live then? Also, it didn't help that Wilhelmina spoke to her harshly, making every conversation an unspoken challenge. It seemed as if Wilhelmina was angry with her, although Theo couldn't figure out why. Theo kept hoping if she denied everything, it would all go away on its own.

Fortunately, Theo's home life was better. It was the safest she had ever felt, despite Aunt Georgia trying her best. Chester, Talim and Mrs Henderson had become her good friends and she loved being with them. Of course, she missed Aunt Georgia all the time but she was relieved to be away from Uncle Ken. Theo felt lucky to have landed where she did and wished it could stay this way all the time. But this happy bubble was not to last. Kiryana's birthday was several weeks away and Mrs Stokes would be returning to the house. She was coming back to plan her daughter's eighteenth birthday party, which was rumoured to be the social event of the season. No doubt, this would change things, and no one, especially Kiryana, seemed to be looking forward to it.

Kiryana continued to be a problem for Theo. She made it very clear that she did not like Theo nor did she want her around. Fortunately, Kiryana didn't spend a lot of time in the kitchen or the common room. For the few meals they shared together, Kiryana maintained a polite détente as long as no one mentioned school.

However, school was a different thing. As soon as Chester dropped the three of them off in the morning, the gloves came off. Kiryana belittled and bullied Theo any chance she could get. Whether the rest of the class felt the same way about Theo as Kiryana, Theo never knew. It didn't matter. As long as Mrs Stokes was the sole benefactor of their education, no one was brave enough to cross her daughter. Theo had knots in her stomach every time she stepped into the classroom. Emma, who seemed to understand what was going on with Theo, tried to be decent to her. But any time Kiryana caught sight of them together, Emma made sure to step away for her own self-preservation. Only

Talim, who didn't give a hoot about his education or what Kiryana thought, did as he liked, and he liked Theo very much. If it wasn't for Talim, Theo didn't think she could have made it through the school day.

"Okay, that's enough for now. Go for lunch and we will continue after."

The morning session was now over. Wilhelmina flew out of the room as if she was being fired from a cannon. No one knew for sure if she ate during the break, or if at all.

Theo put her books in a neat pile on the corner of her desk. She watched the other students file into the break room, chattering as they went. Talim threw his books into his bag and happily swung it over his shoulder. He was leaving before lunch today to help Chester go into Greenstone to pick up some heavy supplies. Theo looked forlornly at him and she wished she could go too.

"Sorry, Theo," said Talim, "it was arranged with Wilhelmina ages ago. I get time off to help Dad with various things. She doesn't seem to mind. Actually, I'm pretty sure she's glad that I'm out of her hair."

"Well, I'm not!" said Theo mournfully. "It's bad enough that you are leaving but do you have to leave before lunch? Who am I going to sit with?"

Talim paused and considered what she said before replying, "Yeah, I forgot I used to eat lunch alone all the time. It's not so bad, really. Just bring a book with you. If you are lucky, they will just ignore you."

"And if I'm unlucky?" she asked tentatively, looking through the doorway to see if she could get a sense of the mood in the other room.

Talim shrugged and said cheerfully, "Chin up, Theo. I'm sure you will be fine. In any case, it's only a half-hour before you are back in class. I'm sure you'll be able to survive a half-hour without me."

Not convinced, she grimly replied, "I'm not so sure."

Theo stood in the doorway of the small break room and spied the little table she and Talim usually shared. Her heart sank when she saw Lola and Emma sitting there, heavily engrossed in a conversation, deliberately ignoring her. Seeing the only available spot was at the end of the long table with the rest of the students, she steeled her nerve and made her way to an empty chair. Sitting only a few spaces away from Kiryana and her friends, she was far enough away to emphasize that she was on her own. She quickly opened a book and began reading as inconspicuously as she could manage. Then she pulled a tomato sandwich out of her bag and began to eat. After taking a few bites of her sandwich, Theo began to relax a little. No one seemed to acknowledge her presence and she was starting to think that lunch would pass quickly without incident. Sadly, this was not going to be the case.

"Hey!" said Caroline. "Aren't we good enough for you?"

Theo glanced up from her book and prepared for the onslaught. Talim was much better at dealing with them than she was, as he had a thicker skin and a better ability to defend himself. She felt very vulnerable without him by her side.

"No, I don't think you aren't good enough for me," Theo replied shakily.

"Then why didn't you sit with us?" continued Caroline, unsuccessfully trying to hide her amusement.

Theo looked into the smirking faces of Caroline, Lauren, Cory and Kiryana. She knew they were setting a trap for her; however, she had no idea of how to avoid it. Not knowing what to say, she just stared blankly at them.

"I mean, come on now," continued Caroline with mock indignation, "you just ran to the table in a way that made us think that you didn't want to sit with us. And we left you a place here." She gestured to the chair that was beside her. "I don't know where you are from, but snubbing people like that is considered rude."

Caroline looked for approval from Kiryana, who deliberately avoided eye contact with Theo. Caroline's grin grew wider as she continued, "I mean the way you ran to your seat, it was like you didn't want to have anything to do with us. And it's weird, because you would think that someone new would try and make more of an effort. Don't you think that's weird, Theo?"

Seeing no other way out of this, Theo hoped that giving her what she wanted would make her stop. "Yes, it's a little weird."

Unfortunately, her acquiescence only fueled the attack. Caroline continued, "A little weird, did you say? No, no, not a little weird. It's really weird. It's really weird that you come in here and just ignored us while sitting at the same table. Where are you from again? The Hinterlands? Don't they have manners where you are from?"

Theo felt unbalanced and unsure of how to deal with this. She had spent most of her life placating her uncle to avoid his outbursts, and generally, this strategy worked. Obviously, things were different with these girls.

"We have manners," Theo replied weakly, trying to get a sense of how to get out of this situation.

"You do, do you?" continued Caroline. "Well then, prove it. What do you do when you offend someone? What would a polite person do?"

Looking around helplessly into their mocking faces, she understood immediately that they were all enjoying it too much to stop. She was at their mercy.

"A polite person would apologize," Theo answered slowly, dreading where this was going.

"That's right. A polite person apologizes. So if you are a polite person, Theo, what should you do?"

All eyes were now on her to see what she would do. Understanding that she was being manoeuvred into this position, she didn't feel the strength to fight them all. Instead, she gave in and replied, "If I offended you, then I am sorry. I didn't mean to."

Caroline flushed with the excitement of her victory and laughed, "Well, I should think so! Imagine any one of us doing that! How rude!"

Then she pulled out the chair beside her. It wasn't an invitation but a command. Theo gathered her book and lunch bag, and made her way over to the chair and sat down. She settled her things again while everyone watched her closely. No sooner had she finished doing so than Kiryana leaned over to Caroline and said, "I don't want her eating with us." Kiryana now turned to look at Theo with venomous glee.

Without missing a beat, Caroline then said, "I'm afraid that Kiryana doesn't want you to sit with us. Would you mind getting up and going back to where you were, please?"

Incredulous that they could be so horrible, Theo slunk out of her chair. Now too much to bear, Theo pushed past the table and raced from the break room. As she ran, she felt the burn of humiliation spread over her face like a brush fire. She was not able to run fast enough to escape the sounds of their laughter. "Hey Theo! Let the light show you the way! The way out, that is!"

Theo ran down the hall into the small cloakroom. She pushed through the coats that hung on a metal rack and collapsed in a heap in the corner. Hidden from view, she allowed the surging emotions to burst through, and her body shook with each sob.

"I hate her! I hate her!" Theo gritted her teeth, face wet with tears. "She is awful!"

Every day Kiryana had found a new way to humiliate her, whether by her own doing or through someone else. How she wanted to scream at Kiryana! What an unfair bully she was! Why was she being so hideous? Try as she might, Theo could not comprehend the reason for Kiryana's cruelty. Was it jealousy? Madness? Frustration? Theo knew she should say something, defend herself, but couldn't find her voice. As soon as she imagined confronting Kiryana, she was immediately reminded of Marley Stark, and how she was mysteriously expelled from the school, sent away and forgotten. And that was enough for Theo to hold her tongue. As much as she hated being tormented by the older girl, Theo was more afraid of being sent away. Again. Chester, Mrs Henderson and Talim had become her new family and her endurance was the price of staying.

"I don't even care about Clarity." Theo's bile tasted harsh and acidic. "Why is it my fault that I have it and she doesn't?" It was true. She didn't care about Clarity, and the more Kiryana tortured her, the more she wished it would go away.

Eventually, she exhausted her tears. She knew she needed to get back to the classroom before they found out she had been crying. But before she could rise to her feet, she heard the sound of footsteps coming in. And more alarming, she heard the door closing.

"Mrs Stokes, this isn't the best time to have this conversation. Perhaps I can schedule a time after class..." Theo recognized Wilhelmina's crisp alto right away.

"No, no Wilhelmina, I'm only here to see you quickly. I must return to Greenstone right away."

"I'm not sure what the urgency and secrecy are about, Mrs Stokes." Theo could hear them cross the room and sit in the chairs beside the clothes rack. Only a curtain of coats separated them, and she pulled herself back farther into the corner and tucked her feet away.

"I'm sorry, Wilhelmina, but I don't want Kiryana to know I'm here. I won't be staying and I would rather avoid a fuss." Wilhelmina replied with something that Theo couldn't hear.

Mrs Stokes continued, "Someone has told me about the Crystal Dragon. I want to know what you thought about it."

Theo heard Wilhelmina rise to her feet and start pacing back and forth. Theo quickly realized this was the real reason they needed privacy.

Finally, Wilhelmina spoke, "I don't think it's a good idea to discuss it. It would be best if you just left now, Mrs Stokes." Even from the safety of her hiding place, Theo winced from the gravity of Wilhelmina's full authority.

Not to be put off so easily, Mrs Stokes continued, "No, no, I'm afraid I need to know what it's all about. Someone told me that it might help Kiryana shift into her Clarity."

Wilhelmina stopped pacing. She then demanded, "Who told you that?" When Mrs Stokes refused to answer, Wilhelmina continued, "The Crystal Dragon won't help anyone, let me assure you of that. It was constructed from the depths of Orfeo Cotswold's demented mind."

"So it exists?"

Wilhelmina sighed. "Yes, it *did*. But it disappeared within the Appal Mountains. That was forty years ago."

"Did you say the Appal Mountains?"

"Yes. This is what the legend says."

"Did you see it work, Wilhelmina?"

Wilhelmina paused a long while before she spoke. "I don't like talking about that time, Mrs Stokes. You know that."

"I know you find it difficult to speak about the man who betrayed you all. But I'm afraid I need to insist upon knowing about the Crystal Dragon - for Kiryana's sake." Something in Mrs Stokes was revealed at the moment.

Wilhelmina returned to her chair and sat down. "Did you ever meet Orfeo Cotswold, Mrs Stokes?"

"I was very young when he was arrested, but I remember the day he vanished from court."

"Yes, he vanished into thin air. He had been doing all sorts of strange experiments with his Clarity. He was trying to figure out how to manipulate the material world. When they discovered his laboratory, they found all sorts of horrible things. You see, all his actions from that time were the product of his madness. The Crystal Dragon was one of them."

Ignoring the warning, Mrs Stokes pressed on. "I understand the Crystal Dragon would open the channel of Clarity for whoever held it. Is this true?"

Wilhelmina stayed quiet.

"Well? Is it true?" Mrs Stokes would not be put off.

Finally, Wilhelmina relented. "Yes, it is true."

"So you saw it work? You saw it yourself?"

"Yes. I saw people pick it up and then have Clarity open up within them. Orfeo somehow put some of his power into the crystal and made it so it would transfer to whomever held it."

Now Mrs Stokes got up and started pacing. "So it is possible to transfer Clarity to someone else?"

"I should be clear, Mrs Stokes, that it is not possible to transfer power to someone else."

"Then what about the Crystal Dragon?" insisted Mrs Stokes.

"Again, that was a product of a mad man's mind. It worked, but only for a moment. You should know that everyone who held it died soon after."

"Died?"

"Yes, they all died. It was part of Orfeo's cruel experiment."

Mrs Stokes stopped pacing. "But what if we figure out a way to harness it? Keep the person safe?"

Theo heard Wilhelmina gasp. "Mrs Stokes, you cannot harness madness. It will drag you in, I assure you. Besides, the Crystal Dragon has been lost for decades. It is mostly a legend these days."

Something in Mrs Stokes voice fell when she asked, "So there is no other way of giving someone Clarity?"

Wilhelmina was firm. "No. There isn't. Either one is receptive or is not."

Theo had heard her say this so many times in class. Everyone knew, including Kiryana, that when Wilhelmina said it, she said it for her.

After a long pause, Mrs Stokes asked, "Do you think Lilith Crowe was lying?"

Wilhelmina was quick to reply, "No, I don't. It wasn't in her nature to give false information. There is no reason I can think of that would make her lie to you. I was there. I saw her give the prophecy."

"Then why hasn't Kiryana's Clarity developed?" Even behind the coats, Theo could tell Mrs Stokes was desperate.

"I don't know. I can't answer that."

"So? It is hopeless then?"

"I wouldn't say hopeless. I just would say uncertain. I knew Lilith Crowe well enough not to discount the possibility. But I don't know how or when. I can't see Kiryana's future."

"So what do we do?"

"Carry on as before, and hope that something opens in her soon. I will go to the Hill and see about the device. They don't let it travel, but they owe me. Then we will see. But after the next Entrance Exam, I'm afraid the Hill won't accept her candidacy any longer."

Mrs Stokes mumbled something which Theo couldn't hear. Then Wilhelmina said, "Mrs Stokes, if you wish your visit to remain unknown, I would suggest leaving now. The students will finish lunch very soon."

Mrs Stokes cleared her throat before saying, "Yes, I suppose I should be on my way. I'd like to see you when I'm back in a few weeks."

"Of course. Whatever you like."

Then the women moved toward the door and Theo couldn't hear any more. Once they left, she unfurled her body and quickly escaped out of the room.

Chapter Nine

Theo came into the kitchen and saw the envelope on the edge of the kitchen island. She immediately recognized the handwriting. She rushed past Mrs Henderson and scooped up the precious letter and pressed it to her chest with joy. It was from Aunt Georgia.

Mrs Henderson watched Theo with concern. Although she was happy that Aunt Georgia stayed in touch, she had seen the pattern often enough to know that Theo's euphoria would soon dissipate into melancholy, when she was once again reminded of their separation. Mrs Henderson had even considered hiding the letters from Theo, especially after the first one had brought on a crying jag that lasted for days. However, she was too aware of the greater harm in keeping them from Theo. She knew it was important for the girl to know she was still loved and missed.

Mrs Henderson sighed and said, "Now try and keep it in perspective this time, honey. Try not to get too upset."

But Theo didn't hear her as she hurried out through the back door. She was too absorbed in her excitement to care about anything else. All she wanted to do was find a private place to go and drink in all the wonderful things she would find inside the envelope.

She decided to go to the walled garden, now a favourite place. Both Talim and Chester had gone into town on a quick errand so it would be quiet. Although they had invited Theo to come with them like she usually did, today she had a sense that a letter would be waiting for her. Premonitions were happening more and more as her intuition was growing stronger.

Theo stepped out into the dingy November afternoon. With only an hour or so of light remaining, she didn't have much time before dark. The small, pale sun already hung low in the sky, and its anaemic light barely passed through the empty branches of the trees. Patches of frost covered the shaded areas of the lawn, and Theo's breathe formed long, cloudy funnels. Snow was on the way.

She skipped down the stone path to the walled garden, knowing the way only too well. She smelled pinewood smoke from the fires that had been burning all afternoon. She knew that Chester had lit the small stone ovens in the alley to heat the stone walls to protect the plants from the cold. Theo smiled. She looked forward to the warmth that would be waiting for her there.

Theo walked through the arch and sighed as she stepped into the lush environment. She still marvelled at how Chester and Talim were able to preserve the growing season as long as they did with their own special form of magic. Although there were fewer flowers than a month before, many of the trees were still green and full, growing fruit and nuts. Theo walked across the quad over to the north-facing wall, and sure enough, the fires from the other side had warmed the bricks with reassuring heat.

A mortar greenman, a wild man with leaves and flowers for hair, welcomed her with his stony stare. The ancient symbol of peace adorned the wall and faced into a trellised arch of twining grapevines. She pulled up a nearby metal chair, slightly cool to the touch, and settled in to savour the news from her aunt. Under the canopy of verdant leaves, she felt nicely cozy and secure.

Aunt Georgia had been writing to Theo ever since she left. At first she was receiving letters every few days but now they had reduced to one every week or so. Theo had been writing back to say she was okay and tell her aunt what she was doing. Of what was happening to her and the stranger changes she was experiencing, however, Theo said nothing.

Theo studied Aunt Georgia's small, tidy handwriting. All her lines were uniform in height and width. Theo's own letters were more scribble than writing, with many alterations to thoughts and words. She wondered how Aunt Georgia could craft such perfection. Then Theo realized that in Aunt Georgia's world, sadly, there wasn't much room for mistakes.

Dear Theo,

First things first —I miss you terribly. It's so awful without you, and I wish you could come back. I wish I could do more for you, too. The house is so empty without you. Your Uncle Ken is keeping to himself. I guess he knows I am still mad at him for making you go. I think he hoped it would make things better between us, but it has made everything worse. I don't like to be forced into things. Neither did your mother. And for that, I am glad you don't have to suffer his temper anymore. Also, I am glad that you are going to a good school. But it's not the same without you here. I hope I can come down and visit you at the Stokes but I don't know how to arrange it without causing a big fuss. I'll see. Take care and write soon!

Aunt Georgia xo

Theo let the letter sink into her lap as she considered its contents. Did she miss her aunt? So much that every part of her body hurt. She thought of Aunt Georgia every day and wished things could be different. Theo was still reeling from the injustice of it all. Why should she have to be uprooted from the only home she ever knew and be accused of things she didn't understand? Try as she might, she could not wrap her head around why Uncle Ken hated her so much. Aunt Georgia seemed to be suffering too, which gave Theo a sadness so pervasive it followed her like fog. Theo wished she knew how to make things better for the both of them.

Was Theo going to a good school? She supposed she was learning lots of new things, well above the grade she would have attended in Kitchie. However, the experience of trying to keep up with the work and keep down the suspicion of her emerging abilities was exhausting. Every night she fell into bed and prayed for a dreamless sleep. Some nights she was lucky, some not so much.

On top of everything, the weird dreams were happening more often. They were getting more vivid, with even greater details and stronger physical sensations, as if Theo was there, standing beside the phantom figure. So many nights she saw this person at the edge of a precipice. Then she would see him fall. Still, she couldn't tell the identity of the person nor alter the outcome of his inevitable death. It was so confusing. Worse, she still believed there was no one she could trust with this information. It would be unbearable if anyone else looked at her the way Uncle Ken did. Theo was convinced that secrecy was her best protection.

Sitting there with her thoughts, she didn't notice two figures enter the garden. and approach the water fountain within the centre of the quad. It was Kiryana and Eddie holding hands. Immediately, Theo dropped to the ground and crouched into the vines. She peeked through the leaves and saw them looking around to see if anyone else was there. Fortunately, they couldn't see her. Satisfied that they were alone, they cuddled up on the smooth, stone lip of the fountain.

Theo cursed at being caught there. She dreaded what Kiryana might do if she discovered her. She had been particularly horrible at school today, and Theo didn't want another encounter. Trapped as she was, she could do little other than stay put and wait it out.

"Isn't Chester around?" Eddie asked with his deep voice. He looked into Kiryana's face and brushed some hair from her forehead.

"No," she sighed as she leaned into him, "no, they are in town picking up groceries. They won't be back until dinner."

Eddie took that as a cue and drew Kiryana into him and kissed her.

Slowly, Kiryana pulled away and said, "My mother will be home in a few days…" Although her voice was low, the sound of it carried easily within the garden.

"Great," Eddie said unhappily, running his hands through his thick hair, "I wonder what new reason she will use to get rid of me this time."

Kiryana looked away and then said flatly, "She won't need a new reason. She has already told me I only have until my eighteenth birthday, then I have to end it."

Eddie, visibly scared by what she said, looked her full in the face and asked, "And? Are you going to do that?"

She shrugged and shook her head, "I don't know. I guess I was hoping for… hoping for something. I thought maybe that things would change, and wouldn't matter about you and me. I don't know, really."

Theo could hear the sadness in her voice. Despite how awful Kiryana had been to her, Theo was surprised that she felt a little sorry for the older girl.

"Kiry, you turn eighteen in two weeks. Are you telling me that you want to break up with me?" Eddie's speech faltered with emotion.

Kiryana turned to face him and said earnestly, "No, no, no - I don't want to end it. But I know how Mother will be, and she will demand that I will do as she planned. By the time I take the Entrance Exam at the end of term, I am expected to step into the life of an Oracle, first class."

"And what about me?" he said as he searched her eyes. "What about us?"

Kiryana couldn't hold his gaze and dropped her chin to her chest. "Being an Oracle is a vocation, a great privilege but there are certain sacrifices…"

Eddie jumped up and walked away from her a few feet before spinning around to face her again. From Theo's vantage point, she had a clear view of him. Every time she looked at the boy, she was struck by how good-looking he was.

"Please spare me your mother's crap," he said angrily. "I know how much being an Oracle really means to you. For goodness sake, Kiry, I know how you truly feel about the whole thing, and how miserable you are about it."

"I'm miserable only because the Clarity hasn't shown up yet! It would be a great honour to serve on the Hill. I worry about it all the time! I worry that it won't happen. I'm afraid of disappointing Mother and Father. I'm afraid of becoming the idiot that couldn't make her own destiny come true!"

Eddie took her hands into his. "There are many, many worse things than not being an Oracle, Kiry."

"Well, not for me there isn't!" she snapped, throwing his hands off. "It has been prophesized since my childhood. Since my childhood! I have spent my whole life preparing for it and everyone expects it. Everyone!!"

Undeterred by her anger, Eddie took her hands again. "Kiry, I don't expect it. I never have. From the first moment I saw you, I knew that you were meant for me. I felt it right away. And you were horrible to me for a long time but that didn't stop, did it? Because I knew, and besides, who can resist me?" He flashed a killer smile at which Kiryana rolled her eyes and huffed with mock disgust.

"You see?" he laughed. "That's why all the girls love me." Kiryana huffed again but with real disgust this time. This only made Eddie smile more. His face became serious as he continued, "Kiry, if you don't accept that we are meant to be together, I don't know what I'll do. And I'm not saying that in a jerk-kind-of-way, I mean, I really don't know how I will get over you and ever have a normal life again. It's like I got the inside information on something I wasn't supposed to know until much later on, and now that I know it, I can't unknow it. You get what I mean? Everything about us being together makes sense to me. I know you feel it too."

Eddie paused and searched Kiryana's eyes for some recognition of what he was saying. But Kiryana, overcome with emotion, could only shake her head. She wasn't able to speak.

Eddie, sensing the weakness of her resolve, moved in closer and continued, "Kiry, I love you. I love you more and more each day, which surprises me all the time, because when I think I've reached the top of it, there is always more to come. I don't say any of this just to say it because I really get the seriousness of it all, but I feel, no, I know, that you are my life. Couldn't you consider me your destiny instead?"

Too overwhelmed to reply, Kiryana let Eddie's hands slip out of hers and stood up. She started walking toward the place where Theo was hiding, which caused Theo to go into a mild panic. Goodness knows what Kiryana would do if she knew Theo was eavesdropping on this very private conversation. She held her breath, frozen to the spot. Kiryana came close enough that Theo could see the tears running down her cousin's face.

Eddie, instinctively aware that he was fighting for his life, followed behind and wrapped his arms around Kiryana. Theo winced as she grappled with the growing precariousness of her situation.

Then, all of a sudden, her left leg began to cramp from the pressure of crouching for so long. It had been growing tired for a while, and now it refused to be ignored. Theo groaned silently and bit her lip.

Fortunately, Eddie took Kiryana's hand and led her back to the water fountain. Theo waited on their return in agony. She decided that she would relieve the pressure on her leg as soon as they began speaking again, to cover up any unintended noises.

Finally, after what seemed like an eternity, Kiryana said, "Eddie, I do love you. I do. To think of not seeing you again, it's all too unbearable. I can't even believe it's going to happen. But my life isn't my own, and I have promises to keep…"

Theo finally shifted her weight but overcompensated and lost her balance. Her hand hit the soft earth with a dull *splat*, not particularly loud, but deafening in Theo's ear. Kiryana turned her head toward the vine leaves hiding the younger girl.

"Did you hear something?" asked Kiryana, tilting her head with mild interest.

Eddie shook his head, "No, not really, but I wouldn't be surprised if there wasn't some silly squirrel in the bushes."

Thankfully, Kiryana was satisfied with Eddie's explanation. When she turned her attention back to him, Theo let out a quiet sigh of relief.

Kiryana opened her mouth to speak again, but this time she was interrupted by the sound of voices approaching from the other end of the quad. Chester and Talim turned the corner, carrying tools they had just bought in town. Both of them stopped dead in their tracks when they saw Kiryana and Eddie sitting on the water fountain.

"You, you are back early," stammered Kiryana, slightly embarrassed to be caught.

Chester angled his head to one side as he studied the couple. He then said without his usual humour, "So it appears- might be a good thing that we did too." He eyed Eddie up and down to emphasize his point.

Eddie said as pleasantly as he could, "Hello Chester, Talim, I was just leaving anyway."

He stood up and kissed Kiryana goodbye in a way to lay claim to his girlfriend, ignoring Chester's scowl. He then strode leisurely across the quad with Chester glaring at him the whole time.

With Eddie gone, Chester turned back to Kiryana and asked, "Are you okay, Missy?"

Overwhelmed with too many conflicting emotions, Kiryana took the opportunity to vent them all on Chester.

"Why would you care how I'm feeling!!!" She then stormed to the other side of the quad.

Once she was gone, Chester said, "Yep, she's fine. Everything's normal. Okay, Talim, m'lad, can you put the new tools in the shed, please?"

Talim, happy to oblige, bounded over to the shed. Returning back, he passed the entrance of the arched trellis and saw Theo. She was now sitting awkwardly on her side, holding her finger to her mouth in a silent plea for Talim not to reveal her. Talim looked at Theo for a second or two, shrugged his shoulders willingly enough, and continued on his way, no questions asked.

"Okay, Dad," Talim said cheerfully. "Let's do this later. I have something to show you."

Chester agreed, and the two of them followed Kiryana's trail back to the house. Theo waited a good five minutes before she felt safe enough to climb out of her hiding place and slink out of the garden.

Chapter Ten

Theo sat at her pale, wooden desk finishing off the last of her homework. Just as she dotted the period in the last sentence of her history essay, she heard Mrs Henderson call from the kitchen to come for dinner.

"Perfect," thought Theo, "finished just in time. Now I have tomorrow free to do whatever I want."

She turned her head to eye with longing a tattered copy of the novel *Anne of Green Gables*. She found it on one of the shelves in a spare bedroom within the guest wing. She didn't often leave the informal quarters as she found the rest of the house empty and foreboding. Every now and then, however, she made her way into the larger rooms and found many interesting and delightful treasures. Still, she was relieved she didn't sleep there. Despite how awful Kiryana was to Theo, she felt badly for the older girl having to stay in a room in the front of the house all by herself.

Theo pushed her chair back and tidied the surface of her desk. She looked around her room and took in the change since her arrival a few months back. Still small and odd in shape, the place now had a totally new look. Pictures hung on the wall and artifacts, found on her many rambles through the woods with Talim, adorned every empty space. Mrs Henderson had allowed her to pick a fabric for curtains and a duvet cover, and the royal blue material calmed the starkness of the white walls and bare floor. Chester had hauled up a petite armchair, which fitted Theo perfectly. It was nestled under the low ceiling in the corner of the room. It had become a favourite nook to escape the pressures of the day, and there she spent hours reading and thinking. Overall, the room had been transformed into a warm and quirky hideaway, reflecting the taste of the young lady who lived within it. If she wasn't here, she probably wasn't in the house at all.

Theo stomped down the stairs on her clumsy, coltish legs and landed at the base of stairs with a thud. "Like a herd of elephants," came Mrs Henderson's usual comment. "It is unbelievable that a slip of a girl like you could be so noisy."

Theo shrugged and hurried to her place at the table, hungry and looking forward to the stew she could smell simmering all afternoon. Talim and Chester, already in their places, stopped talking and stared at her until Theo realized they were trying to make a point.

"What?" she finally asked.

"Um, Theo, honey," said Chester, "Mrs Stokes is home today."

Theo did recall hearing an unusual amount of commotion in the house that day but didn't think anything of it. "So?" she asked, "What of it?"

"Theo, sweetie," replied Chester gently, "Mrs Stokes is eating in the dining room with Kiryana. And as their cousin, Mrs Stokes expects you to dine with them."

All good feelings from the day disappeared in a flash. Theo felt her stomach fall to the floor.

"Oh Chester," she pleaded as the colour drained from her face, "couldn't I just stay in the kitchen with you? I'm sure they won't miss me. Oh please, don't make me go!"

Chester sighed. He understood Theo's reluctance but knew she had to eat with his employer. "Theo, honey, Mrs Stokes specifically requested you join them. I'm afraid you'll have to go." He couldn't help but see Theo's distress, so he tried to say something to help steady the girl, "She is asking you to eat with them as a gesture of belonging, honey. She sees you as one of the family. I'm sure it will be fine. Don't worry."

As Theo realized there was no way out of it, she felt the wind leave her. With a small voice she said, "But Kiryana hates me. And I'm sure Mrs Stokes hates me too."

Chester, fully aware of the tension between the girls, replied as steadily as he could, "Kiryana doesn't hate you. She is just really frustrated, and I'm afraid she is taking it out on you. As for Mrs Stokes, well, that woman does only what she wants. She wouldn't have asked you to dinner if she didn't want you there. Come on girl, buck yourself up. There is no way around it, so you might as well make the best of it."

Chester got up and went over to Theo and pulled her chair away from the table. He took her limp hand in his and gently pulled her to her feet. As they crossed the floor to the hall door, Theo looked back at Talim and Mrs Henderson and took comfort in the fact that they looked sorry for her too.

Theo followed Chester along the same route they took the first time she met Mrs Stokes. Unlike that time, she had a good idea of what to expect which made this trip worse. Chester kept squeezing her hand to show his support; however, there was nothing he could do to alleviate her dread.

Once they reached the foyer, they crossed the marble floor and went to the large, double oak doors that led into the dining room. As they crossed the threshold, Chester winked at her, in his usual fashion, to help raise her spirits. Although grateful for the gesture, it didn't help at all.

"Good evening, Mrs Stokes, Kiryana," Chester's voice rang out clearly, "and here she is." Chester pulled Theo forward and let go of her hand.

"Well, well, well," smiled Mrs Stokes with her perfectly even teeth. Even within her own home, dining with her only daughter, she had dressed impeccably in a blood-red suit. Her platinum hair was loose but styled in gentle waves, matching the elegance of her attire. Theo was struck by Mrs Stokes' glamour and became acutely aware of how shabby she was.

"Hello, Theo, my darling. Here, come and give me a kiss. It's been awhile."

Baffled by her request, Theo glanced back at Chester for guidance. Chester nodded and pointed to Mrs Stokes. Theo stumbled a little as she made her way over and placed a quick peck on the woman's cool and polished cheek. Then she returned to where she was standing before, which was as near to Chester as possible.

"And don't forget Kiryana," said Mrs Stokes with her smooth, commanding voice. "Don't forget to kiss your cousin hello too."

Up until this point, Kiryana had been playing with her fork, ignoring Theo. She looked over at her mother with a silent plea but Mrs Stokes didn't relent and continued, "Yes, it would be good for the two of you to say hello too. In fact, I insist."

Theo froze to the spot. Chester nudged her gently on the shoulder and she made her way around the head of the table to where Kiryana was sitting. As Theo cautiously approached, Kiryana narrowed her icy eyes and clamped her mouth tight. When Theo kissed her cousin's flexed cheek, Theo thought that Chester was wrong - Kiryana most certainly hated her.

"Well, nicely done, girls. Here have a seat, Theo, darling."

Mrs Stokes pointed to a place setting on the other side of her. Theo slipped into her chair and looked across the table at Kiryana, who was now glaring openly at her.

"All right, Chester," continued Mrs Stokes with a wave of her hand, "you may tell Mrs Henderson that we are ready to start." Chester nodded, and after a final glance around the table, he shook his head soberly as he left the room.

Dinner proceeded uneventfully enough. Mrs Stokes was an accomplished politician and was adept at entertaining guests. She did most of the talking, much to Theo's relief, and spoke about events and people Theo knew very little about. Once it became apparent to Theo that Mrs Stokes wanted an audience, not a conversation, she relaxed a little and focused on eating her food as neatly as possible. Even Kiryana put away her claws and settled down to eat her dinner, chiming in every now and then. Once Mrs Henderson brought the apple crumble for dessert, Theo was beginning to believe she would be finished and be back in her room in no time.

"So enough about what I've been doing," said Mrs Stokes, taking a sip of her coffee and looking over the cup's edge into Theo's face. "What has been going on here while I've been away?"

Theo had just taken a bite of her apple crumble and had to chew and swallow quickly before she could answer, "Going on? I'm not sure what you mean."

"Oh, you know, what you have been doing while I've been away? I see so little of you and Kiryana hardly mentions you on our nightly calls, so I'm just wondering how you are settling in. What has been going on since I last saw you?" Mrs Stokes was studying Theo's face with such intensity that she was starting to feel warm from the attention.

Theo couldn't help but glance over at Kiryana who now looked nervous. Although Theo had no reason to protect her, she knew instinctively that the least said, the better. She cleared her throat and replied, "Oh well, I spend a lot of time with Talim in the walled garden. And school is busy."

"Ah school." And like a cat pouncing on a fat mouse, Mrs Stokes jumped in now the subject of school was introduced. Kiryana sighed and squared herself for the inevitable onslaught.

Mrs Stokes cooed. "I was wondering when Kiryana was going to bring it up. But she never does. She never likes to talk about school, do you, darling?" Kiryana's sullen face was the answer to her question.

"So school is busy, is it?" continued Mrs Stokes. "And what programme are you doing, sweetheart?" The endearment felt foreign and forced, and it landed with a thud in Theo's ear. "Are you and Kiryana studying the same material?"

Before Theo could answer, Kiryana interjected shrilly, "No Mother, she is not. But you knew that already, didn't you?"

Mrs Stokes raised an eyebrow and smiled coolly. "Oh Kiryana, darling, I'm just making conversation. It's so rare I get to speak to anyone from your school. I just want to know if she is enjoying it as much as you are." Kiryana cringed from the dig but said nothing.

"So," continued Mrs Stokes undeterred, "are you enjoying school? Are you working hard? How is Wilhelmina as a teacher?"

Theo thought for a moment, and the questions seemed harmless enough, so she replied, "I do like school, ma'am. And we have to work hard to keep up with the lessons, so I guess I am working hard. Wilhelmina is a good teacher. She knows a lot."

"Does she now?" mused Mrs Stokes. "Do you think she knows more than most people? More than Chester? Mrs Henderson? Me, for example?"

"Um," stammered Theo, a little taken aback by the questions, "I'm sure you know a lot, but Wilhelmina is very knowledgeable about all the subjects she teaches, if that's what you mean."

"Well, yes," replied Mrs Stokes, frowning at Theo's comment. She wasn't pleased to hear what Theo had said. "But do you think Wilhelmina can make mistakes? That perhaps not all things unfold the way she sees it. Perhaps, she is not, as she thinks, the final say in all matters!" Mrs Stokes' voice raised until it strained. Theo, confused by her reaction, was too scared to say anything else.

Mrs Stokes got up from her chair and began pacing. Finally, she stopped and faced Theo again. "You see, my dear, Wilhelmina cannot be so knowledgeable if she cannot see that Kiryana will be the next great Oracle of our time. What kind of Seer is she if she can't predict my daughter's great future?"

Again, Theo was baffled by Mrs Stokes' comments and just stared blankly at her. Mrs Stokes studied Theo for a moment then rolled her eyes. She picked up the silver coffee pot and poured herself another cup and returned to her seat.

"So Theo, my darling," continued Mrs Stokes, now modulating her voice back to its usual honeyed tone, "it appears we have a problem, or a puzzle, if you will. Are you good at puzzles, my dear? Yes? Well, let's see, shall we?" She paused for a moment to take a sip of her coffee, leaving a slight trace of her blood-red lipstick on the porcelain cup.

"As you know, the great Lilith Crowe, the great precognitive Oracle predicted that my daughter, Kiryana, would emerge as a great talent. She said she would have Clarity, and this Clarity would show a great truth. Even though these predictions can be vague, it has been interpreted by many, many experts that she was foretelling a great gift for Kiryana. So here is the puzzle: why hasn't this gift, which has been depicted so clearly, not shown any signs of arriving? It is a poser, is it not, Theo darling - a real brain teaser." She glanced sidelong at her daughter who was staring grim-faced into the air in front of her.

Mrs Stokes continued, "What can the problem be? Why isn't Clarity emerging? Is Kiryana studying hard enough, do you think?"

Theo nodded. She had the horrible feeling that she was walking into a trap. Although she owed her cousin no favours, Theo would rather be left out of this conversation altogether. Kiryana continued to sit silently and refused to look at anyone.

"Yes, she is studying then. Well, that's good, I guess. But we both know that studying is not enough for this, now is it? No, no, no - I would imagine that Kiryana is distracted from her real purpose. Yes, I would think that something else has her attention."

Despite herself, Theo looked over at Kiryana and recalled her encounter in the garden with Eddie. Unfortunately for Theo, Mrs Stokes was an expert at reading people and saw that she had hit upon something.

"Yes," said Mrs Stokes knowingly, "something else has her attention, indeed."

"Theo, darling," said Mrs Stokes brightly, now changing gears, "are you aware we are holding a party for Kiryana in a few weeks? It's her birthday, you know. She will be eighteen. Such a grand age, truly. Are you further aware that a few weeks after that, the examiners from the Hill will be coming to your school to test for admission to the Academy? Such a busy and exciting time, is it not? It seems like this has been happening for years – her party followed by an Entrance Exam. How funny. Sadly though, this will be Kiryana's last exam, her last chance, as they don't test girls over the age of eighteen. As it was, I had to pull every last one of my strings to get her into this one. It would appear that by her next birthday, she will be too old to be considered a serious candidate. How funny: too old at eighteen."

But no one was laughing, least of all Kiryana, who sank lower into her chair.

"Well, Theo, this is a puzzle, is it not? How do we help Kiryana achieve her true potential, her destiny that was foretold all those years ago?" She paused and took another sip of her drink. Theo braced for what she was going to say next.

"Yes, something is interfering with her progress, and this obstacle must be removed, don't you think, Theo? Yes? You do?" Despite what Mrs Stokes was saying, Theo was not agreeing with her and was sitting perfectly still. Not that this mattered.

Mrs Stokes then looked over to her daughter, who was gripping the arms of her chair. Ignoring her discomfort, Mrs Stokes announced, "I'm afraid we will have to give up the distraction sooner than we agreed, my love. Even your cousin, Theo, can see how it is affecting you." Theo shook her head in disagreement but no one was looking at her.

"Mother," pleaded Kiryana, eyes brimming with tears, "please not yet! I can't give *him* up yet!"

But Mrs Stokes was unmoved. "I'm afraid I've been a little too indulgent with you, Kiryana. Giving you what you wanted may not have been the best thing for you in the end. I had believed this crush with this boy was just a phase and that you'd move on quickly enough once your Clarity developed. But we are down to the final days, my dear, and I cannot accept failure in this regard. I cannot. Everything that I've done up to now has been to secure this future for you - everything! And the best thing I can do for you now is to help you see this through."

Kiryana began to shake her head wildly to block out what her mother was about to say.

"You must end it with that boy today, right now. You cannot see him anymore, Kiryana. It's over between the two of you."

Kiryana sobbed as she grabbed her mother's hand. "Please Mother, don't be so cruel. Please don't make me give him up. I love him so much!"

"Yes, I can see that you do," Mrs Stokes replied coldly. "Perhaps this correction is a little too late but it must be!"

"Mother, please!" she begged, tears streaming down her face.

But Mrs Stokes took her hand away and rose to her feet, pulling herself up into her full power. "No Kiryana, I will not give in on this. You are never to see that boy again. And I will stay in this house with you to make sure that you don't."

Kiryana dropped her head into the crook of her arm and her shoulders shook with deep sobs. Mrs Stokes placed a hand on Theo's shoulder to pull her up from her chair and firmly pointed her toward the doors.

Relieved to be released from the scene, Theo hurried from the room. Glancing back, she drew in the last image of Mrs Stokes standing over a shattered Kiryana as the heavy doors closed.

Chapter Eleven

The mood of the house changed dramatically after Mrs Stokes returned. Kiryana was withdrawn most of the time yet ready to explode at any given moment. Theo walked on eggshells and did her best to avoid the older girl. Chester, Mrs Henderson and Talim carried on as usual but they felt the strain too. Mrs Stokes kept herself exceedingly busy and took calls and visitors in the Morning Room. Transferring her business from her office in Greenstone to her house didn't affect her schedule at all. Her day began early and she worked late into the evening. She did, however, make time for meals, and Theo now dined with Mrs Stokes and Kiryana every night, a daily ritual Theo dreaded. Chester knew this, but Mrs Stokes refused to change this arrangement, despite his best effort.

Invariably there would be some disruption during the dinners together as Kiryana and her mother fought constantly. Theo did her best to stay out of it, however, Mrs Stokes always managed to draw her in to undermine Kiryana's position. Although it was not of Theo's doing, Kiryana made sure to return each slight with greater ferocity the next day at school. If Kiryana was miserable, she made sure that she would not suffer alone.

Theo sat at her desk in the schoolroom, resting her head on her hands. Her small features were sharper than usual, and dark circles stained the skin under her massive eyes, making them look impossibly large. Theo was sleeping poorly and losing weight. The stress of having dinner with Mrs Stokes and Kiryana made it difficult for her to eat, then the anticipation of the next day's retribution kept her sleepless with worry. Chester did his best to try and ease Theo's mind, and Mrs Henderson made all of Theo's favourite meals, but it did little to ease her anxiety. On top of it all, when she slept, the strange dreams came, and they came often.

School had changed as well. Focus now shifted from the theoretical to the practical. Theo and Talim's non-transmundane curriculum was abandoned entirely, and they were left to read on their own. Now, Wilhelmina's full attention was spent on Kiryana. The teacher spent day after day trying to show the girl how to shift her perspective into Clarity, repeating the same exercises over and over. Although unsuccessful with Kiryana, Emma responded well, while others began showing the promise of lesser ability.

Each day, Wilhelmina began the lesson with the same routine, ignoring the class' need to move on, in the vain hope that today something in Kiryana would open up. Driven to achieve this objective, Wilhelmina no longer showed any interest in Theo. At first, Theo was relieved but then, surprisingly, she began to feel left out.

Theo heard the rustle of everyone coming in from the outer chamber to take their seats, and she shut her eyes to block them out. Noticing that Theo was resting, Kiryana took a wide berth down the aisle and deliberately bumped the table hard. The jolt knocked Theo's head out of her hand, and it took a quick reaction to keep it from banging against the tabletop. Kiryana laughed openly but, like usual, everyone else acted as if nothing happened. Talim, angered by the hostility, shifted to say something but Theo held him back. In the grand scheme of things, it was a small attack and likely to be the only one that day. At least, that is what she hoped.

The class took their seats and waited for Wilhelmina. All tired and frustrated, no one said anything and everyone sat motionless at their desks. Finally, Wilhelmina arrived. She entered the room with her usual flourish of tousled hair and scarves. Once at the podium, she plonked a strange object down on the stand and spoke without greeting the room.

"Does anyone know what this is?" She pointed to the egg-shaped contraption securely mounted on a wooden stand. The students looked blankly at her.

Wilhelmina continued, "This is a very special thing. It has taken me weeks to secure one and have it delivered into my care. This is called a Clarity Beacon. It was created in the early days after the Great Shift to help find other seers. I'm not entirely sure of the mechanics, but in a nutshell, it will find and draw out all those with Clarity. As long as they are within range, it will activate and awaken any latent ability."

Everyone looked at Kiryana. She swallowed hard before asking, "And if it has no effect at all?"

Wilhelmina looked intently at the girl. "If the Beacon cannot stir Clarity, then I don't know what will."

Kiryana took a deep breath. Cory gave her hand a good squeeze for support.

"Okay, class," announced Wilhelmina, never one for mincing words, "I want you to look at the Beacon and start focusing on the light coming from it. I'm not going to tell you what will happen but you'll know it if you see it."

She pulled the oval crystal upwards from its mount to reveal a clear cylinder beneath. She pressed a lever at the top and the Beacon sprang into life. Slowly it began to turn, gaining speed with each revolution. In no time, it was spinning so fast that it looked like a white ball of light.

"Oh, just one more thing," interjected Wilhelmina over the rising hum of the Beacon, "I will be hiding something and I want you to tell me where it is." And she said no more and sat beside the podium.

Fascinated by the device, Theo couldn't help but stare at the whirling vortex of light. She had planned to bury her nose behind her copy of *Great Expectations* for the morning but this intention faded the more she stared at the Beacon. Its buzzing noise was strange, not unpleasant, but odd in a way she couldn't put her finger on. And the more she tried to figure it out, the more she was drawn into it.

She felt a sense of calm she hadn't felt in a long time wash over her, and her breathing slowed as she relaxed. She noticed right away that the buzz had a languid, rolling rhythm, and her breathing started to match its pulse. It was an enjoyable sensation that seemed harmless enough.

Then, like changing gears, the Beacon stepped up the beat. Theo felt the shift immediately. It was an unusual feeling that made her uncomfortable. Soon, to her dismay, she felt something tug at her internal world, trying to dislodge the part that she had worked so hard to keep hidden. Fear rose within her when she realized what was happening. Resolved to keep her ability secret, Theo tried to look away from the Beacon. But try as she might, the connection between her and the device was too strong to break. Fear gave way to panic. The machine reached further in, yanking hard.

Suddenly, the Beacon stopped. It held Theo immoveable for what seemed like an eternity. Then the Beacon cracked with a loud peal, sounding like thunder. The air within the classroom began to bulge then contract, like a creature trying to breathe. It was an unbearable moment for Theo. She could feel a swell of sensations pushing against her. She was helpless against the wave, and she brought her hands to her head to stop the agony. In the end, there was nothing she could do other than let the pressure go.

The Beacon cracked again and the room exploded with colour. All the sensations within Theo rushed forth and spun out of her in visible yellow, blue and crimson spirals. Theo's eyes widened as she took in the strangeness of what she saw. Yes, she was still in the classroom, but it was a different space, a different perspective, and she was seeing something new for the very first time.

She looked about and could see the others still in the room. Talim was beside her reading his book, as calm as could be, but from around him, she could now see a warm, glowing green that clung to him. She tried to call out his name, but her voice stuck like glue. Talim could not hear her.

She looked across the aisle to Kiryana, who sat still staring intently at the Beacon. Theo wished to see her reaction and, magically, found herself in front of her cousin, looking directly into her face. Like Talim, Kiryana had a warm colour radiating from her.

Theo turned to find Emma standing beside her, or at least a version of Emma that she could still recognize. Colours of all sorts were rising from her like steam, floating outward into the air. Emma pointed at Theo and laughed, and Theo looked down at her hands and saw that she too was a swirl of colours. In fact, everything in the room was emitting lines of colour.

Wilhelmina approached them in a mist of indigo and purple.

"Yes," she gurgled within the strange soup, "you are seeing the physical imprint of energy for the first time. Impressive is it not?"

Both Theo and Emma nodded vigorously, spinning around, taking in the kaleidoscopic world.

"It is also a little distracting," she continued. She sounded as if she was speaking underwater.

She walked past the girls and took a long look at Kiryana. She sighed and said, "It was what I was afraid of. She cannot see us and her energy signature is static. She does not have Clarity."

Emma and Theo looked at each other. Both had been trying to downplay their abilities with the hope that Kiryana would develop first. Whatever was happening to them at this moment, both knew that Kiryana wouldn't be happy about it.

Wilhelmina turned away from Kiryana to study the rest of the students. Like Kiryana and Talim, they were radiating energy, but unlike them, their colours moved and stretched into the space around them.

Wilhelmina pointed this out to the girls. "They can't see us. They don't have a transmundane Clarity, but they do have the ability - probably suited to localized work, like that of a physical healer. It is certainly something they can develop."

Wilhelmina walked down the aisle toward the classroom door. She turned to the girls and said, "Before we get too tired, let's see how far your reach is."

Emma and Theo followed Wilhelmina to the door, but Emma stopped short and exclaimed, "I can't go farther than this. I feel myself starting to lose focus."

Not sure of what she meant, Theo nodded and walked through the door into what looked like a Van Gogh painting. The iridescence of the bright, sunny day was powerful, and abundant colours crowded the view. Trees were now resplendent with a mixture of greens and yellows; stones were blurry with overladen shades of grey; the sky was a dazzling stream of blues, whites and purples. Theo stood on the top of the stairs and was too overwhelmed to move. Only when she heard Wilhelmina's gurgling voice did she turn and see the woman walking into the field behind the schoolhouse. She motioned for Theo to follow.

Theo found moving in this world strange. Not difficult to do but it no longer had a concrete feeling to it. Each step felt vague, like a half memory. Theo felt some trepidation about going further into this odd world but, despite Wilhelmina's bluntness, Theo trusted that her teacher knew what she was doing.

Soon Theo reached Wilhelmina, who was pointing at a hole in the tree. She gestured for Theo to look inside. Within the knothole, she discovered a pendant awash with vibrating golds and silvers, nestled among the woodchips.

"I hid this earlier today," explained Wilhelmina. "We cannot move anything in the physical world at this time. We are merely witnessing."

Theo nodded to let Wilhelmina know that she understood, but in reality, she understood very little of what was happening to her. The experience of witnessing this realm was interesting enough, but it made her very nervous. And now she was beginning to feel tired.

Wilhelmina noticed the drop in Theo's energy and quickly said, "Yes, witnessing takes stamina. With practice, you can extend your time, but in the beginning the visits will be short."

Wilhelmina looked about. She scanned the scenery one last time before adding, "I'm going to turn off the Beacon now. Prepare yourself for your return."

And as soon as she said it, Wilhelmina spiralled away in a blur of purples, blacks and reds, back through the schoolroom door like water going down a drain. Too shocked by what she saw to say anything, Theo stood motionless. She didn't have long to wait, however, before she felt something shift again, and the world in front of her swished away in a smear of inky blots and lines. Then all went dark. It took her a moment to realize that she was back in herself, sitting at her desk with her eyes closed. She blinked them open, and she saw

Wilhelmina, looking as severe as ever, watching her and standing beside the Beacon she had just disengaged.

Theo looked over at Emma who was rubbing her eyes, trying to readjust to the static world. Theo looked intently at Emma who caught the silent question but looked away, still too afraid. Theo was neither surprised nor upset by her retreat. Why should this experience change anything? The stakes were still the same as before the Beacon.

Wilhelmina closed the Beacon with a firm click and put the device on the desk behind her. She thought for a moment and took a deep breath. Finally, she faced the class and asked, "So, any thoughts about the Beacon?"

As usual, everyone turned to Kiryana to see what she would do first. She shifted uncomfortably before saying, "It was a great view into the Clarity world. I could see things I had never seen before."

Theo frowned then tried to hide it as quickly as possible. Kiryana was lying, and Wilhelmina knew it too.

Wilhelmina didn't react at all. "Indeed, a great view? Can you tell us what you saw?"

"Well, I saw lots of things," Kiryana said boldly. "But mostly I saw my mother paying for your house."

"Yes," said Wilhelmina with a controlled calm that impressed Theo, "I suppose that you did."

Then she turned her attention back to the class and asked, "Does anyone else have an impression they would like to offer?"

Both Theo and Emma avoided her eye contact. Neither wanted to reveal what they had just experienced. After a moment of uncomfortable silence, Lauren put her hand up. Wilhelmina nodded for her to speak.

"It was a strange sensation, Miss," she said. "I felt myself tingle and being pulled outward. But I couldn't see anything, not like what Kirayana saw, anyway."

"Yes, I felt myself being pulled outward too," chimed in Kiryana, now that she had a hint of what should have happened. Cory, Caroline and Lola also said the same, which for them was true.

Wilhelmina nodded as she explained, "Yes, you will feel a pull out of yourself, which is common. For those who don't have vision, it likely means that your focus will be on things within your physical proximity. Do not fret, though, it is still a beneficial talent to have."

"Anyone else?" Wilhelmina pressed on, looking at both Emma and Theo.

Under pressure, Emma finally gave in, but she underplayed her experience as much as she could. "Miss, I could see in the room but I wasn't able to leave it."

"So you don't know what I hid in the field then?" asked Wilhelmina, already fully aware of the answer. Emma shook her head.

"If I were to ask you what was hidden in the field, Theo, what would you say?"

Kiryana, now suspecting something was up, interjected harshly, "Why would she know what's in the field? She isn't even in the program!" She turned and glowered at the younger girl to keep her quiet.

"Now, now, Kiryana," commanded Wilhelmina, "I want to hear what she has to say. Believe it or not, I am still in charge of this class."

Kiryana, rebuffed, slumped into her chair and folded her arms.

"So," said Wilhelmina again, "If I was to ask you what was hidden the field, what would you say?"

Theo looked over at Kiryana and thought of how hard things were already at the house. She couldn't think of a worse time to reveal herself and couldn't bear the idea of dealing with the inevitable fallout.

She took a deep breath and lied, "I would say that I don't know what was in the field, Miss."

Happy with response, Kiryana smiled smugly. But Wilhelmina pursed her lips. She then said with a heavy voice, "I would say that I am disappointed in you, Theo. You should know that it takes courage to be who you are. Aren't you tired of being afraid?"

Theo looked up with her huge, sad eyes and finally said something true, "Yes, I am tired of being afraid."

Wilhelmina, satisfied with the answer, dropped the subject and moved the class along to a different topic. But Theo was rooted to the spot, left to sit with her overwhelming thoughts.

Chapter Twelve

Finally, the day of Kiryana's party arrived. After careful planning and preparation, everything was ready. Mrs Stokes spared no expense. She hired party planners to organize the schedule and guest list, a crew to decorate the house and gardens, and caterers to take care of all the food. For days, the house was full of strange people, anonymous staff who ran around looking after Mrs Stokes' every demand.

On the day of the big event, Mrs Henderson stood in the middle of the kitchen looking lost. She had no role in the party. Mrs Stokes was tactful about it, however, suggesting that preparing food for hundreds of people would be taking advantage of her good nature. But without duties at hand, Mrs Henderson couldn't settle into her day properly and jumped to her feet every time someone came into the kitchen. Chester had to rescue her from her disorientation and walked her into the sitting room with a cup of tea.

"Enjoy your day off, woman!" he admonished gently. "Goodness knows when the next one will come again."

She laughed in spite of herself crinkling the skin around her bright eyes and said, "I'll be glad when this circus is over and everything is back to normal - well, as normal as it gets in this house." She sank into a floral upholstered armchair and savoured a long sip of her tea.

Theo and Talim had found a perfect spot at the top of the main staircase to sit and observe all the bustling activity. The main part of the house, usually desolate, was transformed into a spectacular ballroom for the party of the season. Groups of people in white shirts and black trousers paraded through the front doors carrying flowers, platters of food, glasses, plates, balloons, instruments, and garment bags. Carpenters were hammering into wood, building a stage for the entertainment and speeches. Technicians were hanging long strings of twinkle lights and hooking up the sound system. Men in red jackets were being given instructions by a woman in a navy blazer who sent them off in whirl. One of them hopped into an arriving car and parked it on the flat part of the front lawn.

A few of the guests who would be spending the night had arrived early to change before the party. One fashionable couple passed Theo and Talim on the stairs, and were speaking to each other, completely unconcerned about being overheard.

The tall man with a crisp accent, not unlike Mrs Stokes, said, "Gloriana has certainly outdone herself this year. I expect she hopes that the lavishness will keep us from noticing that her precious daughter is not, well, how shall I put it, developing as she had hoped."

The thin woman, with blue and white hair, laughed unkindly and replied, "Oh, I wish I could feel sorry for Gloriana, but I don't. She has been pretty high and mighty for a long time, and her fall is going to be grand." The woman turned to look toward Theo and Talim but then looked right past them. "I will say this, though. The house looks wonderful!"

They continued down the hallway, and when out of sight, Talim turned to Theo and said, "A nice bunch of friends she's got there."

Theo nodded in agreement. In fact, there was nothing "nice" about Mrs Stokes' world. Still, Theo hoped tonight was going to be a pleasant break from the regular grind. Looking at the extravagant surroundings she took in the spectacular scenery and felt the excitement building within her.

Things had settled down since the day of the Clarity Beacon exercise. For some reason, Kiryana had stopped harassing her and was giving Theo space. Wilhelmina, satisfied by the results of the test, didn't repeat it or pressure her in any way. Theo, now fully exposed to Wilhelmina, expected more of a challenge from the Oracle and was surprised when none came. Try as she might, Theo couldn't even begin to understand what was going on inside that woman's head.

Theo turned her attention to the hall and watched the arrival of the musicians. Dressed in tuxedos and black gowns, a string quartet carried their instruments to their seats and began tuning their violins and cellos. She didn't often hear live music and was looking forward to it. The string quartet began to play a piece she had never heard before. It was delicate and sad, and she fell under its spell, watching the bows bobbing over the strings. She could have happily stayed there all night if she hadn't been pulled away by the sound of her name.

"Theo," called the woman in a navy blazer, "are you Theo?" Theo nodded.

"Good," she continued with a commanding voice, "Mrs Stokes wants to look at you before the guests arrive."

She took Theo by the hand and led her to the main wing which contained Mrs Stokes bedroom. The bedroom was as large as the Morning Room and twice as ornate. Gold and red dominated the room. A large canopied bed stood against the back wall, and a plush sofa and matching armchairs were arranged around a mahogany fireplace. Oriental rugs lay on top of a cream carpet, and an antique tapestry covered the front wall. The decor made it clear that someone important slept here.

Mrs Stokes stood in the middle of the room with a flurry of white-shirted women darting about her. She was elevated on a short stool as a seamstress adjusted the hem of her floor-length, golden gown. Her platinum hair was pulled high on top of her head, and her white skin gleamed like cream. Wearing red lipstick, which contrasted strikingly with her complexion, Mrs Stokes was going to be the most glamourous woman at the party.

In a chair near her, Kiryana sat sullenly and was playing distractedly with the tassles on her dress. She wore a sky-blue tulle shift with glass beading stitched into the fabric. Her luxurious hair was also piled high, like her mother's, but her make-up was subdued, suiting her age. Theo studied her cousin and once again was impressed by how beautiful the older girl was. She couldn't help but think how strange it was that someone who had so much going for her could be so unhappy.

"Mrs Stokes, here she is," announced the woman in the navy blazer. Mrs Stokes turned to have a look. At first, she glanced quickly at Theo as her attention was divided between Theo and the seamstress, but having settled on what she wanted done, she returned to Theo and studied her more closely.

Seeing Theo in her blouse and trousers, she wrinkled her nose and shook her head, "Oh, no, no, no. That will not do, Theo, darling. Why aren't you wearing your dress?"

Theo looked blankly and replied, "Um, what do you mean? What dress?"

Mrs Stokes frowned and said, "Wh-what dress? Oh for heaven's sake, how come she doesn't have her dress? Can someone look after her, please? And bring her back quickly so we can all go down together."

The woman with the navy blazer rushed to the walk-in closet and hurried back with a garment bag and shoes. "Here it is. Here is the dress. I'm sorry, Mrs Stokes. It was an oversight. I'll correct it myself and bring her back."

"Please ensure that you do. And quickly. I'm almost ready." She turned away to have someone apply a final touch-up to her makeup.

The woman in the navy blazer pulled Theo behind her to an adjacent bedroom. She gave her the garment bag and shoes.

"Here," she said politely, "put these on and I'll come back to fetch you in few minutes. Okay?" Theo nodded and watched her rush out of the room.

Theo draped the bag over the double bed and pulled the zipper open. She lifted out a brown, satin cocktail dress that shimmered in the light. The shoes were of the same rich brown material and had a little heel, to match the elegance of the dress. Theo quickly stripped off her ordinary clothes and pulled the rustling fabric over her head. She just about managed the zipper before slipping her feet into the shoes.

She walked over to the floor-length mirror to see what she looked like. The dress was the most beautiful thing she had ever worn and the colour very much suited her. For the second time that evening, she felt excited about going to the party.

Just then the woman in the navy blazer returned and brought with her a few more white-shirted women. She went to Theo and immediately secured the zipper on the side of the dress. Then looking at Theo in the mirror, she said, "You have to hand it to Mrs Stokes. She certainly has an eye for what works." She smiled and started playing with Theo's wild hair. "Perhaps we can do yours up as well."

She beckoned the women to come over and they began to style Theo's hair and apply a light coat of lip gloss and eye makeup. When done, Theo looked into the mirror to survey the result. Her hair finally looked smooth and stylish, and the subtle eye shadow made her grey eyes look sophisticated. At first, she didn't recognize herself. But when she studied her image a little more, she started to feel pleased. Perhaps she was related to the Stokes after all.

"Okay, Cinderella, let's get you to the ball. I'm sure your "step-mother" is losing her patience."

The woman in the navy blazer hurried Theo back down the hall to the master bedroom. But when they got there, Mrs Stokes and Kiryana had already gone. Only a few of the white-shirted staff were left tidying up.

"Ah well, never mind, Cinderella," said the woman in the navy blazer, squeezing her hand. "I'll take you downstairs myself."

Theo smiled at the kindness of the woman. In truth, she wasn't surprised to be left behind. It was a small slight, but she was accustomed to them. Anyway, it was easy to let it go when she was wearing the most beautiful dress in the world.

Theo followed the woman with the navy blazer downstairs. Talim was no longer on his perch, no doubt shooed away by Mrs Stokes when she saw him. The guests had started to arrive, filling the front hall and adjacent rooms. Waiters in white shirts circulated among them and offered glasses of champagne and hors d'oeuvres. Theo soon found Mrs Stokes standing among a group of people, chatting and sipping cocktails. Kiryana, looking bored and unimpressed, fidgeted near her mother.

Spying their approach, Mrs Stokes smiled widely and welcomed them. "Ah, there she is - my little waif!" She took Theo by the hand and spun her around to get a good look at the dress.

"Yes, yes, much better, much better. I say, I am rather good, am I not? I managed to pick out just the right colour for you."

Confused by the attention, Theo smiled politely and said, "Thank you, Mrs Stokes, for the dress. It's beautiful."

Mrs Stokes, fully aware of her audience, interjected quickly, "Mrs Stokes?! What's with this Mrs. Stokes nonsense? You know you can call me Gloriana, darling - like you always do." And she stared at Theo until she said it back.

"Thank you, Gloriana." It felt strange to say her name but Mrs Stokes was pleased.

"Now let me introduce you to our guests, Theo, darling."

She first gestured to a middle-aged man with a handle-bar mustache and lady with a stout frame and short, grey hair. "This is Eric Marsdon, the leader of the Restoration Party, and his wife Helen, who is also the party whip." Next, she pointed to a younger couple, both tall with athletic builds, who wore form-fitting clothes. "This is Oona and Flinn De Berre, owners of the Peterborough Wind Farm."

Then she smiled at a handsome man, dressed in a slim-fitting tuxedo, who looked somewhat familiar. "And I suppose you know who this is?" Mrs Stokes bubbled with delight. Theo shook her head at which Mrs Stokes burst out theatrically, "Oh Theo, you can't be that sheltered. Surely you have heard of Derrick Mullens, the famous actor?"

To Theo's surprise, she had heard of him. He was the man who introduced the Equinox Celebration at Kitchie. No wonder he looked familiar.

"Yes," began Theo shyly, "I saw you at Kitchie."

Derrick Mullens did a mock bow and said with a flash of his brilliant smile, "Ah yes, that was certainly a night to remember. It was all rather exciting. But I can't imagine not noticing a girl as pretty as you. I'm sure you would have stood out among the crowd."

Shocked by the compliment, Theo's face went pink, which delighted Derrick to no end. Uncharacteristically, Mrs Stokes came to her rescue and said, "Leave the girl alone, Derrick. She is no match for you."

"No, I suppose she isn't," he said as he took a long sip of his whiskey. Then he looked over at Mrs Stokes and asked, "Will Mr Stokes be joining us tonight?"

The question annoyed Mrs Stokes, but she recovered quickly and said smoothly, "Yes, he'll be here in time for the cake."

Derrick looked intently at her and sighed, "That's a pity."

Mrs Stokes gave him a warning look before pulling Theo after her. Kiryana watched them go and her face clouded over. She turned and rushed out of the room.

Like a new toy Mrs Stokes wanted to show her friends, Theo was paraded about and introduced to everyone. Mrs Stokes knew a lot of important people and had a lot to say to each one of them. Strangely, Kiryana's absence didn't seem to bother Mrs Stokes very much. She was wholly preoccupied with the novelty of introducing her new project to her guests.

Eventually, Mrs Stokes became engaged in a drawn-out conversation about recalculating the boundaries of the Capital City. Feeling lost and uncomfortable, Theo asked if she could be excused. Having already made the introductions, Mrs Stokes was satisfied to let Theo do what she wanted.

"Just be back in time for the toast and cake," Mrs Stokes said, taking a pause from her conversation. But having thought for a moment, she quickly added, "Go find Kiryana and bring her back. I'd like to see her before the speeches."

Theo sighed. No doubt Kiryana would be displeased. But looking for her was better than trying to follow along with political conversations with people she didn't know.

Theo headed straight for the kitchen to see if Talim or Chester knew of Kiryana's whereabouts. The kitchen was full of white-shirted staff cleaning glasses and plates and loading trays with new delicacies. The kitchen looked funny without Mrs Henderson in its centre. Then she wondered about Chester and Talim and what they were all doing. She passed through the kitchen, avoiding the rushing waiters with heavy trays held high, and sure enough, she found the three of them in the Sitting Room. They were nestled together watching an old black and white movie and eating popcorn. Seeing them together like this, she suddenly wished she could have spent the evening with them instead.

As soon as she entered the room they looked up but it took them a moment to recognize her. Mrs Henderson was the first to recover and she sprang up and said, "Good heavens, Theo. We didn't even know it was you. My goodness girl, look at you!"

Chester was next. "Theo, my darling girl, look how beautiful you are! I couldn't be more proud of you if were my own daughter."

Even Talim, who was never flustered or at a loss for words, could only stare with a handful of popcorn frozen in front of his mouth.

Mrs Henderson ran over to her and gave Theo a huge hug. "Oh honey, you look so lovely. I trust the party is going well, then?"

Theo, a little overwhelmed by their gushing, could only nod happily. As far as things went with the Stokes, this evening couldn't be better.

"And is everyone behaving?" questioned Chester knowingly.

Theo nodded again but was quick to add, "Yes, they are fine. But I'm looking for Kiryana. We haven't seen her for ages, and her mother wants to talk to her before the speeches."

Chester glanced sideways to Mrs Henderson and said, "Oh, I'm sure she is up to no good. Okay, I'll go look for her too." He rose to his feet, giving the bowl of popcorn to Talim, who couldn't stop staring at Theo.

"Thanks, Chester," said Theo gratefully, "I'm going to run to my room to get a sweater so I can look outside."

Chester waved in acknowledgment as he strode to the back porch and out through the door.

Theo clattered up the narrow stairs a little more clumsily than usual in her fancy shoes and landed with a thud at the top. She loved the way the kitten heels clicked on the wooden floor, making her feel rather grown-up. She tapped down the hallway to her room and stopped short when she noticed a light coming from beneath the bottom of her door.

"That's odd," she thought. "Why would the light be on?" Then she heard shuffling and the sound of something being knocking over, then someone hissing and someone else hissing back.

Theo threw open her door in time to see Eddie MacAvoy climb through her window. She saw him only for a moment before Kiryana slammed the curtains shut.

Theo was outraged. "What are you doing in MY room!" she yelled. She had endured many indignities from the older girl over the past few months, but invading her room to meet her forbidden boyfriend was too much.

Not easily intimidated, Kiryana said haughtily, "Oh, so this is your room. I should have known by all the weird stuff."

"You have no right to be in my room!!" Theo shouted, really upset by the intrusion. Kiryana, surprised by the strong reaction, merely shrugged.

"Well, hey, it was a mistake anyway. I thought the room was empty. So I'll just get out of your way." Kiryana moved toward the door.

She reached for the doorknob but then paused. She warned, "I hope I don't hear about my visitor from Mother."

"All I care about is that you stay out of my room," replied Theo, fully aware of the implicit threat. "Other than that, I don't care what you do."

Kiryana eyed her suspiciously but decided not to press the issue further. She was almost out the door when Theo said, "And by the way, your mother is looking for you. She wants to see you before the speeches."

Kiryana nodded to show she understood and left. Theo looked around the room to survey for damage. Only her desk lamp had fallen in Eddie's hasty escape, so she placed it upright. Happy to be alone, she went to her bed and flopped backward, releasing a huge groan as she fell.

Chapter Thirteen

Theo lingered in her room for a while after her encounter with Kiryana. She needed a moment to shake off Kiryana's rancour before returning to the party. She arrived in the main foyer just in time to meet Chester coming in from the other side.

"Did you find her?" he asked urgently, his face red from rushing.

Theo nodded and said, "She was in my bedroom with Eddie MacAvoy."

Chester sucked in his cheeks as he said, "That girl is just looking for trouble. Mrs Stokes certainly has her hands full." He paused for a moment. He was going to say something else but he became distracted by the sound of tinkling of glasses.

Mrs Stokes was on the stage with a glass of champagne in one hand and a microphone in the other. Kiryana and a distinguished, well-dressed man stood behind her.

"Who is that?" asked Theo, wondering why the man was holding Kiryana's hand.

"That, my dear, is the elusive Mr Stokes," said Chester in awe. "I haven't seen him at the house for some time."

Theo craned her neck to see above the people in front of her. She desperately wanted to have a good look at him. Obviously a bit older than Mrs Stokes, he was extremely good looking and had a sharp air about him, like he knew what you were going to say before you said it. He had the same bone structure as Kiryana, but his eyes were smaller, darker, more intense. Seeing them together, it was obvious that they were father and daughter. Kiryana looked happy, beaming up at her father, nestling close to his side. Suddenly, Theo felt sad. She had to look away to let the feeling pass.

Mrs Stokes waved to get everyone's attention and said, "Ladies and gentlemen, ladies and gentlemen, thank you for coming tonight to help celebrate our daughter's eighteenth birthday. We are so thrilled you all made the journey to our little country house."

The crowd tittered at the deprecating description of the grand mansion.

"And I'd also like to thank my darling husband for facing his "agoraphobia" and leaving the security of the city for the wilds of the Hinterland."

Again the crowd laughed even though Mr Stokes frowned slightly, obviously not amused.

Not bothered by his reaction, she continued with even greater joviality, "So thank you again for coming all this way. Seriously, it really does mean a lot to Jon and myself - to have so many of you, our friends, here with us tonight."

The crowd applauded to show their appreciation before she motioned for them to quiet down so she could continue, "We are so happy you are all here. Our only daughter, Kiryana, is our pride and joy. We've done all we can to help her achieve her remarkable potential, and she has surpassed all our expectations. She has grown up to be this wonderful young lady you see before you." Mrs Stokes stepped back and brought Kiryana forward, despite her daughter's reluctance to leave her father's side. Mrs Stokes wrapped her arm around her Kiryana's stiff shoulders and walked her to the front of the stage. When in place, she cued someone on the side who wheeled in a three-tiered cake covered with sparklers.

"Friends and family, before we burn down the place, can you help us sing "Happy Birthday" to our beloved birthday girl - who is today eighteen years old!" And she began to sing, encouraging the crowd to join in.

"...*happy birthday to you*! Happy birthday Kiryana, darling. We are so proud of you!" She kissed her daughter on the cheek, leaving behind a scarlet imprint. Then she drained her glass of champagne.

"Thank you for singing along; however, I would encourage singing lessons for some of you…"

Again the crowd laughed a little but then mumbled. Before they settled down, someone called out, "Gloriana, has Lilith Crowe's prediction come true?"

Mrs Stokes' smile faded quickly, and Kiryana stepped away from her mother and hurried back to her father.

Accustomed to the line of fire, Mrs Stokes was not easily rattled. "Oh, she is coming along fine," she insisted, planting the smile back on her face. "Her Entrance Exam to the Hill is in a few weeks, and we expect her to pass with flying colours." She looked back at her daughter, but Kiryana wouldn't look her mother in the eye. Sensing doubt in the crowd, Mrs Stokes scanned the room until she found who she was looking for. "But why ask me this question when you can ask her teacher, the great Wilhelmina Van Dorne," she said too loudly, deflecting the quesion to the other woman.

Wilhelmina was at the bottom of the staircase and had been there for some time. But she said nothing and stood rigid and tight-lipped, with her usual aura of mystery cloaked about her.

"Wilhelmina," insisted Mrs Stokes, not able to keep the desperation entirely out of her voice, "wouldn't you say Kiryana is coming along fine and should do well on her entrance exam?"

Wilhelmina absorbed the question for a long time. Mrs Stokes fidgeted a little as she tried to curb her impatience. Finally, Wilhelmina cleared her throat and said without emotion, "Kiryana has done as well as she could. The Entrance Exam will determine where she belongs."

Not entirely happy with the response, Mrs Stokes tried to smile again and say as confidently as she could muster, "Th-there, you heard it from the source. The exam will gain her entrance to the Hill." And before she could be challenged further, she quickly added, "There is cake being served at the side tables, so please help yourself." She clicked the microphone off and hurried to the side of the stage and down the steps.

Spying Mrs Stokes approach, Chester leaned over to Theo and whispered urgently, "I know that look. If I were you Theo, I'd make myself scarce right now."

Not needing to be told twice, Theo rushed across the large foyer and down the hallway. She opened the first open door she found and stepped into the dimly lit room. It was a small study filled with bookcases. An old-fashioned desk dominated the space, and two large, overstuffed leather armchairs were to the left of it. She could not see any of Mrs Stokes' elaborate taste in this masculine room. It had to be the office for her husband, Mr Stokes.

The room was still, with the stagnant air of a place that didn't see enough movement or natural light. Theo walked over to the desk and saw that it was neatly arranged with only a few stationery items on top. She curiously flipped through the unused stack of legal pads and opened the desk drawers to find boxes of pens and paperclips. If this was Mr Stokes' private study, there was no evidence of him in it at all.

"Find what you are looking for?" sounded an unexpected but familiar voice.

Startled, Theo looked up to see Wilhelmina ensconced in one of the large leather chairs. Given the dimness of the room and the darkness of Wilhelmina's attire, it was easy to see why Theo missed her when she came in. It appeared they both had the same good idea about avoiding Mrs Stokes.

"I didn't know you were coming to the party tonight," said Theo, coming closer so she could see Wilhelmina's sharp face better.

"No excuse was good enough to avoid it," replied Wilhelmina with shocking candour. But then having said it, she softened her voiced a little and added, "I thought it was the least I could do for Kiryana."

This was the first time that she and Wilhelmina had been alone together. In fact, this was the first time she had ever seen Wilhelmina outside of the school. Given the strangeness of the situation, Theo felt brave enough to sit beside her in the other chair.

Wilhelmina studied Theo for a moment and having noted the changed appearance said, "I see you are dressed up for the occasion. I take it that you are enjoying yourself then?"

Theo, feeling unusually secure in the no-man's land they found themselves in, decided to be as open as her teacher. "I liked some bits of it, but it mostly feels uncomfortable to me. I don't know what I'm supposed to do with these people."

Wilhelmina nodded knowingly and smiled, which caused her face to crack unnaturally. "Yes, it is hard to pretend to be like everyone else, when, in fact, you are…not." She stared intensely at Theo, and Theo, for the first time, didn't even try to pretend she didn't know what her teacher meant.

"How old were you when you knew?" Theo asked. And just like that she let the veil drop.

Wilhelmina raised an eyebrow but offered no other acknowledgment of Theo's step.

"Well, let me think," sighed Wilhelmina, and she uncrossed and recrossed her legs. "In some ways, I always knew when I look back on it. But Clarity started showing up in obvious ways when I was about thirteen or fourteen. Which is your age now, is it not?"

Theo nodded vigorously, enjoying the relief of having a real conversation about what was happening to her. It hadn't occurred to her until this moment how wonderful it would be to share her secret with someone who understood. All of a sudden, she felt so much lighter.

"Do you like being an Oracle?" Theo asked, tentatively. Fully aware of how unpredictable Wilhelmina was, Theo wasn't sure how long the conversation would last.

Again Wilhelmina sighed and replied thoughtfully, "It's a strange life, that of an Oracle. Everyone sees the privilege and makes assumptions about it. So many Statics envy us the gift because they want to be special too. But being special can be a hard thing when you don't fit into most normal places. I suppose I do like being an Oracle because that is what I am, and it's much easier being what I am than what I am not. Is this not the case, Theo?"

Theo looked down into her hands and let Wilhelmina's words wash over her before she could reply, "I've lost so much because of Clarity – I'm sure my Uncle Ken saw it in me before I knew. And if I were to reveal myself here, I'd likely lose the family I have now. How can Clarity be a good thing when I keep losing so much because of it?"

"I'm pretty sure Clarity is indifferent to most human relationships, Theo. As for those, I can't always explain why people do the things they do even though I can see the results long before they happen. Over the years, I have learned to keep my visions to myself and let people find out on their own. It's less… explosive."

"Is that why you haven't exposed me?" asked Theo as she leaned in closer.

"And Kiryana also," she reminded Theo with a bitter laugh. "You are a strange family: one is as gifted an Oracle as I've ever seen, and the other has no Clarity at all. And yet the two of you keep pretending to be something you are not – all because you are trying to keep someone else happy." Shaking her head with the absurdity of it all, Wilhelmina rose to her feet and went to the other side of the room.

Taking a deep breath, Theo finally allowed herself to say what she truly felt, "I'm afraid no one will like me if they know." The sound of her voice rang loudly in her ears.

Wilhelmina looked straight through her and replied bluntly, "I'm not sure I like you now."

Theo, not expecting her harsh response, reeled back a little and took a moment to refocus.

"Listen, the life of an Oracle can be difficult. If you don't even have the backbone to acknowledge what you have, then you won't stand a chance; it doesn't matter how much native talent you possess. You are not an Oracle so you can be popular. Telling the truth is a tricky business, and it takes strength and skill to do it. If you are more concerned with what people think of you, you are not going to do that job very well, are you? Fear has no place in this craft."

Wilhelmina pulled herself to her full height and lifted her head high. Theo fell backwards into her chair, now in awe of her, fully aware of the power of this woman. Wilhelmina came closer and pierced Theo with the intensity of her black eyes.

"This is a serious thing, Theo, my girl. And you will have to decide what you will do with your own life – I'm not going to tell you. Nor is anyone else, not really."

Having finished what she wanted to say, Wilhelmina went to the door. Before leaving, she turned to look at Theo one more time. "That's it. I'm done with this charade. After the exam, I'm gone – blast the stupid house. It was a foolish idea to think that I could live in this world anyway."

She pulled the door open and, just like that, she was gone.

Theo crept up the back staircase to her room. She managed to go from the study through the kitchen without running into anyone. She was grateful for this as she was too deflated to handle small talk. Closing her bedroom door behind her, she kicked off her shoes and let the dress fall to the floor. In an instant, she was dragging the covers over her head, safe in her bed. She squeezed her eyes tight and waited for sleep to come.

Elsewhere in the house, a lone figure crept down an empty hallway. The sound of music and laughter wafted up from downstairs. The party was now in full swing and would continue late into the night. The figure continued quickly until he reached the intended door. Once there, his hand turned the doorknob and he deftly slipped inside. The figure moved about freely, looking at the owner's possessions. A wavy shadow fell over a photograph of Kiryana and her parents, all smiling happily for the camera. A gloved hand held a package with Kiryana's name on it, and reached to place it on the night table beside the bed. The hand hesitated as people passing in the hall alarmed the intruder. But when they carried on and their voices drifted away, the hand relaxed and dropped the package. Once done, the figure hastily retraced his steps out of the room, and ran into the darkness of the night.

Chapter Fourteen

Theo sat on the smooth lip of the water fountain within the walled garden. She was soaking up the sallow sunlight on the chilly winter's day. Since the night of the party, everything had changed within the house. Without the distraction of Kiryana's birthday, the focus was now upon the Entrance Exam. Theo and Talim had been excused from class for weeks during the preparation period, and word had come from Wilhelmina that they would not be accepted back after the holidays. Both Theo and Talim would need to find a place in the local school as soon as possible.

At first, Theo was relieved to be released from attending class. But, surprisingly, this gave way to feelings of disappointment and sadness that Wilhelmina didn't try to persuade her to stay. Theo was deeply unsettled by her conversation with Wilhelmina on the night of the party. She was now even more confused and didn't know what to do. Also, the strange dreams were coming in increasing waves, still showing a person falling, still obscuring his identity. More than ever, Theo wished she had told Wilhelmina about the dreams when she had the chance.

Finally, the day of the Entrance Exam arrived. Knowing that the examiners from the Hill were at the schoolhouse, Theo felt anxiety grow within her, not unlike what she experienced in Kitchie during the Equinox ceremony. Despite trying to think of other things, she could not distract herself from the fact that the exam was going on without her.

Talim was thrilled to be excused from school. He thoroughly enjoyed his time away from his studies and took the opportunity to spend more time in his garden. Over the past few weeks, he amused himself with trying new growing techniques. This morning, he was attempting to splice different fruit trees together. Chester had managed to knit lemon branches to an orange tree some years ago, and the result was stunning. Interested in duplicating the same effect,

S A McDonald

Talim happily hacked into the trunk of a mature orange tree. He had already selected a robust and leafy bud to be the lemon scion. He wiggled the stem into its new home and wrapped the delicate bark with tape to support it while it healed.

Theo sat quietly watching Talim. She marvelled at his concentration as he worked diligently on shaping the various cuts on his rootstock trees. Less a seasoned gardener and more a mad scientist this morning, he was given permission by his father to try as many combinations as he wanted. Although he understood that trees from the same family worked together better than more distant varieties, this knowledge didn't stop him from experimenting as he pleased.

Unlike Theo, Talim's movement from thought to action was almost instantaneous. He never hesitated. At this moment, he was joining a cherry bud to an apple tree. In his usual way, he studied the elements thoroughly then set about solving the problem. When he noticed trouble with the fit, he discarded his first plan and tried an apple bud instead. Although not as exotic as the cherry graft, he knew the apple bud was the better, more practical choice. Like his gardening, he moved through life in much the same way.

Every so often, Talim looked up as he stretched his sturdy back. He wrinkled his brown eyes with pleasure and smiled at Theo. Theo tried to take an interest in what he was doing, but gardening was not really for her - despite how much she enjoyed sitting among the trees and fragrant flowers. Instead, she was more interested in studying Talim, to understand why he took so much joy in working elbow-deep in the dirt. Talim certainly tried his best to involve her, telling her the common names of the plants and flowers, and the Latin names as well. But the information just washed over her like water running down a hill. She really had no desire to know these things.

Despite their different interests, she loved spending time with Talim. He was as grounded and sturdy as any of the ancient oaks trees within the walled garden. Being around him made Theo feel rooted and serene. Talim took everything in his stride and was constant in his mood and opinion. Unfortunately, he didn't think much about Clarity and had no respect for the Oracle craft. He was quick to dismiss much of what was going on within Wilhelmina's class. "It's such nonsense," he would often say to Theo, thinking she felt the same way, especially given how she was treated. Why did you need another way of seeing the world when the ordinary way was good enough? Perhaps Talim had a point, but that did nothing to change her circumstances. It made her worry what Talim would say if he knew the truth about her.

Too nervous about what was happening this morning at the schoolhouse to stay quiet, she finally edged the topic into conversation. "Have you ever seen any of the previous entrance exams?" She held her breath to see if he would be receptive to the question.

"Huh?" he grunted, trying to dig a hole into the slender trunk of a young plum tree.

Theo cleared her throat and tried again, "Were you allowed to watch any of the exams? During previous years?"

Still focusing on what he was doing, he replied without much thought, "Um, no." He continued cutting the correct diameter for his next bud.

Not to be put off, Theo pressed on, "So? Do you think they would mind if anyone watched, if they were interested to see what happens."

"Um, I'm pretty sure they would...mind. I think that's why we've been excused from school." Talim walked over to a wheelbarrow to pick up another roll of tape. He tore off a long piece and began wrapping it around the new graft.

"I know we've been excused," said Theo, as she drew an invisible picture on the stone lip. "But do you think they would let people watch if they just showed up."

"Um...I don't know. Probably not," he replied bluntly, completely uninterested in this line of conversation.

"Yes, but say Mrs Stokes showed up, would they let her stay and watch?" Theo wasn't even sure where she was going with this idea.

"Well, then, yeah, I'm sure Mrs Stokes could stay," he replied blandly as he cleaned his pocketknife and began shaping another bud.

"So if Mrs Stokes could watch, why couldn't someone else?"

Finally, having enough of this strange conversation, Talim looked straight at her and said, "Theo, what are you talking about? Do you want to go to the schoolhouse and see the Entrance Exam?"

Theo, feeling shy, still didn't want to reveal herself. Not yet. "Well, yes, I think it would be exciting. Not everyone has this rare opportunity." She couldn't look Talim in the eye as she spoke.

"Rare opportunity?" said Talim. "What are you talking about? When has any of this been a rare opportunity?"

Talim snapped his pocketknife shut and stepped closer to look at Theo. He wiped his dirty hands through his golden-brown hair to move it out of his eyes. He studied Theo a good while before he asked, "Theo, what's going on?"

"Going on? I don't know what you mean."

Exasperated by her reply Talim retorted, "Okay, I'm imagining it. Have it your way." He turned around to go back to work.

Theo watched him tend to the small tree and wondered how he was able to shift from one thing to another as easily as he did. She wished she could let the whole thing drop, but something inside of her was pushing her hard.

She took a deep breath. And before she could stop herself, she heard herself say, "Talim, I have Clarity."

Talim stopped what he was doing. He raised himself to face her and looked at her hard. Finally, he said, "Well, I guess that makes sense."

Amazed by his reaction, Theo couldn't keep the shock out of her voice, "What! Are you saying that you knew?!"

Talim shrugged his shoulders and said matter-of-factly, "I didn't *know* know but it explains a lot. I mean, yeah, it would explain why Kiryana hates you so much. And why Wilhelmina is always on your case."

"Wilhelmina knows, Talim. When she used the Beacon, she could see me on the other side. She says I have a lot of talent, but other than that, she hasn't said much else. I'm not sure what I'm supposed to do. What do you think I should do?"

Talim started to laugh, "Of all the people to ask…" When Theo didn't laugh in return, he sobered and continued, "Listen Theo, I don't know anything about Clarity. Not a thing!" Talim looked about and noticed his newly grafted orange and lemon tree.

"I know gardening – that's my thing. Like today, an orange-lemon tree is not a natural tree, but it can exist. But Dad says there is only so much we can do to make it work. At some point the bud has to attach to the trunk. It has to decide to do this on its own. So there you go, Theo. I think some of this growing has to be done by you. If you want to do it, *you* have to do it. No point talking or complaining about it."

And at that moment, Theo was astonished by what Talim said. Not unlike what Wilhelmina had said the other night, she was impressed by the simplicity of his advice. Again, Theo admired how clear and straightforward things were for him.

"So?" she asked slowly. "Should I go to the schoolhouse?"

Talim shrugged as he said. "Well, Theo, that's really up to you. But there is no point a in tulip pretending to be a tomato. If you have Clarity, then maybe you need to find out what that is – if that's what you have."

Theo was thrilled by Talim's easy acceptance, and she clasped her hands together with relief. She sighed happily and said, "Oh Talim! I was so scared to tell you. I thought you would hate me if you knew."

Talim widened his eyes and smiled shyly, "Ah heck, Theo, I could never hate you. I always knew you were interesting."

Theo beamed at Talim. Then she began to think about what she needed to do next.

The yellow bubble car sped up the driveway and screeched to a halt in front of the schoolhouse. All its occupants, Theo, Talim and Chester, jumped out and rushed up the stairs and through the front door.

Before going into the classroom, Chester pulled Theo aside and said to her, "Good luck, my lovely. You stick to your guns and you'll do fine. Just remember that we are rooting for you." He gave her a bear hug and squeezed some of the air out of her. Theo gasped but smiled as she pulled away.

Talim stepped close and gently punched Theo on the shoulder before saying, "I can go in with you if you want."

Theo was very tempted to take him up on his offer, just for moral support. But given that she was entering a world he didn't understand, she realized this was something she needed to do on her own. Grateful for the offer, she put her hand on his arm and said, "Thank you, Talim. You are a good friend, but this is something I should have done a while ago."

Talim smiled and stepped away to let Theo pass.

"Good luck, Theo," he said.

She took a deep breath and stepped into the classroom.

The examiners, all seven of them, stood in a circle within the centre of the room. They wore the same ceremonial red robes she had seen in the Kitchie ceremony. With the hoods raised, they seemed more specter-like than human. They were mumbling something inaudible and were waving their hands in a way that added to their strangeness and menace. As soon as she saw them, Theo doubted her decision. Did she really want to claim her place among them?

Upon seeing her enter the room, the examiners stopped and waited for someone to acknowledge her. No one said anything, at first. Finally, Kiryana couldn't take it anymore and hissed, "What are you doing here! Get out! How dare you interrupt the exam!"

Having been harassed by Kiryana for months, Theo felt strangely unperturbed at this moment. Not at all interested in what Kiryana thought any longer, Theo held her place and ignored the comments.

Kiryana, annoyed at being ignored, was about to continue her tirade when Wilhelmina raised her hand to silence her. "Enough, Kiryana!"

Wilhelmina moved forward into the room until she stood in front of Theo. "So?" she asked. "You have decided then?"

Kiryana, not accustomed to being dismissed, wasn't ready to give up so easily. "Decided?! Decided what?! She has no right to be here! She doesn't belong here!"

Theo looked straight into Wilhelmina's eyes and could see the depths of her wisdom laid bare. Without hesitation, and oddly, without fear, Theo nodded and said, "Yes, I have decided. I have Clarity, and I've come to be tested."

Wilhelmina smiled with satisfaction and led her to centre of the room. One of the examiners broke from the circle to meet them.

Kiryana stood with her mouth hanging open, too shocked to speak. Finally, she sputtered, "Sh-sh-she can't be tested!! She can't!! I won't allow it!!"

However, neither the examiner nor Wilhelmina seemed to be able to hear her. The examiner dropped her hood to reveal an older woman with pristine white hair.

Wilhelmina began the introductions. "Theo, I'd like to introduce Sarah White Horse. She is the lead examiner today."

Sarah leaned in to look closely at Theo and crinkled her ice-blue eyes with approval. "Yes, yes, I see what you mean, Wilhelmina. I certainly see."

"Can we test her today? She is not officially registered and hasn't been taking the transmundane classes," said Wilhelmina officiously.

Sarah White Horse replied with utter confidence, "There is only one real requirement for this entrance exam. And if she possesses it, she has the right to be tested."

Wilhelmina took Theo by the shoulders and studied her face as she said, "Are you ready today, Theo? So you know, once you take this step, there will be no turning back."

Theo was a little overwhelmed by the severity of what Wilhelmina said. But she realized there was only one direction for her. She had to step forward into her own life.

"Yes," declared Theo, "I understand."

"Very well, then," said Wilhelmina with full authority, "go and have a seat with the others and ready yourself. We are preparing and will call you in turn."

Kiryana, no longer able to contain herself, jumped to her feet and ran over to Wilhelmina and placed herself in front of the taller woman to demand that she deal with her.

Wilhelmina looked down at Kiryana and regarded her with an uncharacteristically sad look.

Less enraged and now more desperate, Kirayana stammered, "W-what is going on here? W-what is happening? W-why is SHE here? Why is SHE being tested?"

Unable to pretend any longer, Wilhelmina spoke as gently as she possibly could. "Kiryana, I think you already know why Theo is here. And I think you already know why you should go."

Kiryana shook her head violently to block out what Wilhelmina was saying. "No, no, no! It can't be! It can't be! This is not how it's supposed to be!"

Wilhelmina now decided to stand with the truth and could not be moved from her position. "Kiryana, I'm afraid this pretense has gone on long enough. We cannot build your candidacy on something that will never happened, despite our best intentions."

Sensing what Wilhelmina was about to say, Kiryana began to gasp uncontrollably and look around the room wildly. "No, no, no! This can't be happening. This isn't supposed to be how it ends. No, no, no!"

Wilhelmina had to grab hold of Kiryana to steady her before she said, "Kiryana, I'm afraid I cannot recommend your candidacy to the Hill. I'm really sorry, my dear girl, but it is not to be for you."

Stunned by the pronouncement, Kiryana pulled herself away and staggered backward a few steps and whimpered, "So you are not even going to let me try?"

Wilhelmina shrugged her shoulders and said with a deadpan expression, "What would be the point?"

Kiryana spun about to look around the room, but no one dared meet her eyes.

Wilhelmina gathered herself together and said firmly, "Kiryana, you are now excused."

Unable to find the words to express her desolation, Kiryana turned and ran sobbing from the room.

After a few moments, Wilhelmina said to the class without any emotion in her voice, "Enough distractions. Prepare yourselves. This will not be an easy exam."

Chapter Fifteen

Theo sat quietly as she watched the other candidates take their tests. Having been added to the list at the last minute, she would go last. She was grateful to be at the end of the queue if only to glean any hint of what she was supposed to do. Unfortunately, not much was revealed from watching the others.

Caroline was taking her turn. The examiners reformed their circle and she stood in the middle of them. The exam always started the same way - the Oracles were silent at first, then slowly they would begin their chant, gradually raising the volume and moving their arms. When they reached the right pitch, Sarah Whitehorse would ask each candidate to shift into the realm of Clarity, if she or he could. Following the request, all stood planted to the spot, swaying gently like seaweed under a high tide, until the session was complete. From the outside, the exam looked rather dull with not much going on; however, when the students returned to their seats, each looked exhausted and disappointed.

Caroline's exam had been going on for a while. Theo was trying to calm her own nerves as she was up next. She had already waited for hours while Emma, Cory, Lola and Lauren made their attempts. Now finished, they had been excused from the room and only Theo was left. Based on the timing of the other sessions, Theo had settled in for the wait and tried to get as comfortable as she could, ignoring the butterflies in her belly. When a hoarse screech came from the centre of the Oracle ring, she looked over to see Caroline staggering around, clawing the air with her hands. She shrieked again before she flopped into the arms of Wilhelmina, who tapped the girl between her eyes until they fluttered open. Happy to be out of the trance, Caroline let out a sigh of relief and let the teachers steady her.

"Okay Caroline, that will do for today. We will let you know the results this afternoon," said Wilhelmina, and pointed the girl toward the door.

Caroline hurried to the wall to gather her belongings. Caroline's usual olive complexion was ashen, and Theo felt her stomach tighten when she looked at her. Caroline mouthed the words "good luck" before she scurried out of the room, more than happy to put that experience behind her.

Wilhelmina and the examiners spoke for a good length before they were ready to call upon Theo. She had no idea what to expect and not a clue what to do. She had watched each of the candidates slip into their trances, into the Clarity realm, yet Theo didn't know how to make it happen on her own. After all the fuss about getting to this point, she might just falter at the start and have the shortest exam ever.

"Theo, can you please take your place in the centre of the ring," requested Wilhelmina curtly.

Theo slowly rose from her chair and walked into the circle. The examiners closed around her and she felt the power of their presence immediately, like a magnetic field. Theo looked down at her hands and saw that they were shaking. Adrenaline was surging through her body and she could taste the bitterness of it in her mouth. Wilhelmina, not a part of the circle, stood on the side and watched Theo closely.

"Okay Theo, we are going to start the trance momentarily. Are you ready to begin?" she asked. Her voice was higher than usual.

"Um, um, I'm not sure," Theo stammered, feeling panic starting to rise within her. "I'm not sure how to move into Clarity. I don't know what I'm doing!"

Wilhelmina nodded gently. "Listen Theo, you'll be fine. You will. Just imagine you have a muscle that you have never used before. The call from the Oracle ring will pull on it and you will feel the tug. Trust me, you will. And when you do, just let it go; let it flex. It will know what to do. You'll be pulled over into the other realm. Like the day of the Beacon. Once you are there, we will provide instructions. Okay?"

Theo was grateful for the guidance and smiled weakly. She was still scared but nodded to go ahead anyway.

Wilhelmina signalled to Sarah White Horse to begin. Without hesitation, the circle began to chant with low discordant tones that filled Theo's head with a buzzing fog. The pull that Wilhelmina spoke of began instantaneously, like that of a gentle current pushing and shifting her about, and a part of her, unknown to her, like a hidden pair of eyes, began to open wide.

When the circle sensed the connection, it shifted into a higher modulation. The gentle pull transformed into a surprising grip, which almost knocked Theo off her feet. Theo's first instinct was to resist the hold. She had to push down the desire to flee. But like Wilhelmina had promised, the secret part of her already knew what to do. Theo took a deep breath and just let it happen.

Theo slid from the static classroom into the bright, colourful parallel world once again. Unlike the explosive push from the Beacon, this entrance was smooth and graceful. It was as easy as Wilhelmina had promised. Theo was still standing in the middle of the room, but now the examiners were no longer there. Only Wilhelmina stood in the room with her, looking very pleased.

"Welcome, Theo," said Wilhelmina brightly with that funny, gurgling voice, "that didn't take long at all."

Theo, still not certain about this realm, tried to smile back but felt a little unsure of her motions.

Without wasting any time, Wilhelmina stated, "The examiners are set up at different stations and I will take you to each one. I can't offer you more information than that, but I'm sure you will do fine. Okay?"

"Okay," she replied with her own garbled voice, still not confident in her ability.

The first station was set up outside the school house. The first examiner, a young man with blue hair, stood at the edge of the field. He also looked pleased to see Theo.

"Ah, you've made it outside. Splendid! I had to go back into the schoolhouse for the last four!"

"Yes," replied Wilhelmina. "I expect this one to go farther."

"Very good," the young man's voice vibrated with each word, "this is a simple test, Theo. I've hidden an object in the field and I need you to find it."

"Okay," replied Theo tentatively, "but how will I know what I'm looking for?"

The young man glanced at Wilhelmina questioningly, but she interjected quickly, "You don't know these things yet but the object has been inscribed with an energetic signal. If you are sensitive to it, you should be able to see it. Understand?"

Theo nodded. She climbed up the slope and into the field, as she had done the last time she was in this realm. Instantaneously drawn to the same tree, she could, in fact, see silver waves pulsating from inside the familiar maple. She went there directly, and sure enough, she found the same silver necklace that was hidden there before. She reached in to try and pick it up but the image shimmered and weaved itself around Theo's hand, unwilling to stay solid and firm.

Theo called out to the examiner and Wilhelmina, "I've found the silver necklace but I can't pick it up."

The blue-haired man nodded with satisfaction as he said, "Very good. I would have been amazed if you could move a solid object so early on, but well done. Next station please."

Theo sloshed her way back through the eerie and beautiful yellows, oranges and greens of the grass. She managed to move about easily enough, but the sensation was strange and vague, like trying to tie her shoes wearing rubber gloves.

Once she reached the driveway, Wilhelmina, without a word, pointed her in the opposite direction behind the schoolhouse. Theo did her best to keep up with her teacher, who seemed to float rather than walk. They approached the next examiner who was standing near a wooden box within the field.

"Hello Theo," said a young woman with short, platinum hair and a pierced nose. "Within the box is a hive of bees. Your next task is to tell me what is troubling the hive. Good luck!"

Theo glanced over at the wavy blue, yellow and black image of Wilhelmina, but she merely smiled enigmatically and revealed nothing.

Theo waded through the blinding yellow and gold rapeseed flowers until she arrived near the box of bees. Immediately she could see that the bees were flying about haphazardly, and she could hear the distress in their buzzing. She approached the hive gingerly, uncertain of how the bees would react. She could tell, somehow, that the insects were not troubled by her presence. In fact, they started to swarm about her and seemed to calm down a little when she came near.

Amid the swirls of darting blues and yellow lines, she moved her hands around the box to see if she could find what was causing the trouble. After finding nothing, Theo stood there baffled. As she looked around, she became more alert to the buzzing sound as it grew stronger and more prominent within her awareness. Now she began to sense that there was a rhythm to it. Once she focused on the emerging pattern of the sound pulses, she suddenly, and surprisingly, noticed that the sound held meaning. Now concentrating on this rhythm, an image started to form in her mind's eye. From a dark fade to a strong focus, the image of a bee formed clearly. In her mind, this bee was much larger than the others and held a great importance to the hive.

"The queen bee," Theo whispered to herself, not entirely sure if this was the problem. Finding her voice, she decided this was the best answer she had. "Are they looking for their queen?" warbled Theo through the strange, blurry air.

The platinum-haired woman nodded and smiled broadly. "Yes. Very good! Now do you see the small box to your left? Go over to it and see if you can tell the hive where she is."

Turning to her left she saw another box about 30 feet away from her. Wading through the inky flowers, she arrived at the box and looked inside. Within the box was a ventilated jar holding a large and agitated queen bee.

Theo was pleased that she managed to solve the problem, but for the life of her, she had no idea how to tell the hive where their queen was. She knew she couldn't open the jar, which would be the easiest solution, so she felt rather stuck. Theo stood there helpless until Wilhelmina, sensing her trouble, called out to her. "How did you find out it was the queen? Try and retrace that step and see what happens."

Still uncertain, Theo remembered how the image of the queen bee came into her mind's eye. So, she tried to put into her mind the image of the queen in the jar to see what would happen. Also, she began to concentrate on the buzzing to find the particular vibration that alerted her to the hives' plea. After a little of while of searching, she found the right groove. And then it made sense: the buzzing fell into place with her mental image. To her delight, a buoyant drone landed on the lid of the jar. Soon another arrived. Then another until all the bees had followed her call and swarmed about the box that held their beloved queen.

"Well done, Theo!" called the examiner, "Well done. You are free to move to the next station."

Wilhelmina approached the box and reached in and, to Theo's astonishment, undid the lid of the jar. A happy queen shot straight out and a whirring cloud of bees chased after her.

Wilhelmina said, "You do understand that you are physically still in the class room? Yes? Manipulating the physical world in this state can be done but it is a learned skill. For another day, I think."

They next approached the back of the schoolhouse. Unable to see the examiner, Theo gave a questioning look to Wilhelmina. Instead of answering, Wilhelmina pointed to the top of the building and Theo saw the examiner waiting there for her.

"Good afternoon, Theo," called out a jovial, round-faced man, "I'm so pleased that you made it this far. For this test, I just need you to come up and see me. Simple."

Simple?! Not so simple. The examiner was balanced on the crest of the roof like a weather vane. Looking about, Theo saw no way of climbing up to him.

Again noticing that Theo was at a loss, Wilhelmina said, "Theo, you are still standing in the classroom. Why do you think you need your feet to move about here?"

Of course, what Wilhelmina said made sense but it didn't help Theo understand how she was to get to the top of the building. She moved to the wall and tried to see if there was any way she might climb up. Wilhelmina just tutted and pulled her back. The touch was odd and faint, but strong enough to draw her in.

"No, no. You won't need to climb. Again, right now you are just a projection of yourself into this realm. The physical rules no longer apply to you. Moving around and speaking and whatever else you are doing is an act of will. To get to the top of the building you merely need to will yourself there. Do you understand?"

Theo wasn't entirely sure what Wilhelmina meant. She tried saying, "To the top of the building, please," as if she was giving directions to a taxi driver.

With no hint no movement whatsoever, Wilhelmina sighed and offered more specific advice. "Theo, I want you to imagine yourself on the roof already. I want you to see yourself there as if it already happened. Can you tell me the details of what the view looks like, how strong the breeze is, what can you see from the top? To move from here to there, you must simply see yourself there as if it is a done deal, already in the past. Do you understand? Can you try that?"

Theo nodded. And despite dreading the height of the perch, she closed her eyes and began seeing herself looking down from above. She held this image until it became stronger and stronger, and then feeling as if something had shifted, she opened her eyes. To her surprise, she saw that she was beside the examiner on the roof. Pleased, she began to look around. But when she looked down and saw her feet balanced on the slight beam of wood, the implausibility of being there hit her. She immediately lost her balance and fell, bouncing all the way back to the ground.

Deflated, Theo picked herself up and looked at the examiner, who had at this point decided to come down. Worried that she had failed the test, she was pleasantly surprised to be greeted by his large smile. He nodded the go ahead to move on to the next station.

"Not the most graceful levitation I've seen but I'm sure you'll have time to perfect that on the Hill," he said.

Next, Wilhelmina took Theo away from the school. She led Theo down a road, turning back to look at her now and then. Finally, they arrived at a clearing a good way away from the schoolhouse. As they entered into the clearing, Theo saw another examiner standing by a table with a two-layered chocolate cake on top of it.

Wilhelmina looked at Theo. She asked her, "Are you feeling tired, Theo?"

Theo had been feeling a little drained during the last bit of their walk. Nodding, she said, "Yes, I do feel a little tired."

Wilhelmina acknowledged her reply but said nothing more. As they approached the table, the examiner, a middle-aged woman with grey hair, greeted them with a faint and unsteady voice.

"Hello, Theo. This is a stress test. We just want to see how you perform under pressure. I'm going to give you a problem to solve and you'll only have a minute to do it. Are you ready?"

Flagging already, she hated the idea of trying to figure out a puzzle. But she smiled weakly and nodded.

"Alright, here is the problem. You have this cake in front of you. I would like you to give me eight equal size pieces by using only 3 slices. How would you do that?"

Theo walked over to the cake and looked down. She imaged slicing the cake from end to end but could only achieve six equal slices. As she pondered the puzzle, she found herself feeling even more tired, which made it difficult to see. Studying the cake, she became frustrated that the answer wasn't obvious. To her surprise, she found herself slipping away from the table and out of the clearing. It took her a moment to steady herself and clamber back to the table to try again. She wrapped her hands around the edge of the table in an effort to anchor herself there, but she forgot that her presence wasn't a physical one, and her hands passed straight through the wood.

"Ten seconds, Theo," the examiner prompted.

Feeling the panic of not being able to complete the test, Theo lost her concentration again and found herself slipping backwards out of the clearing and farther down the road. By the time she regained control and returned to Wilhelmina and the examiner, her time was up.

Frustrated, Theo blurted, "It's not possible, is it?"

"Really?" questioned the examiner, who picked up the knife on the table and cut the cake from above into four even quarters. Then she sliced the cake along the side, separating the two-layer cake in an upper and lower half.

"If you count the slices, I'm sure you will find eight."

Having seen it done, it made perfect sense. Theo immediately felt annoyed for not being able to solve it. She began to berate herself, which seemed to drain her all the more.

"No matter," the examiner quickly interjected, "please move onto the next station."

Wilhelmina, wasting no time, motioned for Theo to follow her back down the road toward the school. As they neared the school, Theo began to feel more energized and was able to see things much better. As they rounded the last bend, the blue-haired examiner once again came into view.

"Hello, Theo," he said, "do you remember Sarah White Horse? Yes? Good. She has walked to this point with me and has left and gone somewhere else. I want you to see if you can follow her trail."

Blankly she looked to Wilhelmina for some guidance, as she was once again uncertain how to perform the task that was asked of her.

Wilhelmina looked down the road and thought for a moment before replying, "Theo, can you see how the colours move in patterns? Can you see when something collides with an object how the energy shifts direction? If you look down the road, you will see a synchronized shift of energy away from the path of Sarah White Horse, much like ripples in water. If you concentrate hard enough, you should see a path that will show you the way."

Grateful for the explanation, Theo began to study the way the light and colour floated about. As Wilhelmina had said, she began to notice a slight pattern. At first it was difficult to make out as she wasn't sure what she was looking at. But once the pattern emerged, the edges of the Sarah's trail became very clear. Excited to see what she was supposed to see, she hurried down the road chasing after her quarry with Wilhelmina and the examiner rushing behind to keep up.

Soon she arrived back at the schoolhouse. But instead of going into the classroom, the path led Theo upstairs into Wilhelmina's private quarters. Under normal circumstances, Theo would have never dared entering Wilhelmina's space. But she she was concentrating so hard, she didn't much register where she was.

As she neared her target, she noticed the ripples were getting stronger, letting her know that Sarah White Horse was near. Theo raced up the stairs and through the rooms until she found the Oracle, who was facing outward, looking through a window.

"I've found her!" exclaimed Theo, feeling pleased with her success.

"Yes, you have," said the examiner, fully satisfied with her performance. "Well then, only one last test remains. And it's the hardest one I'm afraid. This will be about handling what you see, especially given the malleability of this realm." Then the examiner looked knowingly at Wilhelmina before continuing. "If you are ready, Theo, approach Sarah for instructions, please."

Theo was now feeling trepidation about this test because of the examiner's warning. Theo slowly approached Sarah White Horse, thinking it strange that Sarah wasn't facing into the room and hadn't acknowledged them at all. Theo crept up until she was standing directly behind the woman but Sarah White Horse did not move. Theo worried about what was coming next. She held her breath and braced herself. She cleared her throat and softly garbled, "Sarah White Horse, may I have the next instructions, please?"

Even before Sarah White Horse turned around, Theo could tell something was wrong. Slowly, Sarah turned her head and Theo screamed. Sarah's face had been removed. In its place were large, writhing worms with gaping razor-teethed mouths. Unlike anything Theo had ever seen before, the grotesque image was more than she could stand. She turned and ran. With each step, she lost focus, and the realm about her swirled away until she fell into blackness.

Theo became aware of the sensation of someone tapping on her forehead. She opened her eyes and looked at Wilhelmina, who was cradling Theo's head and studying her intently. Now back into the classroom, Theo quickly refocused and looked about her. All the examiners were watching her patiently, some with an air of amusement, others with concern. Feeling stiff, she slowly climbed to her feet. She waited nervously for someone to say something.

Sarah White Horse came forward to speak. Although Theo knew it was just an illusion before, she couldn't resist the urge to recoil a little from her. "I'm sorry about that, Theo, but it will become necessary to control your reaction in those situations."

Then standing tall she announced, "Unless there are any objections, I would like to offer you, Theodora Yates, a place in the Academy right away. I haven't seen a candidate as strong as you in some time."

Theo didn't quite absorb what the Oracle said, for she was distracted by the rare occurrence of seeing Wilhelmina smile.

Chapter Sixteen

Theo had to shake her head to make sure she heard Sarah White Horse correctly. Was she just invited to join the Academy on the Hill?

"I'm sorry," she said. "Can you repeat what you said again, please?"

Sarah White Horse laughed heartily and replied, "No Theo, you didn't imagine it. Yes, I'm offering you a place at the Academy and would like you to start immediately."

Not knowing if she could trust this woman, Theo looked to Wilhelmina for confirmation. It was an odd thing to look to Wilhelmina for support but she always told the truth.

"If I were you," Wilhelmina said, almost gaily. "I would hurry home right now and start packing."

Really? Was this really happening? Was it going to be this fast? Still trying to recover from the strain of the Entrance Exam, she felt overwhelmed by the urgency of the moment. Her thoughts went straight to Talim, Chester and Mrs Henderson, and she suddenly realized she wasn't ready to leave them yet.

"Um, um, that's great. Thank you very much," Theo managed to say. "But why so soon? Why does it have to be right away?"

Wilhelmina tilted her head as she spoke, "No, it doesn't have to be right away. But have you considered the climate of the house when you get back? I don't imagine Mrs Stokes will be as welcoming as before."

Of course that made sense. Theo had been so focused on acknowledging her gift that she hadn't considered the possible fallout. Of course Mrs Stokes and Kiryana will be angry with her. More so now since Kiryana was refused the right to test. Fair or not, they will perceive the whole situation as Theo stealing Kiryana's last chance. Still the thought of leaving for the unknown world of the Hill frightened her. Theo wished that things could slow down just a little.

"It just seems a bit much, to move to the Hill so soon," Theo said meekly. Deep down she knew it was the chance of a lifetime but she didn't want to leave her only friends behind.

Wilhelmina approached Theo and uncharacteristically placed a thin, bony hand on her shoulder. "I know leaving here seems scary - I know it is. But I want you to think about what it would be like to be surrounded by people who understand exactly what you are and what you can do. I'm sure Talim will be happy for you. Despite his lack of interest in academics, he strikes me as the sort who understands why things are the way they are. I'm sure it will be okay."

Theo was so astonished by Wilhelmina's gentle support that she was speechless. Having no other excuse at hand, she finally agreed by nodding and smiling weakly. Wilhelmina, too pleased to hide it, smiled again and shook Theo's shoulder.

Thrilled by the acceptance, Sarah White Horse clapped her hands loudly and said, "Excellent! We shall all leave in the morning!" She began to undo her ceremonial robe, and while slipping off the garment, she suddenly was struck by a thought. "Theo, as you weren't really prepared for the test, are there any questions you would like to ask at this time?"

Ask any questions? Was she kidding? So many that it caused her brain to clog with the volume of them all. She managed to regain some equilibrium and started to think about what was really distressing her right now. And she remembered her dreams. With the new realization that she could now unburden them to people who knew better, she had to steady herself from sinking into the floor with relief.

"Yes, yes I do have questions! I need your help, please!" began Theo with great excitement. "I''ve been having these dreams for months…."

Sarah White Horse couldn't contain herself when she heard this. "Wilhelmina, you didn't mention that the girl could divine the future as well!"

Wilhelmina looked genuinely shocked by this revelation. She shook her head as she spoke. "That's because I didn't know. She never said anything before now."

Sarah White Horse walked over to Theo and looked her fully in the face as she said, with a hint of awe in her tone, "Well, aren't you full of surprises? You are much more than we were led to expect. So you are having predictive dreams, are you then? What can you tell me about them?"

Theo had seen the dream so many times that it was etched in her memory. It always unfolded in the same way: she walks into a cave with a large pool of water. Someone is sitting by its edge holding an object, but she can't tell who the person is or what the object is. The scene then shifts to a cliff's edge and she can see the back of this person being struck by a blue light. The figure falls over the edge and crashes into the rocks below, dead on impact. After conveying the dream, Theo added, "I've been having this dream every night this week. And it's really troubling me when I'm awake too."

Sarah White Horse and Wilhelmina exchanged a worried look. Then Sarah said, "The increased frequency indicates that the incident is getting closer. But the fact that the character in your dream hasn't become clear to you means that a key decision hasn't yet been made. I would say, however, that it is fast approaching. Theo, for your own good, getting you to the Hill right away would be the wise thing to do."

Realizing that she would be protected, being cloistered might not be such a bad thing after all.

It didn't take long for Theo to pack as she didn't have many clothes, not that she cared about that anyway. She was more concerned about her letters from Aunt Georgia and the treasures she found with Talim. Having secured them in a safe place within her bag, she sighed and took a long look about her funny, little room. How odd it would be to wake up after tomorrow and not see its overhanging, crooked ceilings. She was happy here, and she was going to miss walking through the doorway and slipping into the safety of this space.

She stomped downstairs to the kitchen in her usual manner which caused Mrs Henderson to lament, "Oh, how I'm going to miss those elephant feet of yours, dear girl." Already a little red-eyed from crying, she sniffled as she went about preparing the evening meal.

Talim and Chester were sitting at the table, each lost in his own thoughts. Neither were particularly glad to hear of Theo's immediate departure, even though they were thrilled she did so well on the exam. Caught up in the rush of trying to get Theo to the test in the first place, they hadn't considered what would happen should she pass. Too late to do anything about it now, they both sat with their sadness and kept their feelings to themselves.

Chester and Mrs Stokes already had a run in earlier that day while Theo was packing in her room. As much as Theo tried to ignore it, she couldn't help but hear the enraged shrieks from the woman downstairs. Theo didn't need her Clarity to understand what she was saying. Theo smartly stayed upstairs until she heard Mrs Stokes storm out of the kitchen. It was unlikely Mrs Stokes would return again that evening to say goodbye, so Theo relaxed and tried to savour the time she had left with her friends.

Pushing his food around his plate, Chester was pensive and lacked his usual zest for eating and conversation. Talim, too, was sombre and unenthusiastic about the meal. The strange silence made Theo uncomfortable.

Unable to take it anymore, Theo finally blurted out, "Listen! I'm only going into the city. I haven't died or anything!"

Chester looked up from his plate and finally mustered a small, crooked smile. "Yes, Theo. We know it will be good for you to go to the Hill. But we are going to miss you, my dear. I know you are Mrs Stokes' cousin, but you are like family to us." Talim nodded and then plopped his head into his hands.

Theo hoped it wouldn't happen at dinner, but her feelings began to well up inside of her. "Oh Chester, you are my family too. I didn't want to go because I didn't want to leave you or Talim or Mrs Henderson." And Theo jumped from her chair and ran over to Chester and threw her arms around him and squeezed him tight. Chester leaned into Theo and couldn't speak for a moment or two.

Finally he managed to pull away and, in spite of himself, started laughing. "Ah, you are right, Theo, my girl, you are only going to the Hill. Off to be a grand Oracle. My goodness, Talim, she is going to be famous, and we knew her when she was just a slip of a girl." Talim, not at all impressed by Theo's prospects, could only focus on his own loss. He sniffed at his father and looked away.

After hearing Chester, Theo widened her eyes and asked, "Do you think I really will be famous, Chester?"

Chester nodded emphatically and replied, "I have no doubt, my sweet girl, if only for the fact that you pipped Kiryana to the post. That story will have legs, I'm afraid."

Theo thought for a moment and then said honestly, "I didn't do it on purpose, you know. In fact, I feel rather bad about how it all happened. What's going to happen to her, do you think?"

Chester shrugged his shoulders as he replied, "That remains to be seen. I'm sure it's been quite a blow to her ego, and that of Mrs Stokes. But if she didn't have the gift, what did they expect? Anyway, Kirayana has lots of real talents, and she and her mother will be better off if they focus on those."

"Do you think they will let me come back and visit?" Theo asked. She hadn't seen either Kiryana or Mrs Stokes since the exam, and she truly wondered if she would ever see them again.

Chester took Theo's hand in his own and looked into her eyes, "I know Mrs Stokes is a vain woman, Theo, and she has her faults, but I've never seen her act so cruelly as to keep people apart. I think she just needs time to calm down and get used to how things are now. Who knows, she might even wave you off tomorrow morning."

Strangely enough, the thought of Mrs Stokes and Kiryana coming to say goodbye really pleased Theo. Despite it all, she was sad to be at odds with them after all that had happened.

Mrs Henderson plonked a large piece of chocolate cake in front of Theo and Talim. "Here, you two, this should cheer you up." Unable to resist Mrs Henderson's extraordinary chocolate cake, Theo and Talim dug in.

"Okay," mumbled Talim through a mouthful of cake, "this almost makes up for you leaving… almost."

"I doubt if you"ll have food as good as this on the Hill," sighed Mrs Henderson. "I've done a good job at fattening you up a little, Theo. Make sure you eat while you are there, honey. I don't want those people to undo all my good work." Theo, compelled by Mrs Henderson's concern, went over to her and gave her a good squeeze.

"No one will be able to replace you, I'm afraid," said Theo warmly. "I will be at the mercy of their awful cooks."

"Well," sniffed Mrs Henderson, dabbing her eyes. "Just make sure you come back every now and then so I can fix whatever damage they've done."

"I'll come back as often as I can," promised Theo solemnly. She fully intended on making that prediction come true.

Theo entered the cave as she was drawn by the light emanating from within. A deep pool of water filled most of the basin, and a smooth rocky shoreline rose towards the edge. There, sitting on the bank was a wet figure holding a large crystal. Then Theo and the figure were sitting outside. The crystal was glowing like it was on fire and the brilliance of its light obscured the details of the figure's face. Theo chased after the figure. They rushed up the side of a mountain and stopped on a plateau that looked over a deep gorge. The figure stood on the precipice and ranted "I can see! I can see!" And from over the lip of the ledge a strange, blue sphere appeared. At that moment, the figure's head turned, flipping long, brown hair over her shoulders. Sad, amber eyes came into quick, sharp focus, as did all of Kiryana's striking features. Kiryana! Then, to Theo's great dismay, Kiryana fell into the gorge, like she always did. Before Theo could do anything, she swirled away from the cliff's edge and landed back within the darkness of her own room.

Theo sat bolt upright in her bed, now fully awake from her dream. Still in her tiny room during her last night at the Stoke's house, she let out a sigh as she fully absorbed what was just revealed to her. So it had been Kiryana all along!

Thinking of what Sarah White Horse had said about waiting on a key decision, Theo wondered what decision Kiryana had made to prompt this line of fate. As she pondered this question, she inadvertently said her cousin's name out loud.

"Kiryana," she whispered to the air around her.

In response to the call, Theo heard a rustling noise from a dark corner of her room and suddenly realized she wasn't alone. Icy fingers of fear tickled her spine. She held her breath and stared into the blackness. She could make out the shape of a figure, just outside the ambient glow of light that seeped in from under her door.

"Who is there?" Theo quavered. "Who are you?!"

And as if Theo's call had magically conjured her, Kiryana stepped into the low light. But before Theo could speak, Kiryana rushed to the bed and covered Theo's mouth with her hand.

"Don't make a sound!" hissed Kiryana. And from behind her, Eddie appeared, wringing his hands.

"Kiry, are you sure you want to do this?" he moaned. "It's not too late to stop."

Barely able to see Kiryana's features in the dim light, Theo still could tell by the way she held herself that she was resolute. "The Crystal Dragon is my only hope, Eddie. And Theo is the only one who can read the map."

And then without further conversation, Kiryana gestured for Eddie to come forward. Kiryana took her hand away from Theo's mouth only long enough to stuff a musty rag into it. Too shocked to react at first, she then tried wiggle free. Now fully committed, Eddie groaned and placed a large, mouldy canvass bag over Theo's head and scooped her up and slung her over his shoulder. Kiryana grabbed one of the packed bags and quickly opened the door and motioned for Eddie to follow.

The couple moved very quickly, bounding down the stairs. In no time, they crossed the kitchen to the back door. Theo managed to spit out the rag and began to shout. Unfortunately, by the time she found her voice, they were away from the sleeping household. It was too late and no one could hear her cries for help.

Before she knew it, she was being flung into the back of a car. Kiryana and Eddie jumped into the front and slammed the doors. In a flash the car jumped forward and sped down the driveway into the night.

Chapter Seventeen

Theo struggled against the mildew–infested sack and finally threw it off her head. She sat upright in the back seat and took in where she was. Eddie was hunched over the steering wheel watching the road intently. Still no happier to be part of this abduction, he focused on getting to where they were going as fast as possible. Kiryana sat rigidly beside him and refused to acknowledge anyone. Theo grabbed either side of their bucket seats to demand their attention.

"What are you doing?!" Theo shouted, finding a volume she had never used before. Something within her had changed, and she no longer felt intimidated by her older cousin.

Ignoring the new tone, Kiryana carried on as usual, "Be quiet, Theo. It will take hours to drive to the Appal Mountains. Then we have a long hike."

Theo shook her head in disbelief. Kiryana spoke as if they were just out on a Sunday drive, not even registering the severity of the crime she just had committed.

"Long hike!!" Theo shrilled, letting her outrage out. "Appal Mountains! What are you talking about?! I don't want to go to the Appal Mountains! Turn this car around and take me back now!"

Kiryana sat stonily for awhile. Finally, she said, "I'm afraid I can't do that. Try and get some rest as tomorrow will be a long day."

Astonished by Kiryana's reaction, Theo couldn't contain her emotion. "Get some rest! Tomorrow will be a long day! Are you mad? I'm supposed to be leaving for the Hill tomorrow morning, Kiryana! I can't be here with you doing goodness knows what!"

Kiryana looked over her shoulder, very much like what Theo had just seen in her dream that night. All of a sudden, she felt scared for her cousin.

Deadpan, Kiryanan said, "I have a map to find the Crystal Dragon. It is hidden in one of the caves in the Appal Mountains. Unfortunately, I need you to read the map."

Theo was bowled over by the statement. Immediately, she was back on the floor of the cloakroom, overhearing the conversation between Mrs Stokes and Wilhelmina. The Crystal Dragon! The Appal Mountains! The madness of Orfeo Cotswold! Theo's throat tightened. Kiryana was in danger and the Crystal Dragon was the reason.

"Kiryana," Theo's voice hushed so not to alarm her cousin, "you can't go after the Crystal Dragon. It is cursed, I assure you."

Kiryana looked at Theo with curiosity, and then to Theo's surprise, she began to laugh, "What are you talking about? Cursed? How would you know anything about it?"

"I overheard your mother talking to Wilhelmina. The Crystal Dragon was made by Orfeo Cotswold as a cruel experiment. Anyone who touched it came to no good."

Kiryana's face twisted with uncertainty. "What do you mean no good?"

"Wilhelmina said that once they got Clarity, they all died soon after. The last person to have it ran away with it into the Appal Mountains."

Eddie turned to look at Kiryana, and Theo could see his grave expression. "We can turn back now, Kiry. I'm sure Theo won't say anything about tonight."

Theo quickly added, "Eddie's right, Kiryana. I won't say anything to anyone about it. I know how upset you are about the exam."

Unfortunately, her attempt to placate her cousin didn't work. Instead, Kiryana snapped, "I don't need *you* to feel sorry for me, you little liar. So what are you now? Wilhelmina's protegee? Don't need the rich girl anymore?"

Theo shook her head. "No, no. That's not how it happened. Wilhelmina was trying her best to help you along. She wanted it for you too."

"Sure, she did. She just wanted a nice house away from it all. She had her reasons too."

Kiryana's voice was flat and cold, unlike anything Theo had heard before. Worse, she gave no indication that she understoon the seriousness of what she was doing. Eddie's guilt was obvious, but Kiryana seemed to be completely disassociated from the gravity of the situation. She appeared more strange than menacing. Theo then realized that Kiryana was so broken that she was capable of anything.

"I can't be here with you, Kiryana," said Theo cautiously. "I have to leave in the morning. Do you understand this?"

Kiryana slumped down into her seat, and Eddie placed his hand on her knee to reassure her. Finally, she said, "You see, Theo, that's just the thing. I'm afraid I can't read the map to find the Crystal Dragon. And neither can Eddie nor Cory nor Caroline. Only Clarity will reveal the energetic lines embedded in the fabric. Only an Oracle of sufficient calibre can read it. And the Oracle has turned out to be you… and not me…" Kiryana let the last word drop off and fall to the floor. Crushed by the truth of her failure, she had become smaller.

Theo shifted her weight as she listened. She couldn't think of what to say to make her cousin feel better. It was unfair that Kiryana didn't have the ability but what could she do?

"I'm sorry it didn't work out for you," Theo tried gently.

"Yes," laughed Kiryana bitterly, "it didn't work out for me. Everybody knows it didn't work out for me. And everybody knows what a great prodigy you turned out to be. You - pretending to be this sad, lost girl, while just waiting for your chance to swoop in and steal my place. Why did you have to come here at all? I mean, you could have done this anywhere. Why did you have to come here and flaunt your success in front of me? Did it make you feel better? Did it make you feel smarter? All this time, acting like this pathetic thing while knowing you had the gift ten times over any of us. Did you laugh at my every feeble attempt? How cruel are you, really?"

Theo had not considered how the situation would appear from Kiryana's point of view. In fact she had been too absorbed with her own struggle to consider how it would look to others.

"No, no," Theo insisted earnestly, "I wasn't mocking you, any of you! I wasn't doing anything. I was just trying to find my way, Kiryana. I was so afraid of losing what mattered to say what was happening to me."

"Losing what mattered?" Kiryana repeated with disbelief. "There is only everything to gain by becoming an Oracle. I don't believe a word you are saying. Or are you still mocking me?"

"No, no, I'm not, Kiryana. Truly I'm not!" pleaded Theo. "Only *you* wanted to be an Oracle. Only *you* wanted to take that path. Your parents supported that! Everything I've ever cared about was taken away from me because of Clarity. Uncle Ken hated me because he knew before I did, and Aunt Georgia was taken away from me. I knew you would hate me too, as would your mother, once you found out. As weird as it seems, you are the only family I have left, and I was more afraid of losing that than gaining anything to do with being an Oracle."

Kiryana studied Theo a long time then glanced over to Eddie, who was nodding gently to her. Kiryana softened her demeanor a little and replied, "Well, I do know a little something about being afraid all the time. But it still doesn't change the fact that I need you to read the map."

She sat straight in her seat and turned back to look out of the car window at the road ahead. "I'm afraid I can't let you go."

Theo slunk back into her seat and tried to make sense of all her jumbled thoughts and feelings. Still uncertain of how much she could trust Kiryana in her current state, Theo decided it was best to wait things out a little and hope her cousin would come to her senses. Theo didn't feel unsafe, but she didn't have a good feeling about it either. At some point, she was going to have to reveal her dream to her cousin and make Kiryana understand just how dangerous this journey was going to be.

After a few moments of strained silence, Kiryana finally said, "We are going to the Appal Mountains, and that's it. You can make this harder if you want. That's up to you. Eddie is going to drive until we get there, so I'm going to take the opportunity to sleep. I suggest you do the same. You may want to put on some heavier clothes as it's going to be cold when we get there."

Deciding it was best to leave it alone for awhile, Theo found her bag and pulled out some jeans, a thick sweater, socks and sturdy shoes. She put the clothes over her pajamas and positioned herself on the seat as comfortably as she could manage.

Too unsettled to sleep properly, Theo drifted in and out of semi-consciousness. She remained aware of the movement of the car, feeling every twist and bump in the road. At one point, she felt the car turn off the main highway and weave around the curves of a regional road. Every now and then, Kiryana would shift from her sleep and ask Eddie a question to which he would reply with "soon." Finally, the car slowed down and came to a stop. Theo wrinkled her eyes and blinked in the dim morning light. They had driven through the night, and she sat up to see where they had landed.

They were in the parking lot of a national park. She looked up to see the rounded foothills of an ancient mountain range. The sun was just beneath the horizon, and the hills were backlit with low light.

Covered now with towering pines and maple trees, the forest had recovered from the desolation of the Great Shift. Birds called hopefully in the pre-dawn light as they flitted about from tree to tree. Theo marvelled at the scene before her until she remembered the reason for being there.

"We are at the park's entrance," Eddie announced, stifling a huge yawn. "It's just dawn now, Kiry. I'll need some sleep if I'm going to be of any use today."

Kiryana nodded but added grimly, "Okay, but only a few hours, Eddie. It won't take long for the house to realize that Theo is missing." She then looked back at Theo. Her expression warned the younger girl to stay put.

Eddie dropped his seat back a little to make himself comfortable and was snoring gently in a matter of minutes. Kiryana continued to stare intently at Theo until Theo realized she too had to go back to sleep. Once she acquiesced and slipped back into her resting position, Kiryana shuffled back into hers. However, unlike Eddie, Kiryana only rested quietly, too afraid to drop her guard entirely.

Without the movement of the car to disturb Theo, she slept more deeply although not peacefully. Her mind was alive with images of amber eyes and crystal claws.

The slam of a car door woke Theo from her sleep. Stiff and uncomfortable, Theo blinked into the bright light while she tried to regain her sense of where she was.

Kiryana was coming back from the public toilet at the park's entrance. Eddie had just climbed out of the car and was going to meet her. They spoke in strident tones before he gave up and continued to the bathroom. Kiryana returned to the car and opened up the trunk and pulled out several, heavy backpacks and dropped them to the ground. She rummaged through one of them and took out some bottles and cereal bars. Yanking the car door open, she threw a few of the cereal bars in Theo's lap and gestured for her to take the water bottle.

"Drink as much water as you can. There is a water pump here, and I want to refill the bottles before we start."

Still not fully awake and unprepared for the demand, Theo just stared at the bottle thrust into her hand. Not looking for a response, Kiryana turned and grabbed the hiking boots lying near the backpacks and went over to one of the picnic tables to put them on.

Theo took a long swig of water and started chewing on one of the cereal bars. Not the most delicious thing she ever tasted, but it did the job. Now fully awake, Theo became aware of how uncomfortable and grotty she felt. She stretched a little and climbed out of the backseat, intent on going to the bathroom to clean herself up. She reached back into the car and got her bag and started to walk. In a second, Kiryana was by her side.

"Just to make sure you come back," Kiryana warned.

Theo looked at her cousin's determined face but could only see the desperation underneath, so she said nothing.

They walked through the empty parking lot and past the shaded picnic sites. If she wanted to, Theo could have easily run away from Kiryana. It wouldn't be hard to disappear into the woods and lose Kiryana among the trees. Although it would be frightening to be on her own in the strange forest, Theo was confident she could use her new skills to find her way back home. But, strangely, she found that she couldn't leave her cousin. With the vision revealed, Theo now felt responsible for Kiryana. Not entirely sure why she had the information she possessed, Theo knew she must help Kiryana understand the danger she was in. The challenge was finding the right time when Kiryana would listen.

Stepping out of one of the bathroom stalls, Theo pulled the zipper up on her jeans. A little more comfortable out of her pajamas, Theo felt better prepared to face the journey ahead. Kiryana leaned against one of the walls and watched Theo wash and dry her hands. Except for the time within the stalls, Kirayana hadn't let Theo out of her sight.

Uncomfortable with the scrutiny, Theo blurted out, "Look, I'm not happy about being here, or how you pulled me out of bed in the middle of the night. But I have no intention of running away, okay? I've decided to help you. So can you just relax? Please?"

Kiryana blinked, uncertain of what to make of Theo's announcement. "Why should I believe you? Why would you want to help me?"

Theo looked her cousin full in her face and said, "Who knows why? But what other choice do you have? You are either going to trust me or not."

Kiryana steadied herself and said, "I'm not sorry, you know. I did what I had to do. Unfortunately, you are the only compass available, so that's just how it is."

Theo studied the older girl. Something about Kiryana's defiance made Theo worry about her all the more. She approached her cousin and looked into her eyes. "Kiryana. I'm afraid I've had a vision about you and about the Crystal Dragon. You are in danger. This will not end well."

Kiryana stepped back as if Theo had slapped her. "W-w-what did you say?"

Theo stepped closer and continued gently, "Kiryana, last night, I had a vision about you. In it, you are holding the Crystal Dragon. It's true – it does give you Clarity. But you see something that makes you very upset. Then you run to the edge of a cliff, and something terrible happens. You fall to your death."

Kiryana studied Theo's face for a moment before breaking into a long, hysterical laugh. Baffled by her reaction, Theo stared in stunned silence as her cousin shook with spasms.

When Kiryana finally quieted, she straightened up and said, "Hasn't my life already been cursed by a vision? What is one more?"

Unsure of what to make of this, Theo felt the need to convince Kiryana of the impending danger. "Did you hear me? I believe this vision is telling me, telling you, that to search for the Crystal Dragon will kill you. Can't you understand that?"

Kiryana rolled her eyes with disgust. "See what? Do I believe the vision? I have no reason to believe ANY vision. And for that matter, I have no reason to believe you either." She began to pace back and forth.

"Oh, you are a clever girl, you are. For a moment, I was starting to think that you really wanted to help me. But you don't, do you? Visions? Ha! There are no visions, are there? Just a clever way of getting me to take you back home. But hey! No worries, huh? Just a reminder of what a clever liar you are. And you, Theo, my girl, are the best liar in the world."

Kiryana picked up her gear and strode to the outside door. She stopped at the threshold and practically spat out the words, "Just so YOU know, I will be keeping my eye on you. So you just try and relax!"

She stormed out, leaving Theo to stare into the bathroom mirror. She looked into the reflection of her over-sized eyes and mumbled, "Good job at picking the right time, Theo. Gold star."

With her gear in tow, Theo followed Kiryana back out into the parking lot. The sun was high in the sky, but the winter light wouldn't last for long. Kiryana was hoisting a heavy backpack on her shoulders, and Eddie was finishing lacing up his hiking boots. Noticing her approach, Eddie stood up and came over to the younger girl. Albiet being the most handsome boy Theo had ever seen, his anxiety had drastically changed his appearance. For the first time ever, she wasn't in awe of his beauty. Instead, she felt sorry for him. She stood patiently and waited for him to speak.

Eddie shifted his weight back and forth until he finally said, "I'm not sure how to apologize for throwing a sack over your head and kidnapping you in the middle of the night..." Hearing how awful it sounded made him stop mid-speech. Theo knew it wasn't his idea and that he was helpless against Kiryana's demands. He was lost in his own predicament and unable to act in his own best interest. At that moment, Theo feared for him too.

"You know this won't end well, Eddie," Theo said. Unlike Kiryana, he snapped to attention and waited for her to say more.

"I've had a vision. Although she finds the Crystal Dragon, it will drive her mad. She runs to a cliff's edge, and from what I've seen so far, I'm pretty sure she throws herself over it."

125

Eddie studied Theo's face and decided she was telling the truth. He rubbed his forehead with his hand before he spoke.

"I know this is bad. I do. And I'm so sorry to involve you. But Kiryana is beyond reason, and she would have done this with or without me. At least if I help her, I can try and protect her. Something in her broke, and I'm afraid to let her out of my sight. What you say comes as no surprise to me. I know there are dangers ahead. But if I keep close to her, keep her in my sight, perhaps there is a chance." When he finished, the pain distorted his beautiful features.

Unable to resist the impulse to soothe him, Theo reached out and took his shaking hand in hers. "It's okay, Eddie, I don't blame you. Really, I don't. You just love her too much."

Eddie smiled a little at Theo's comment and squeezed her hand. When the moment had passed, he pulled back and looked into the sky to see the placement of the sun. "We better get a move on if we want to make it to the rock ridge before nightfall. The woods are full of timber wolves, and we want to be high out of the trees before dark."

Without another word, he returned to the car, leaving Theo to ruminate upon the dangers of wild, hungry animals.

Chapter Eighteen

Theo gingerly approached the car where Kiryana and Eddie stood now fully geared for the hike. Eddie had a padded, yellow coat in his hand which he offered to Theo.

"There are gloves and a hat in the pockets," he said kindly to her. "Unfortunately, I don't have boots for you but your shoes should do the job."

Theo nodded and quickly put on the thermal coat and gloves. They immediately took the chill away.

Unaffected by Eddie's generosity, Kiryana said bluntly, "You won't need a change of clothes so you can leave your bag in the car. The knapsack on the ground is yours."

Theo put her bag in the car and went over to pick up the backpack. Her first effort to lift it was cut short as the bag slipped out of her hands. It was much heavier than she thought. Seeing her struggle, Eddie quickly came to her aid and helped lift the knapsack on to her. As soon as the bag touched her shoulders, her eyes narrowed with strain. She couldn't believe she had to carry this weight up the side of a mountain and rush to the top before dark. Shaking her head in revolt, she blurted out, "I won't be able to carry this – it's too heavy!"

Unimpressed by Theo's complaint, Kiryana rolled her eyes with impatience. Eddie said nothing but took the bag off her. He opened it and pulled out the heavier equipment, and placed it back in the car. Satisfied with the adjustment, he closed the bag again and helped put it back on her. It was significantly lighter, and Theo smiled with relief.

"I guess we are not really camping, are we?" Eddie said sombrely. "I left all the camping gear and thermal blankets. The bag will get lighter as you drink the water."

Theo smiled at his consideration. Annoyed with the pleasant rapport between Eddie and Theo, Kiryana snarked, "Are we finished *making friends*? Can we go now?"

Not wanting to upset her any further, Eddie nodded and pointed them toward the main trail marked by a faded sign, placed there long before the Great Shift. "There is only one way up from here. Once we hit the mid-section, there will be a series of trails that branch off that we need to look for. For now, we just follow this trail upwards for a few hours."

Eddie steeled his expression and started forward. Kiryana gave Theo a gentle nudge to push her along after him. The three of them marched into the dense tree cover and began their climb up the long slope.

The trail had been carved out of the woods long ago, and very little work had been done to maintain it over the years. The farther they moved up the mountain, the less obvious the trail became. Low shrubs, tall ferns and young saplings had grown over it obscuring bits of the path from view. Eddie carried a trail map and a compass which he used as best as he could to keep them on course.

However, a lot of the time was spent trying to find the next section of the trail. In some places they were lucky; ancient trail markers still hung on trees and pointed the way. In other places, it wasn't so clear. Eventually, they arrived at a section that had no markers and no sign of the trail. They clambered over low bracken in the hope of finding the path hidden underneath.

Annoyed and impatient, Kiryana complained, "I can't believe this! After all that we've planned, we are going to get stuck in this stupid forest!"

Eddie, scratching his head underneath his woolly hat, stood holding the compass and studying the trail map. "From what I can see, we haven't gone too far off course. We aren't high enough to hit the main trunk trail, so we haven't overshot the mark. Well, as far as I can tell."

Tired from the difficult hike so far, Kiryana leaned against one of the bare trees to help support her weight. She looked at her watch and wrinkled her brow. "We are losing time, Eddie. If we don't find our way soon, we"ll have to spend the night in the woods."

Theo perked up her ears when she heard this. No one looked happy with the thought of spending the night in the trees. Although they hadn't encountered wild creatures of any variety so far, the idea of running into a pack of timber wolves was never far from anyone's mind.

"Okay, you guys wait here. I just want to have a look over this crest and see what's on the other side." Eddie said before he bounded off into the distance.

Happy for the rest, Theo dropped her bag and shuffled through her pack until she found a bottle of water and another cereal bar. Despite the delay, Kiryana also seemed grateful for the stop. She pulled her bag off her shoulder and let it sag to the ground.

Theo munched quietly as Kiryana sat with her own thoughts. When it became apparent that Eddie was going to be awhile, Kiryana reached into a sachel wrapped around her waist and pulled from it a packet of papers. She read the first page with deep absorption and then studied a large, parchment leaf. After a minute or so, she sighed, frustrated, and dropped the document onto her lap. She grimaced and looked over at Theo.

"This is the map to the Crystal Dragon. Can you have a look?" Kiryana asked without any graciousness.

Theo hesitated. She wasn't sure if she wanted to look at the map. She was certain that she should prevent her cousin from going any further. And yet a part of her was curious. Despite it all, she wanted to know what was written on it.

Theo nodded and scrambled over to her cousin. Kiryana handed over the parchment leaf but held on to the other papers. Despite the parchment paper being old and faded, Theo could tell that the information on it was newer. The images of the Appal woods and several mountain peaks were illustrated in an old-fashioned way. There were no other markings other than the symbol for North.

At first glance, the map looked as if it had been made as a prop for a game. For this reason, Theo seriously doubted its validity. "Um, Kiryana, I'm not sure what to make of this. If you ask me, it doesn't even look real."

But instead of becoming annoyed by her comment, Kiryana nodded in agreement. "It is odd, I know. But the letter that came with it assures me that a proper Oracle would be able to read it."

Theo thought for a second and said, "Perhaps it would be helpful to read the letter. Maybe it can help me understand what I'm supposed to do."

Kiryana blanched. Obviously not happy with the request, she sheepishly offered the letter to her younger cousin. She said, "This letter and the map were placed in my room the night of my birthday party. I don't know who did it."

Theo absorbed what Kiryana said and hesitated again. Without knowing who provided the map, how could they trust it? She had anther reason to stop the journey.

Handwritten with ink, the letter said the following:

Dear Kiryana, my Friend

I cannot stand by idly and see your potential come to naught. It is a harsh trick by Lilith Crowe to set you up for such humiliation, and for that, she should pay in her afterlife. I cannot imagine why anyone would be so cruel, but the world is full of twisted people, made so by the harshness of their own lives. Perhaps at death's door, Lilith was angry about what she sacrificed to serve her profession. Perhaps her last gift to this world was to pass her bitterness to you. I cannot fully understand her motives, but I can certainly see the impact of her actions.

It enrages me to see a creature as great as you passed over for those less deserving. It is an unfair twist of fate that puts you in this place. It is wrong, and I cannot let this happen. I can help you. I possess information that can bring about the destiny you were supposed to have.

The enclosed map is a very special one. It holds the location of the Crystal Dragon. Kept hidden on the Hill for decades, I managed to acquire the information needed to find it and help you possess the talent you were meant to have. One look at you, and it is evident that you were made for great things.

Entwined into the fabric are energetic lines that point to the Crystal Dragon's location. Anyone with Clarity will be able to see them and will know how to navigate to it. Find yourself the right guide, and you will be on your way.

There are many negative stories about the Crystal Dragon but do not believe them. Power is a great thing, and it is jealously guarded by those who have it. You'll see this once you possess your own Clarity.

An Admirer

Theo took in the information and let it sit with her a moment before commenting. "Um, Kiryana," said Theo tentatively, "it's very flattering and all that, but you don't even know who sent it to you. How can you trust what it says?"

"You haven't read everything yet," replied Kiryana. "There is more. This was sent to me two days ago." She handed over another sheet of paper for Theo to read.

Dear Kiryana, my Friend

It is with a heavy heart that I write this letter to you. A difficult thing is about to happen to you. I take no pleasure in telling you this, but I say this so that you can trust the information that I have given you. Without warning, you will be denied the test for entry into the Academy on the Hill. And instead, another, who has no right, will come from nowhere and usurp your position. To make it worse, this upstart will be claimed a prodigy, having hidden her ability for her own reasons. Once this comes to pass, you will realize that you must seek the Crystal Dragon to rightfully return this honour to yourself. Better still, force the prodigy to go with you and let her be the instrument of your own glory. I cannot sit silently and let you be passed over.

An Admirer

Shocked by the content of the second letter, Theo was stunned by the accuracy of its prediction. Not many knew of her abilities, and few would know of the events during the examination. Sadly, Theo's mind went straight to Wilhelmina Van Dorne. She would be the only one who could have possibly predicted that outcome. Other than her, Theo didn't know of anyone else who would hold such knowledge.

The thought of Wilhelmina setting her and Kiryana up like this shocked Theo. She felt deeply betrayed. But knowing Wilhelmina as she did, it wouldn't be outside of her unpredictable character to do something like this.

Kiryana broke the silence. "Yes, it is eerily on the mark. So you can see why I have reasons to act on it." She then brought up other pieces of paper before continuing, "With the map came the instructions on how to find the park's entrance and where to start climbing up into the mountains, which we have done. But once we find the main trunk trail, we won't have any more to go on other than what I'm hoping you can see in this map."

Still trying to make sense of it all, Theo looked at all the pieces of paper. However, she couldn't ignore her concern, "Kiryana, it is still a huge risk to trust what is in these letters. You don't know who wrote it, and you don't know why they are sending you on this hunt. Even if they predicted what happened on exam day, it doesn't mean they are giving you good information about the Crystal Dragon. This could be a dangerous waste of time!"

Kiryana was quiet for a few moments before replying, "That is what Eddie said as well. And you both could be right. However, if there is a chance, no matter how slim, that I might acquire Clarity, then I'm willing to risk everything for it."

Now very alarmed about the situation, Theo continued, "And have you given any more thought about my vision, Kiryana? This admirer of yours may know what is waiting for you in that cave and is sending you to your death." Theo, who had been sitting cross-legged while reading the letters, jumped to her feet.

"You know, I was willing to help you find the cave and was hoping that we could figure out a way of helping you and protecting you at the same time. But I really think that we are being set up for a disaster. I don't feel good about this, Kiryana. If you were in your right mind, you wouldn't either!"

Kiryana, who had been sitting as well, also jumped to her feet. "I don't care what you or anyone thinks. I believe the letters are guiding me to my destiny. I won't be stopped by you or anyone else!"

"We will see about that, now won't we?" retorted Theo, now too outraged to be bullied into a fool's errand. "Good luck finding the Crystal Dragon without my help."

Kiryana was completely unprepared for Theo's rebellion. Theo had been pliable for months while living in the house. Kiryana assumed she easily could push her cousin into giving her what she wanted. Kiryana stood open-jawed facing Theo, now with arms crossed and feet planted into the soft earth.

"W-what do you mean you won't help?" sputtered Kiryana. "Do as I say, or else!"

"Oh yeah?" snorted Theo. "What can you do to me that you haven't already done? Um, kidnap me in the middle of the night and drag me into the middle of nowhere?! You've already done that!! Geez Kiryana, you have no concept of how horrible you have been to me. For someone who needs something from me, you haven't a clue on how to ask for it!" Theo paused and took a deep breath and continued. "You know, I'm done with this. Whether you believe me or not, I'm actually doing you a favour by not helping you."

Theo picked up her backpack and threw it over her shoulders while Kiryana watched helplessly. She thought hard, desperate to turn the tables back. "You can't leave! You can't leave when we are so close! You can't be that heartless, Theo! You must help me! It's only fair. It's only fair for ruining my life!"

"Ruining your life!" laughed Theo. "Your life was ruined long before I showed up. I'm sorry you don't have Clarity, Kiryana. But I'm tired of apologizing for who I am and what I can do."

Feeling more and more defeated, Kiryana sank to the ground and said weakly, "You see, that's the thing. I do want Clarity. It is my dream. Everyone assumes it is all my mother's doing but it isn't. It's something I want too."

"And what about Eddie?" asked Theo. "You know if you get what you want you'll have to give him up. Are you ready to throw him away?"

Kiryana whipped her face up and glared at the younger girl. "Never, never say that! You don't know, you don't know how hard it's been! Each moment we have is precious, and it breaks my heart when I think of leaving…" She couldn't finish as she burst into tears.

Theo softened a little and walked over to Kiryana and offered kindly, "You do believe me when I tell you that you are in danger? I'm not lying, Kiryana. It's a bad thing for you to chase after the Crystal Dragon. Why don't you just let it go and go back home and be with Eddie?"

"The risk doesn't impress me at all," replied Kiryana, sniffling. "And I can't explain it other than to say that I believe my destiny is within one of the caves. I know that as strongly as the air that I'm breathing."

Theo, too frustrated to reply, stared at the top of Kiryana's head until the sound of running footsteps drew her attention. Eddie raced into view and rushed to the girls, collapsing breathless at their feet.

"What on earth…" began Kiryana but Eddie cut her off.

"Shhhhhhh," he hissed. "If you two would just shut up and listen!"

They listened for a minute or so, scanning the thick wood in the late afternoon light for any sign of activity. The girls soon grew restless when they couldn't hear anything.

"What are we listening for?" asked Theo but Eddie just gestured for her to be quiet a bit longer. And then it came. Far in the distance, they could hear it. It was a long, lonely yip that echoed along the hillside. Another yip answered from across the other side. The hairs on Theo's neck rose as she knew this was bad news.

"How long has it being going on?" asked Kiryana apprehensively.

"I guess about five minutes or so - or as long as the two of you have been screaming at each other," replied Eddie as he scowled at the two of them. "Anyway, it's not good. These howls are closer than the first ones. I'm worried that they got our scent."

"What are we going to do?" Theo couldn't control the tremble in her voice.

"The sooner we make it out of the woods and to the rock ridge, the better off we will be. They won't have the chance to surround us, and we can climb out of their reach."

"So you found the trail again, did you?" asked Kiryana hopefully. But Eddie shook his head. "I know we aren't far from the edge of the woods, but I can't figure out which direction to go or how far away we are from it."

"Oh great," moaned Kiryana, "we could be walking in circles all night."

133

Another howl called into the air. The three of them looked wide-eyed at each other as it became obvious that the wolves were getting closer.

"Okay, we need a plan, Eddie," said Kiryana. "Can you pick a direction?"

"Yes," said Eddie hesitantly. "but without the trail, we could be walking into deeper forest."

"What other bright ideas do you have?" replied Kiryana on the verge of panic. "We just can't sit here and wait for them to find us!"

Eddie scanned his map and compass once again, praying that some piece of information that he missed would jump out at him. He was about to suggest going the way he just came from when Theo took a deep breath and said, "Give me the map."

Too frightened and overwhelmed to react quickly, both Kiryana and Eddie just stared at her. Impatient, Theo repeated her demand, "You heard me. Give me your crazy Crystal Dragon map before I change my mind!"

Galvanized by the hope of what the map might reveal, Kiryana scrabbled into her bag and pulled out the parchment and handed it over to Theo.

Theo took the map and studied it again. It felt denser than it looked. It held something else, and she suddenly was intrigued by its composition. Still not sure how to read it, she decided to use what she already knew. She took another breath and went to the part of her, the newly revealed part, and flexed that muscle once again. Within seconds she had shifted into her Clarity, and was seeing the world again with kaleidoscopic colours and energetic lines.

Immediately the flat map came alive. Ghost images grew from the centre of the page and sprung into the air around her. Trees came first, then a trail, then a mountain with a craggy crest. A phrase wafted outward, repeating over and over - "Old Man's Hall, Old Man's Hall"- until Theo was saying this aloud.

The mountain grew and grew until it covered the air above Theo's head and floated in the opposite direction from where Eddie had come. The image sailed out of sight, but it left behind a trail of sparkling blue lights, like glowing breadcrumbs to follow. Satisfied with what the map revealed, Theo shifted out of her reverie and was relieved to see that the trail of lights was still visible to her.

"This way!" shouted Theo and ran in the direction of the blue lights.

Another wolf barked, even closer than before. Too frightened to argue, Kiryana and Eddie jumped forward and followed.

They ran at full speed over brush and fallen logs, under low branches, getting scratched and bumped along the way. Fortunately, the guiding lights were patient and waited for them to catch up. They ran hard until their lungs were about to burst and could run no more. The three of them stumbled into a clearing and stopped to catch their breath. Eddie looked up and shouted with joy, "The trail! It's the main trunk line leading to the ridge!"

The trail opened before them, carved deeply and unmistakeably into the hill, winding upward and toward a rising ridge on the right side.

"Thank goodness," sighed Kiryana with relief.

But the relief was short-lived when a series of yips called out. Their panic grew when they could hear the sounds of bushes rustling not very far behind them.

"This way! Hurry!" shouted Eddie.

They ran and made it to the ridge which protected their right side. Theo, who was last in the group, felt a nip at her shoe, and she lost her balance and fell. She screamed and turned to face a shaggy, lean wolf, the size of a large dog. Behind it were many others, hunched and ready to pounce.

Eddie dropped his bag. He shoved his hand in and pulled out a long, cylindrical tube. In a heartbeat, he set it on fire. The burst of light and fizz frightened the animals, but they backed off only a little. Eddie stormed forward and brandished the flare in their faces. It was enough to keep them away but not enough to drive them off. Eddie helped Theo to her feet and pulled her behind him.

"Keep going, you two. We can't be far from the top!" he shouted as he walked backwards, keeping his eyes on the pack.

The timber wolves, keen for a kill, followed at a safe distance. Eddie, Kiryana and Theo watched the flare with growing anxiety as it shrank. As the wolves grew used to the light, some became brazen enough to approach. But they were soon sent back when walloped with a stick by either Kiryana or Theo.

"Do you have another flare?" asked Theo hopefully as she watched the light dim. Of course, she knew the answer already before Eddie shook his head.

Kiryana looked up the trail and saw a bright opening through the trees. "We are almost at the top!" she yelled.

"Keep going!" said Eddie, unable to take his eyes of the pack.

Up they crept along the trail, bracing their backs against the smooth rock of the growing ridge. Step by step, they advanced until they came out onto a wide plateau. The wolves, undeterred by the open space, followed fearlessly. As the last of the flare sputtered and died, all stood their ground uncertain of what would happen next.

Eddie was the first to act. He threw the empty cartridge at the nearest wolf and ran shouting at them, waving his arms like a madman. "ARRRRRRR go away, go away you stupid wolves! Go away!!!!"

At first, not very impressed, the pack didn't move. But then suddenly, unexpectedly, the timber wolves whined and ran off. Eddie, at first shocked by their reaction then pleased by his success, began to laugh with huge guffaws, "If I hadn't seen it myself, I would never have believed it!"

To his surprise - and everyone else's - a deep voice from behind them echoed Eddie's sentiment, "I wouldn't have believed it either if I hadn't seen it as well."

The three of them spun around to find themselves facing a large group of men and women. The speaker was the man in front, extremely tall and thin, dressed in a short black jacket hanging open over his loose, brown cotton shirt and trousers.

"Look what the Goddess has brought us today," announced the man with a wide grin, revealing a large, gold tooth.

Theo, Kiryana and Eddie looked grimly at each other, sensing that perhaps they had escaped the frying pan only to fall into the fire.

Chapter Nineteen

The tall man stepped forward and swooped low with a gallant bow, pulling his black tube hat off his shaved head.

"Salutations strangers," he said, grinning to show all of his teeth, "I am Phineas MacNabb but you can call me Mad Dog or Rufus. Actually, I'm more partial to Rufus these days, so please call me Rufus. We, all these wonderful people here and myself, are the People's Freedom Group - or PFG (pretty flipping great, ha, ha). We have been living free in nature's truest manner, and we welcome you to our fold." When he finished, the many men and women, of various ages and manner of dress, all mumbled and shuffled as they greeted them.

Theo, Kiryana and Eddie, baffled by the welcome, stood frozen to the spot, uncertain of what to make of the man and his tribe.

Finally Eddie, after looking from Kiryana to Theo, cleared his throat and said, "Thank you, um…"

"Rufus," guided the man, stretching his thin cheeks as far as his skin would permit.

"Um, yes, Rufus," said Eddie tentatively, "thank you for scaring off the wolves. I heard they could be a problem, but I didn't expect them to be so fierce. I don't know what we would have done if you hadn't come along."

"Yes," nodded Rufus, "they didn't used to be so bad. They had to become shrewder since the Great Shift and some winters are leaner than others. We've had our battles, the Grey Alpha and I. The long and short of it, he has learned to keep his distance. But no offence to any of you, they are merely being the animals the Goddess intended, and food is food. In their minds She brought you to them. But indeed, it is for us that you are intended!" He punctuated his speech with a jubilant clap of his hands.

Unnerved by the second reference of being delivered to these people by this unknown Goddess, Theo stepped forward and asked, "What do you mean the Goddess delivered us? Are you planning to eat us?"

No sooner had she asked the question than Rufus and many of the men and women with him starting laughing. After finishing, Rufus clasped his hand warmly onto Theo's shoulder.

"No, no, my sweet, little one, we are not going to eat you, although you might be as tasty as any plump rabbit. No, no, nothing like that. We have been praying to the Goddess all morning to satisfy a lack, and now here you are. Prayers answered."

Kiryana knitted her brows and worried how these strange people's intentions would interfere with her all-important search for the Crystal Dragon. She pushed past Theo to get the man's attention.

"Hello Rufus," she said, flashing her perfect smile, "and hello to the rest of you too. Thank you very kindly for saving us from the pack. I'm sure we can find the perfect way to thank you. But we are up here looking for something rather important, and we need to be on our way before night fall so we can set up camp."

Rufus eyed her over, slowly taking in all of her beautiful charms. Obviously very smitten with her, he leaned toward her with such interest that Eddie felt the need to drape his arm over her shoulder to establish the nature of their relationship.

"Ah," Rufus noted graciously, "I can see that you are spoken for, my young lovely. And what a pair you make! For those like me who bow at the altar of beauty, I can only stand in awe of what nature has rendered. It is as it should be, of course. But please don't refuse me the pleasure of admiring what I see."

Kiryana, well-accustomed to people staring at her, widened her smile and said with a practiced diplomacy, "I am only sorry that I am not available." Eddie raised an eyebrow at the audacity of her lie.

Delighted to be considered by Kiryana, Rufus reached out and took her hand and kissed it. He lamented, "Such is the way of love, but what a delight it is to stare into those golden eyes of yours."

Kiryana let Rufus take his time looking at her which made both Eddie and Theo very uncomfortable. Finally, Kiryana broke the moment and said as casually as she could, "Thank you again for your help. We are truly indebted to you. However, as much as we would like to stay and chat with you, we must be on our way."

She made a gesture to move but Rufus stepped closer and took her hand again, with less chivalry than before. The smile on Kiryana's face faded quickly and was replaced with an expression of mild alarm.

"Ah, my young beauty," said Rufus sadly, "if only I could let you go. No, no, I'm afraid you must come with us back to our camp."

Kiryana began to shake her head, but Rufus ignored her refusal and stated firmly with his full authority, "I'm afraid I must insist. We all must. It would be disrespectful to refuse any gift from the Goddess." Then he looked back at his group and gestured for them to come over. In a matter of moments, they were completely surrounded.

Now feeling the full sense of threat, Eddie pulled Kiryana behind him and stood toe to toe with the older man. "Just what do you intent to do with us?" he demanded.

Realizing that the situation was escalating quickly, Rufus raised his hands and gestured for his people to back off a little. He softened his tone and said, "Now, now, calm down, young man. It's not as horrible as you might think. We have no intention of harming you."

"Then what do you want from us?" replied Eddie, keeping his guard up.

"Well, it's how we live," explained Rufus. "We have rejected the unfair bonds of regular economic structures and have returned to nature. We live on what the benevolent Goddess provides us: fish from the stream, berries from the bushes, milk from our goats. But sadly, the Goddess favours the cycle of feast and famine, and there are times when we don't have enough. Sometimes, we need to supplement our supplies." The group of people behind him started to grumble unhappily.

Now speaking to his people, Rufus announced, "Not every system is perfect, and there are times we must make compromises. And I still insist it is better than starving!"

From within the crowd, a young woman with blonde dreadlocks called out, "You are selling out, man! You always give up too soon!"

Fully annoyed by the comment, Rufus raised his voice and yelled, "We have only lasted these few winters because of the supplements. I am willing to risk an imperfect execution of our philosophy for the luxury of lasting until summer."

"You have no guts!" shouted back the young woman. "You are a hypocrite and a sell-out."

Rufus gritted his teeth but resisted replying, and deliberately planted a mad grin back on his leathery face. Theo, Kiryana and Eddie looked helplessly at each other and wondered what they had walked into.

Rufus took a deep breath before continuing, "So we needed help with our supplies to survive the winter. We prayed to the Goddess to help us. And then you showed up. So you are here to help us."

"How?" asked Eddie, still no clearer about what was happening to them.

"Ah yes," said Rufus, "we know a man in the village who does some dealing with us. We bring you to him, he pays us in supplies and he'll contact your families in search of…"

"A ransom," interjected Kiryana as she quickly gleaned the implication.

Shaking his head gently, Rufus corrected her, "No, no, more like a reward. He's done it before and he negotiates fairly. Anyway, our rice and beans stocks are dangerously low and we need something of value to barter. And here you are: sent by the Goddess with love."

"And we give credence to the economic structure we have avowed to reject!" shouted the young woman again, very angry about having to compromise her ideals.

"Yeah, yeah, we are doing what we must to avoid starving. I can live with that!" shouted Rufus back at her.

"And what about our trip?" asked Kiryana. "We have come specifically to explore the caves. We can't leave now."

Rufus replied gently, "My beauty, there are thirty-five men and women who rely on these supplements to survive. I'm afraid you'll just have to come back another time. You would have my word as a devout believer in the Goddess that we will never trouble you again."

Feeling despair at the idea of abandoning her quest, Kiryana thought for a moment and said, "I'm sure you are wrong about what your Goddess wants. And I can prove it! Here is an initiate Oracle, due to train in Greenstone as soon as we get back. She can tell you what your Goddess truly wants for you!" Kiryana grabbed Theo by the arm and thrust her forward. She landed in front of Rufus with a thump.

Surprised and mortified at being put in this position, Theo stood awkwardly as Rufus studied her intently.

"An Oracle? My goodness you are just a child. I haven't seen an Oracle in person since I was a young man. How extraordinary to find one of you out of cloister." The awe in his tone was sincere.

"Um yes, well, my powers have just developed this year, and I haven't started my training yet," said Theo shyly.

Seeing that she wasn't making the strong impression she needed to make, Kiryana quickly spoke up, "She is very modest, I tell you. But don't let that fool you. She is a prodigy of the highest degree and will be able to tell you to what your Goddess truly wants. Go on, ask her! Ask her!" Both Theo and Eddie's jaws dropped a little as they couldn't believe what she was doing. Fortunately, no one else seemed to notice.

Rufus, now open to the idea that an audience with an Oracle might be the reason for their meeting, rolled back on his heels and looked solemnly at Theo. "Can you tell me the Goddess' will?" he asked softly, worried she might disappear into thin air.

Kiryana slyly smirked to see her ploy working. Of course, Theo wouldn't dare let her down.

Theo looked at Rufus and then at the people surrounding him, all thin and underdressed for the cold in bizarre, hand-made clothing. She didn't need to access her Clarity to know that they were kind but desperate folk who were starving. In an instant, she felt compelled to help them.

She looked over at Kiryana and remembered their fight from earlier on. Again, Theo didn't need an extra sense to know that someone was setting Kiryana up for a disaster. Her own vision confirmed that her cousin was in danger, and it was very much in Kiryana's best interest to prevent her finding the Crystal Dragon. Who knows? Perhaps this Goddess that Rufus spoke of was acting on Kiryana's behalf too. It might be serving a greater good if Theo just went along with what these strangers wanted.

"I can see a sign coming in, a sign is on its way," said Theo, as she pretended to go into a trance. Rufus and his followers all leaned in closer, fascinated by what she might say. Kiryana grew excited at the prospect of being set free. "Yes, yes, I can see a sign forming. Yes, I can see the edges. Yes I can see it! I can see it!"

"What? What is it that you see?" asked Rufus, unable to contain himself and widening his eyes.

"I can see it! I can see it now! I can see bags and bags of rice and beans!"

"What!" cried Kiryana, realizing that Theo had pulled a fast one on her.

Pleasure rippled through the crowd and Rufus smiled with great delight. "Bags of rice and beans! Great Goddess' girdle! So it's settled then. Alright, let's go back to camp and have a wonderful meal, a good night's sleep, and we'll take you down first thing in the morning!"

Furious, Kiryana whispered into Theo's ear as they started marching forward, "Just so you know, this isn't over yet!"

Despite herself, Theo couldn't help but smile with satisfaction as they walked into the dimming light, away from the ridge's edge and away from the Crystal Dragon.

It was an easy walk to the camp. Despite having their plan interrupted by these people, it was a relief to be surrounded by them and protected from the wilder aspects of the mountains. Even Kiryana, who refused to look at either Theo or Eddie during the walk, softened her disposition when she saw the circle of canvas tents and small yurts. A large bonfire sat in the middle of the camp and cushions were scattered about as an invitation to join and warm up.

Theo, Kiryana and Eddie were directed to take a seat. They dropped onto large cushions and sighed as the heat began to seep back into their hands. Soon they began to relax, letting the toll of the previous night's drive and harrowing hike unravel. They released their weariness and sank fully into the comfort and warmth.

Noticing their sleepy looks, Rufus rushed over to them and said very loudly, "No, no, we can't lose you yet! Wait, wait! Dinner is about to be served."

No sooner had he said it, when men arrived carrying steaming bowls of rice and lentils and placed them in their laps. The smell of it was so good that Theo thought she would swoon from the delight of it. She began to salivate with anticipation of her first bite as she realized she was much hungrier than she thought. Kiryana and Eddie had wasted no time and already thrust their spoons into their bowls and were eating with gusto.

"Our diet is not that varied," said Rufus as he began to eat his own dinner. "But I think the cooks do a good job with what they have to work with."

With their mouths full, Theo, Kiryana and Eddie could only nod in agreement.

It didn't take long for them empty their bowls and place them down on the ground. As soon as they did, someone came along and picked them up. Then they were then given a slice of flavoured bread that was closer in texture to cake. This was even more delicious than the rice and lentils, and the three of them gobbled it up in no time. Lastly, they were served a cup of steaming sweet tea whose aroma swirled delightfully about them. They took small sips as the liquid cooled.

Now with the meal over, all the members of the group took their place around the fire and began to talk buoyantly. The knowledge that more food was coming raised the spirits of the commune and they started telling funny, familiar stories that even Theo, Kiryana and Eddie found amusing. Rufus, who was so dominant at their first meeting, now slipped into the background as others from the group stepped forward to entertain. At one point the young woman with the blonde dreadlocks, who was called Shoshanna, came forward with a guitar and began singing. Soon others joined in with instruments and voice, singing pretty and sad songs. Despite the unsavoury reason for being there, the People's Freedom Group treated Theo, Kiryana and Eddie like honoured guests to the party.

A young man with beautiful long hair and a thin, reddish beard leaned over and offered Kiryana some more of the sweet-tasting bread. He had been sitting near her all evening, stealing glances at her when she wasn't looking. While this would normally irritate Eddie, he too was busy with all the looks he was receiving from many of the women. Clearly Kiryana and Eddie were being admired. Strangely, neither of them felt overwhelmed nor uncomfortable with the attention.

Rufus, who had been watching them quietly for a time, spoke up and said, "We must take it easy on our guests; they are not used to our ways. You see, we believe in the wisdom of our instincts and in the freedom of choice. We believe that we should be allowed to satisfy our desires. If done with kindness and respect, of course. It shouldn't be unpleasant for anyone."

Eddie, who was being given more tea from a pretty, young girl with thick, golden braids, looked past her to nod at Rufus that he understood. Then he smiled warmly at the girl who beamed under his gaze. "I'm afraid that we come here to explore some of the caves. And you should all know that Kiryana and I are a couple," said Eddie clearly announcing his situation.

"Are you very much in love?" asked the girl with the braids.

"Yes," Eddie replied looking into her wide eyes, "hopelessly so."

"Too bad," said the girl as she moved away and found her seat on the other side of the fire.

Rufus laughed a little as he said, "Ah, youth. I can't decide which is better: young love or the freedom to explore. But it doesn't matter, does it? We each have our own way in the world. So which caves were you set to find?"

Eddie looked blank and tried to come up with some name that would sound convincing. But he didn't need to think long before Kiryana piped in confidently, "Old Man's Hall."

Theo, surprised to hear this coming from Kiryana, didn't realize that Kiryana had heard her when she had been in the trance.

"What's this?" asked Rufus. "I haven't heard of Old Man's Hall."

Relieved to hear this, Theo relaxed thinking that the phrase from the map was nonsensical. Kiryana was no closer to finding the Crystal Dragon.

Suddenly the young man with the red beard spoke up with a clear, animated voice, "I know of Old Man's Hall." Excited to have Kiryana's rapt attention, he continued, "Old Man's Hall is part of the Bluebeard Beacon. Normally cave explorers go to the higher entrance on the front of the mountain, but there is a lesser known one lower down at the back. It was called Old Man's Hall as a joke for those too feeble to climb to the main entrance. Anyway, I don't think there is much in the Hall – I've only seen the one cave myself."

"So it exists, does it?" asked Kiryana with a flirtatious smile which caused the young man to shine with delight.

"Yes it does! And it's not hard to get there from here…" he continued.

Rufus stopped him and said, "Thank you, Noah. Your helpfulness is much appreciated but sadly our guests won't be seeing the cave on this trip."

Noah stopped and understood to say no more. He did sneak a glance at Kiryana whose amber eyes sparkled with appreciation. She got from him all the information that she needed.

Rufus raised himself from his cushion and made his way to the bonfire. It was a signal the tribe understood well and all settled in their places. Everyone waited for him to speak. Even Shoshanna, still visibly annoyed, focused her attention squarely on him.

"And so it goes - the wheel turns. What is up will go down, and what is down will have its day. The Goddess is fair, but not to everyone at the same time. What is better? To have no power in the world, or to have power then have it taken from you? The lessons of the Goddess are time-enduring and universal, and our corporeal stay is brief." Rufus riffed with his eyes closed. Then he opened them and asked the group, "What story tonight? What are we in the mood for?"

There was a rumbling of suggestions but none of them made any sense to the new comers. Finally, the name Finnegan could be heard echoing around the bonfire.

"Finnegan it is," said Rufus, as he planted his feet wide into the ground. He cleared his throat and began:

Finnegan was a good man. He gave to his brothers, and lived a life he earned. One day, he crossed an evil man. This man beat Finnegan and left him for dead by the side of the road. Too weak to move, he was at the mercy of the world. When the rain came, he was grateful for the water to wash his wounds and ease his thirst. When the sun came, he was grateful for the warmth. When a passerby came, he was grateful not to be alone.

"Please help me," Finnegan said. "I have been beaten and left for dead."

The passerby, a young man in a fine suit, had a long look at him but there was so much blood everywhere.

"This is terrible," said the young man. "Surely, he who did this to you must be punished."

"Yes, I suppose so. Still, can you help me up and take me to a hospital?"

The young man looked at his own fine clothes and hesitated. "Yes, I can. But first let me chase after your assailant. Someone must make sure he doesn't get away with this crime."

And before Finnegan could reply, the young man was gone.

When the rain came again, Finnegan was grateful for the drink, and when the sun came back, he was happy for the light. Soon another passerby approached.

A young mother with a baby stopped and asked, "Are you still alive?"

"Yes, I am weak but I am still here," said Finnegan and gave the woman a smile.

The woman climbed into the ditch and tried to lift him up, but he was too heavy and one arm was already full with her child.

"I can't manage it," she gasped.

"No matter, just go for help. I can wait."

But the woman did not think Finnegan could wait, and she would be wasting her time. Sadly, she continued on her way.

The rain did not come again and the sun was starting to set. The night would be cold and Finnegan knew he wouldn't see the morning. Still, he was grateful not to have been alone and called to the heavens with his thanks.

"Who are you thanking?" asked a voice. It was another man who had just approached.

Finnegan turned to the stranger and offered his hand to him and clasped it tight.

"Do you need a doctor?" asked the stranger.

"No, I need a friend," said Finnegan. He closed his eyes and sighed. The stranger held him tightly until he couldn't hold on any more. And for that, Finnegan was grateful.

"And this is Finnegan," said Rufus. And the group replied "Finnegan".

Rufus finished and everyone sat quietly. Theo, Kiryana and Eddie felt soft, reassuring touches on their arms from the people sitting beside them.

Then Rufus clapped his hands and said, "Alright, my lovelies, I'm sure our guests are tired, and tomorrow we will start early as we head into town. Nothing can't be faced with a good night's sleep afore it!" Rufus walked over to Theo, Kiryana and Eddie and motioned for them to stand and follow him.

He led them to one of the smaller yurts and showed them inside. Three camp cots covered with large, woven blankets filled the space. A small lantern sat on a short stand, casting a warm glow against the canvas.

"I think you'll be comfortable here," said Rufus. "If you need anything, please just holler."

He passed through the canvas flap but then stopped and poked his head back through again. "I'm very sorry to have to do this but there will be shifts of people sitting outside your tent making sure you stay the night. It is unfortunate but it can't be helped."

Not really needing a response, Rufus pulled his head out and called from the other side of the flap, "Sleep well, my angels, and see you in the morning!"

Chapter Twenty

As soon as Rufus walked away, Kiryana ran to the canvas door and threw it open. Two tall and lanky men dressed in hiking gear stood in front of the tent and turned around to face her.

"Anything we can help you with?" the shorter of the two asked with a crisp politeness.

Kiryana shook her head and dropped the flap. Turning, she found Theo and shot her a scathing look. Theo, fearing for her safety, ran and hid behind Eddie who had already raised his hands to try and calm his girlfriend down.

"Bags and bags of rice and lentils!" yelled Kiryana as she barged into Eddie, trying to reach around and grab any part of her younger cousin.

"Now, now Kiry," grimaced Eddie as he caught Kiryana's flailing hands. "Cool it! Flipping out isn't going to help anyone."

"Sure it will!" Kiryana shouted. "It will feel good just to strangle her!"

Grabbing her wrists, Eddie said, "I'm not going to let you hurt her. I don't care what she has done. You and I are in enough trouble already just by bringing her here."

After fighting futilely against Eddie's firm grip, Kiryana finally stopped struggling. "All right, all right. I give in. Just let me go."

After studying her face for a moment to judge whether or not she meant what she said, Eddie relaxed his grip enough for Kiryana to pull her hands away. She rubbed her wrists as she went to the other side of the tent.

Feeling utterly defeated, Kiryana approached one of the camping cots and slumped onto its edge. Theo came out from behind Eddie and turned to look up at him.

"Have you read the letters, Eddie?" Theo asked. "Don't you think it is highly suspicious that a stranger is sending her on this ridiculous treasure hunt? And considering what I have seen in my vision, it's crazy to go after this Crystal Dragon!"

Theo, exasperated by the older girl's inability to acknowledge how dangerous the journey was, now directed her comments to Kiryana, "You know, given all that you've done to me, no one would blame me for keeping my mouth shut and letting you fall off the edge."

Kiryana shrugged and ignored Theo. Instead she looked pitifully at Eddie and lamented, "Fat load of good you did, Eddie. You said nothing and let them keep me here. How can you let it all end when I'm so close to finding what I want?"

Eddie, visibly hurt by Kiryana's comment, went to her side and put his hand on her back. "Kiry, honey, I don't know what you expected me to do? It's not as if I can over-power thirty people."

"Well, you don't have to look so happy about being here - hanging out with pretty girls with braids."

Eddie ignored the insinuation and continued gently, "You know, Theo has been pretty adamant about what she has seen in her vision. It is starting to make me think perhaps it would be wise to end this now before something bad happens."

"Finally someone is talking sense!" said Theo as she flopped on her own cot.

"Are you saying that you are now on Theo's side?" accused Kiryana as she stood to her feet.

"I'm not on any one's side. I mean, I am on your side, of course, Kiry, but I don't want to do anything that might cause any harm. Maybe it's just time to see this for what it is and call it a day." Eddie followed Kiryana and wrapped his arms around her. "I love you more than anything and there is very little I wouldn't do for you. But I won't help you if it's going to hurt you."

Angered, Kiryana broke from Eddie's hold and glared at him. "So that's it then? You're out?"

"I think it's the wise move. And I think over time you'll see it was the right thing to do."

"Don't count on that!" cried Kiryana. She ran to her cot and threw her covers over her head to shut out yet another person who had let her down.

Eddie looked helplessly at Theo. She felt sorry for him. Then she sighed, "Best to leave it for now. She'll be angry for a while."

Eddie nodded sadly as he stared at the blanket over Kiryana. Then he walked over to the last cot, threw himself upon his back and covered his eyes with his arms.

"Good night," Theo said to the room after settling herself under her own covers. No one said anything back.

Exhausted, Theo was asleep in minutes and didn't move until loud shouts and banging noises outside of the tent woke her up. She opened her eyes in time to see Shoshanna bursting through the canvas flap and command, "Get up and come with me!"

Theo rubbed her eyes as she swung her feet over the edge of the cot and stuck her feet into her heavy shoes. As she hurried to throw on her coat, she noticed Eddie standing at the foot of Kiryana's cot.

"Kiry? Are you coming?" He asked tentatively, unsure of where he now stood with her. He had already put on his coat and was ready to follow Shoshanna.

However, Kiryana didn't reply. In fact she hadn't moved at all since last night and still hid beneath her covers.

Considering what happened yesterday, neither Eddie nor Theo were surprised that Kiryana was still sulking. Eddie sadly shrugged, and he and Theo rushed through the canvas flap. It was easier to let sleeping dogs lie.

Although it felt like Theo had only been asleep for minutes, she in fact had slept through the entire night. A weak winter dawn was creeping over the horizon and a thin, pale light had started to illuminate the camp. Everywhere people were rushing about in alarm, pulling down tents and packing up cushions and pots.

Shoshanna rushed them through the camp and toward the ridge's edge. Finally, they rounded a bend and arrived at a stone platform that overlooked the valley. A few men and women stood about looking worried while Rufus stood precariously near the edge holding an old-fashioned spy glass to his wrinkly eye.

Noticing them, he smiled tersely and demanded, "Um, would either of you know why the police are searching the parking lot below?"

Theo and Eddie approached the edge and looked over. At first they were taken back by the height. Once they got past the shock, they saw lights spiralling around in the area where they had left their car.

Eddie, having nothing left to hide, said matter-of-factly, "Oh, I guess they found our car."

"And why would the police be looking for your car?" asked Rufus now realizing that something might be wrong.

"I guess for a number of reasons," replied Eddie, taking his time, enjoying the moment. "Perhaps it's because Kiryana is the daughter of the Stokes, who both serve in the High Council in Greenstone, and she ran away from home. Or perhaps it's because we stole the car to get here. But I really suspect that it might be because Kiryana and I kidnapped Theo, who was scheduled to leave for the Oracle academy yesterday morning."

Rufus stared with his mouth agape at Eddie while Shoshanna groaned out loud. Then, after processing what was said, and to everyone's surprise, he began guffawing loudly and heartily, "Well, I guess the Goddess didn't send you after all," he laughed without irony. "My, that minx is one tricky creature." He said something to one of the men near him, and the group of them, with the exception of Shoshanna, rushed back down the path toward the camp.

"So what are you going to do with us now?" asked Eddie.

"Do with you?" Rufus repeated. "Do with you? Why, nothing. In fact, we would like to be as far away from you as soon as possible."

"You mean you are going to let us go?" chimed in Theo with disbelief.

"You are no good to us now, are you? Any association with you is only going to bring the arm of the law down upon us. And quite frankly, there a few of us who haven't been in their good graces over the years. We all would rather prefer they didn't know we were here."

"So we can leave now?" asked Eddie eagerly.

"Yes, now, yesterday, last week," said Rufus with a wave of his hand. "We will be finished de-camping in twenty minutes so you better get your stuff."

Then he looked over at a grim-faced Shoshanna and raised his hands in defence as he said, "I suppose you are going to let me have it now, aren't you?" Shoshanna, not amused, crossed her arms and silently glared back at him.

Eddie and Theo didn't waste any time and ran back along the path to the small yurt. They burst through the canvas flap to find two of their backpacks had been returned. Eddie, excited to tell Kiryana the good news, rushed to her cot and pulled the covers off. But instead of finding a sullen girl curled beneath, they discovered a pile of cushions shaped to look like her.

"What the…" gasped Eddie. He spun around in confusion but it didn't take long for him to realize that Kiryana had taken off. Of course, she wouldn't have given up so easily.

"I can't believe she left us behind!" cried Eddie, who was very hurt to have been abandoned.

"Eddie, how did she get out?" asked Theo. "She can't be too far ahead."

Grabbing their gear, Theo and Eddie rushed out of the yurt, in time to miss the collapse of the canvas, as it was the last tent to fall. Now that there was more daylight than darkness, lanterns and flashlights were turned off and packed away. Given that they had been up for only fifteen minutes, both of them were amazed at how the sparse the camp now looked.

Theo and Eddie ran back the way they came and met Rufus who was speaking to various people. Eddie rushed over and took hold of his arm to demand his attention.

"Kiryana has run off in the night. She was determined to go to Old Man's Hall so we think she headed there. But there is no way she would know how to find it on her own. Someone would have to take her there."

Rufus looked surprisingly concerned. "Those Beacons can be dangerous, especially if you don't know what you are doing." He thought for a moment, then walked over to one of the tall hikers and asked, "Who was watching the yurt after you last night?"

The man stopped packing his duffle bag and replied, "It was supposed to be Josiah, but Noah volunteered instead."

Having heard enough, Rufus turned to a woman in a rainbow-coloured head scarf standing near him and said, "Find Noah."

A few minutes later a sheepish Noah stood before them, unable to look any of them in the eye. Noah was the same ruddy-haired young man that was paying so much attention to Kiryana the night before. Eddie, filled with rage, pushed forward and took Noah by the scruff of his coat.

"What did you do with her?" he shouted. "If anything happens to her, I'll break every bone in your body!"

Rufus and another the tall man pulled Eddie off Noah and held him while he struggled and grunted. Theo, fearing this approach would only make matters worse, stepped in and said, "Eddie, stop it! This isn't helping. We need to hear from Noah what happened."

Realizing that Theo was right, Eddie stopped struggling. Once he relaxed, the men let him go and he stumbled forward. But he continued to glower at Noah.

"Okay, Noah," asked Rufus sternly, "what part did you play in this nonsense?"

Obviously regretting what he had done, Noah started speaking hesitantly, "When I started my watch, I looked in the yurt to make sure everything was okay. These two were asleep but Kiryana was wide awake. When she saw me, she begged me to take her to the Hall. She said that she wasn't the important ransom, that people would want the guy as he was the son of a powerful politician and the girl, who was a prodigy Oracle. If she left, no one would miss her."

"And you believed her?" sneered Eddie. "Or were you just hoping to get her to yourself, alone!"

Rufus shook his head and motioned for Eddie to stay quiet. "Ignore that Noah. What else happened?"

Shifting from foot to foot, he tried to defend his actions, "She seemed so sad so I wanted to help her. She said she needed me to show her the way. When she looked up at me, it was impossible to say no. So I got cushions from the fire pit, found her backpack, and we headed out a few hours before dawn."

"So she is at the Old Man's Hall now," clarified Rufus.

"Yeah, she is there. I don't know why she wants to sit in a damp cave by herself. I stayed with her for a little while, but as soon as we got there she completely ignored me."

"Did she find what she was looking for?" asked Theo anxiously.

"No. She didn't find anything. She got fed up and told me not to bother to wait for her. That it would be best if I left."

"So she got from you what she wanted and then she didn't need you anymore. Sounds like Kiryana." Theo said, but she was relieved to hear that Kiryana hadn't found the Crystal Dragon.

Noah looked at Theo and nodded his head to show he understood. "I guess I've been a bit stupid about her, haven't I?"

"Yep!" snorted Eddie, "a complete idiot!"

"Now, now," interjected Rufus, "he is no more foolish than any man trying to please a beautiful girl. So she was safe when you left her?"

"Yeah, she seemed fine," replied Noah.

"Okay then, seems your friend is alright for the moment, and Noah has learned a valuable lesson," said Rufus.

"So what happens now? You have to show us where the Old Man's Hall is so we can find her," demanded Eddie, overwhelmed with worry.

Rufus began to shake his head as he spoke, "I'm sorry, Eddie, but we can't risk having any of us being found by the authorities. In fact, we should have been off this site already. I'm sure Noah can give you good directions but you guys are on your own."

Suddenly Noah was reminded of something and said, "Wait! Kiryana wanted me to give this to Theo." He reached into his coat pocket and pulled out a familiar, leather sachel.

Theo took the leather purse and opened it. Sure enough the map was safely inside. Eddie heaved a sigh of gratitude when he realized that Kiryana had sent back a way for them to find her.

"Thank you, Noah. It's fine. We can find our own way now," said Theo.

Rufus smiled and clapped his hands loudly together. "Okay people! Our Goddess loves to be entertained but we have gotten there in the end! Time for us to be on our way!"

Theo, remembering Rufus' predicament, felt concern for him and his crew. What would they now do for food? "Rufus, what are you going to do without the reward. Will you be okay?"

Rufus wrinkled his eyes as he said, "Aw sweetheart, are you worried about us? Well, don't be. We will just have to leave the mountain for the winter and busk for money in the lower towns. We've done it before and we've been fine."

Upon hearing this, Eddie reacted, "What! You could have busked for money all along? And you were going to sell us for ransom?"

Without any hint of remorse Rufus laughed and mischievously replied, "And give up this view without a fight? Are you crazy?"

Then he picked up some canvas bags near him and began to march forward across to the other side of the clearing. Soon the others did the same, taking every possession they owned on their backs. In a matter of minutes everyone had cleared out with military precision leaving no trace of the People's Freedom Group ever having been there.

Theo and Eddie now stood alone with only the sound of birds twittering in the early morning light. Looking around at the empty space, Eddie said with amazement, "Did we imagine them?"

Theo smiled as she replied, "Maybe. Maybe we did."

Realizing there was no time to waste she pulled the map from the leather sachel and opened it up.

"I guess she hasn't totally given up on me," sighed Eddie as he looked sombrely at the map.

"Aw, Eddie she is just mad at you," offered Theo kindly. Eddie placed a hand on her shoulder and gave a good squeeze.

"You know with all that you had to put up with, she really doesn't deserve you."

Theo looked up into Eddie's soft brown eyes and said, "I could say the same about you too." And in that moment they connected with a shared knowing.

Eddie turned his attention to the map. "Will it take us to Old Man's Hall?" he wondered.

"Only one way to find out." Theo shifted into her Clarity once again, now comfortable with the knack of it. She watched the images grow from the map once again. Immediately she felt relief that the information was still there.

Once again Blackbeard Mountain rose up from the parchment and lifted high above her head. And as before, it floated in the direction of the ridge leaving behind pretty blue ripples of lights for her and Eddie to follow. Without wasting any more time, Theo and Eddie hurried on in the hope of finding Kiryana before anything terrible happened.

Chapter Twenty-One

It didn't take long to arrive at the clearing where they first met the People's Freedom Group the night before. From there, the path of lights took them onward toward the impressive mountains called the Towers. The Towers were a group of seven peaks all about the same height that dominated the landscape with their sharp and jagged points. Stark and brooding, these peaks were devoid of any vegetation except for scrub and weeds. Ragged rocks and large boulders were scattered about as if left behind after a giant game of marbles. As Theo and Eddie came closer, the charcoal dirt began to thin before disappearing entirely, revealing hard granite and gneiss stone slabs. Then the even surface gave way to the slowly rising slopes of the mountain's base. Now they began to climb.

It was a slow ascent but an easy one as there were many accessible footholds. The sparkling blue lights hovered in the distance, always spurring them on, always waiting for them to catch up.

Eddie climbed up first and made sure he had a good grip before reaching behind and pulling Theo up behind him. They climbed like this for some time. The blue lights were taking them around to the unprotected side of the peak with a long, harrowing fall into the deep valley below.

Theo looked up to see the blue lights disappear over a large rock edge and panicked when they fell out of sight. Still a good way from the rock edge, she called up to Eddie.

"We'd better hurry!" she shouted. "I can't see the blue lights anymore!"

Eddie nodded and hoisted her up behind him and lifted himself up to another ledge. Again, he reached back for Theo but lost his leverage as he rushed to secure a firmer hold. As he scrambled to keep from falling, he let Theo's hand slip from his. Skidding a little down the slope, Theo quickly regained her control and caught hold of a spikey bit of scrub.

"Are you okay?" Eddie called to her and she nodded back, trying not to look down. Taking better care, Eddie and Theo moved up the rest of the way as quickly as they dared. Finally, they crested the rock edge and landed on a flat plateau that lay outside the wide mouth of a cave. Theo sighed with relief when she saw the blue lights twinkling from within the depths of the entrance.

"This is it!" said Theo as she rose to stand. "We've made it!"

"So Kiryana is in here?" asked Eddie with uncertainty as he looked into the grim opening.

"As long as she stayed put, she is," replied Theo.

Theo crossed the threshold and followed the beckoning lights, which now shone brilliantly within the darkness of the cave. The cave receded into a narrow hallway that led deep into the underbelly of the ancient peak. When the reach of daylight ended, darkness covered everywhere.

Eddie dropped his knapsack and pulled from it two head lamps and a couple of powerful flashlights. He gave Theo her equipment and quickly turned on his own. He spun around and tried to see what the cave looked like within the narrow beams of artificial light. The walls were smooth and barren of any discernible features.

Theo, still focusing on the blue lights, noticed that they weren't moving any longer even though she was getting closer. The main passage of the cave led downward yet the lights remained resting on one of the walls. Curious about the change of movement, Theo approached the wall to see what the twinkling lights wanted her to find.

They had gathered in a small space and united to create a brightness that was hard to see past. When she was near enough to touch them, they spun together to form a single beam. They spiralled from their resting place down into the wall itself. She aimed her flashlight to see where they went and discovered a deep hole, like a chimney, which burrowed into a lower chamber of the cave.

"Eddie!" she shouted excitedly, "have a look at this!"

Eddie rushed over to see what the fuss was about. At first, he couldn't find the opening as a protrusion of rock hid the hole from view. It would be very easy to miss even if he knew what to look for. He shone his light down into the shaft and flipped the light back and forth to see the tunnel.

"Oh, this is interesting," he said. "If you look at the sides you can see chip marks as if someone had carved it out. This isn't a natural vent."

"Yeah, it's strange," agreed Theo. "And it's where the map wants us to go. We are supposed to climb down this tunnel."

Again Eddie shone his light around the hole and shook his head dubiously. "It's a really small opening, Theo. But sure, if that's where we are supposed to go. Here, help me with this."

Eddie pulled out a long, nylon rope from his backpack, and Theo helped wrap it around him. Once in place, he clipped it expertly so it was snug and secure. Positioning his headlamp for the descent, he climbed up to the opening and swung his legs into the tunnel. However, once his waist passed the rock, his shoulders caught on the solid sides and wouldn't budge. He pulled himself out and tried head first but his shoulders, wide and firm, wouldn't fit through. Frustrated, he finally climbed out.

"I can't fit, Theo," said Eddie as he rubbed a few sore spots that got bashed in his attempt. "Are you sure this is the way in?"

"I can only tell you what I see. The guiding lights went down this hole."

After thinking a moment, Eddie looked at Theo and stated the obvious. "Theo, I'm too wide to fit. And I think it's important that we continue to follow the lights. They are leading us to Kiryana."

Theo, sensing where this was going, started shaking her head vehemently. "No, no, no," she resisted. "No, I'm not good in small spaces or in the dark."

"No, listen," insisted Eddie, "I don't think that shaft is very deep and you wouldn't be in it for very long."

"How do you know it's not long?" asked Theo. "What makes you think that? All I can see is unending darkness!"

"Wait," he replied. "Let me prove it." Eddie bent down and picked up a few loose pebbles. Going over to the tunnel, he dropped the pebbles down the shaft. A resounding clatter echoed back in no time. Eddie smiled with satisfaction.

"See? It's not that long, and you'll be in the next cave in no time."

Feeling extremely nervous about the prospect of being squished by the weight of a mountain, Theo still wasn't convinced.

"How did Kiryana and this Noah guy get down there if it's so small?"

"What can I say, Theo? I'm a big guy. And I'm sure eating rice and lentils all the time isn't bulking up these PFG folks. Come on, it won't be so bad. I'll tie a rope on you and hold you as you slide down."

"Well, I don't know…"

"Theo, you are the only one here who can. When you are down there, maybe you can see if Kiryana found another way in. Okay?"

"As long as you hold on tight to the rope," conceded Theo hesitantly.

"As tightly as if the world depended upon it," he promised. "You are my favourite Oracle after all." Despite the odd shadows that were cast on his face from his head lamp, Theo could see the sincerity of his smile.

Eddie took the rope and tied it around Theo's waist. He lifted her up to the opening and guided her in head first. Securing her headlamp and shifting the straps around so they sat in the right place he gave her a gentle pat on the back as he slowly let her slide out of his arms.

"Once you can see the opening at the bottom, it will feel a lot better for you."

Theo was as frightened as she had ever been. Sliding down head first into a dark tunnel was an adventure she rather would not have. There was hardly any room and she was constricted right away by the cold stones pushing back. Theo struggled to breathe as she imagined the walls falling inward. Cold, strands of fear began to twist through her. All she wanted to do was run away, but she was trapped, pinned by the narrowness of the chute. She felt helpless and afraid, and she wanted to cry.

"Eddie, Eddie!! Pull me up! Pull me up! I can't do this! I can't breathe! Let me out! Let me out!" she tried to scream, but she couldn't get enough air to achieve volume.

"Theo, I'm sure you are almost at the bottom. Can you see anything?" Eddie called, still lowering her down, little by little, unaware of her panic attack.

Theo shook her head to block out his question. All she wanted to do was to get out of this insufferable hole. She was starting to feel as if she was suffocating; her mouth opened wider to gasp in dank air. Never in her life had she felt so awful. Normally when frightened, she would jump to her feet and run the fear out. But she was trapped in a small space, and the fear whirled inside of her like a tornado. Unable to thrash or scream, she was stuck in the centre of her own storm.

"Theo, just a few more feet and you'll be there. Be brave a little longer!" Eddie said, hoping to spur her on.

"I can't! I can't! I can't breathe! Please just pull me back," she whimpered. "Please, just let me out!" While she was thinking this was the worst thing that had ever happened to her, her shoulder hit a rock that jetted out from the side. In an instant, she was stuck.

Eddie felt the rope go slack when Theo stopped dropping. Thinking she had reached the bottom, he yelled down hopefully, "Are you down? Are you out?"

Theo couldn't believe what was happening. She was so overwhelmed with terror that she thought that she might actually die. She started to squirm about in her rock cocoon but the motion merely knocked the head lamp off her head. It fell to the bottom, rolled out of sight and turned itself off. Now, on top of it all, she was in the pitch black, stuck.

"Eddie, Eddie, Eddie," she wailed hoarsely, "I'm stuck. I'm stuck!"

"What?" he called down, as he could hardly hear her. "Are you at the end?"

Tighter and tighter the rocks pressed in, and all the blood in her body pooled into her head.

"I'm stuck! I'm stuck! I'm stuck!" she tried again, much louder than before.

Finally Eddie heard her. In an instant he was pulling hard on the rope. But in the process of wiggling about she had managed to wedge herself against the protruding rock on the other side of the wall. As Eddie pulled, he dragged her further into the unyielding surface. Theo cried out in pain for she was truly jammed in the hole.

"I can't move! There is a rock sticking out!" she said again. Eddie stopped pulling at once. He peered into the vent to see what she was pinned against. But all he could see were the soles of her shoes. Her body had completely plugged the chute.

"Oh God, Theo," he said, now beginning to panic himself, "can you try and lift yourself upward to push back against the rock?"

She tried to use her hands to lift herself backwards, but because of her position, she couldn't get any leverage. "No, no!" she said. "I can't! I can't! I'm going to die in here!"

Eddie thought for a moment, and then said as calmly as he could, "Okay, Theo, I want you to be as brave as you can. I think you are very near the bottom. I'm going to go into the main gallery and see if I find the end of the tunnel. I'm sure I'll be able to reach up and pull you out. Hang in there. I'll be there in a second." Eddie took the bags and the flashlights, and ran into the belly of the cave, clattering over loose stones in his haste.

The thought of being left alone in this predicament was the element that pushed her over the edge. "Don't leave me!" she screamed.

When Eddie didn't answer back, making it clear that she was on her own, Theo finally lost it. With the burden on her body and spirit, she couldn't stand anymore and passed out.

When she came to it felt as if she had been unconscious for hours. At first she forgot what had happened and felt blissfully safe in the warm dark. But soon she realized where she was and the dread returned.

Theo stopped struggling while she was passed out and her breathing returned to normal. Noticing that the space didn't feel so tight, she found that she could move about a little more. Realizing that staying calm would help her in this tight spot, she tried to relax against the immoveable granite. Although miserable within her stone cage, she had passed out and survived. She didn't die after all, at least, not yet. She softened her body as much as she could and tried to take deeper breaths. "At least I won't suffocate."

159

The air felt cool and moist. She could focus on the problem of being stuck without the worry of suffocation. Although she didn't feel as constricted, the weight of her body hanging against the hard rock was painful. She had no idea how long she had been suspended like this or how long it would continue; she only knew she had no control over the situation. Accepting this fact made her relax a little more – what else could she do? As she relaxed, the pressure on her back subsided a little.

Unable to find a way out, Theo was left to battle her own thoughts. She had heard that a person's life unravelled before their eyes just before dying. Perhaps she would die after all. She braced herself for the unfolding narrative of her short life, but nothing came. No early memories of her mother or of walking or of learning to talk. She searched for something else to preoccupy her mind but her thoughts were jumbled. It took an effort but eventually she recalled a memory of the time she went to the beach with Aunt Georgia. It had been a lovely, warm summer day, and they stayed until after sunset, happy and relaxed. Theo hadn't thought about her aunt in a while, and she felt a little guilty for the neglect. Would she ever see her again? Would she ever get out of this hole? She felt panic trying to dig in its claws, but she was able to resist and forced herself to think of something else. Her mind drifted to Kiryana.

How ironic it would be if it was her and not Kiryana who didn't survive this trip, after all the fuss made about the visions. Would Kiryana enjoy having the last laugh? Theo let out a sigh that sounded strange to her ears. Left in the vent long enough her skin and muscles would rot away, and her bones would clatter all the way to the bottom like rolling dice. Roll them bones. She wondered how long it would take for everything to melt away. At least she was already in her tomb and perhaps would be preserved liked the ancient Egyptians. How old were they again? A civilazation long gone before the Great Shift. Their remains had been shown in museums, she had learned. Would her remains find their way into a museum of the future? Would they take her bones and put them in a jar?

So much for being a prodigy when she only was able to embrace it for, what, a week? No, no, it was less time than that. Her exam was when? Only two days ago. Might as well have been a hundred years ago. She was so afraid of letting people know about her gift. Now it all seemed like another life. Yes, she had been free since the revelation, despite being kidnapped. How funny. Yes, that's right. She used to be so afraid all the time hiding a secret that meant disaster to no one, not even her. How strange was that? All that fuss about nothing.

Eddie should have made it down into the main body of the cave by now. How long had she been there? Minutes? Hours? She decided to count to a hundred, and when she finished, he'd be at the bottom, reaching up to pull her out. "One, two, three…"

"…ninety-nine, one hundred!" She strained her ears to hear any sound of Eddie. But she could only hear the rustle of her clothes and a random drop of water from below. "Okay, let's try one thousand then. One, two, three, drip, drip, drip…"

A sharp pain throbbed in her shoulder as it grew fatigued from her weight. She wondered how long the muscle would hold before it split apart into pieces. Would it be a race? Who would find her first - Eddie or her Maker? She was beginning not to care as long as one of them arrived soon.

A song rose from the depths of her mind. It had been years since she heard it and she wasn't sure who sang it to her - her aunt, her mother? Theo had a picture of her mother taken before she was born. She had been looking at that picture of her mother for so long that it formed a false memory, and Theo was convinced she was there that day, watching her mother pose for the camera. It was the only way she had known her.

Mama, sing me a song…Rock a bye baby, in the treetop, when the wind blows, the cradle with rock, when the bough breaks, the cradle will fall, and down will come Theo, broken and all! Again! Sing it Again! Rock a bye baby…

Theo looked down the tunnel into the blackest dark she had ever seen. At first, the emptiness of it had girth and presence and felt like another creature – a greedy demon ready to pounce if you dared to look at it. But as she stared at it, the darkness didn't threaten her or morph into a beast with sharp fangs. It stayed silent. It stayed still. And it could be trusted to remain that way. For whatever it meant to her, ultimately, it didn't matter; it was what it was. There was nothing she could change about it. Surrendering to this simple fact was the only thing she could do. It was inevitable. What sense did fighting any of it make anyway?

As another spasm of pain shot through her, she cried to the unknown about her, "Please, please, help me. Help me now, I beg of you." And she held her breath until the pain ebbed away.

Her mind went to the bonfire the night before - that bright, warm bonfire. What was the story Rufus told - about Finnegan? How he was left to die by the side of the road, and all he wanted was a friend to keep him company. Theo, only a young girl, now understood the story. In some ways it would have been better if Eddie had just stayed with her instead of trying to rescue her. She didn't want to die alone. No one does. But the thought didn't last, and her mind's eye went back to the bonfire – that bright, warm bonfire.

She squeezed her eyes and tried to hold on to what light looked like. Could she still remember the sun? Was light now in her past? Would she die never seeing colour again? What was her favourite colour? Blue? Green? No, she believed it was yellow. Yes, she loved a cheery yellow. Could she see yellow in her mind? What was yellow- a lemon, a car, a sunflower? Yes, a sunflower resting against Talim's garden wall. What a beautiful thing, so very beautiful. She formed the shape of the petals in her mind, and the yellowness of it rose up from her imagination until she could see the brightness under her shut eyes. It grew stronger and stronger and stronger…

Theo flickered her eyes opened and realized she wasn't imagining the yellow. From below came a brilliance that filled the narrow tunnel with light. Finally! Help had arrived!

"Eddie! Eddie!" she shouted with joy. "Up here! Up here!"

But to her surprise, he didn't reply. Had she thought about it long enough it might have worried her. But she was so thankful to be able to see again that she didn't question his silence.

Able to view the tunnel clearly now, she noticed that the rock protrusion was slight and that another followed shortly after the first. But they were the only ones. Past them the chute widened considerably and gave clear passage to the bottom. Eddie was right. She had travelled a good deal of the tunnel already and only a small portion remained.

She looked at the jutting rock carefully. She decided that if she shifted her body flat against it, there would be enough room to squeeze past it. She wiggled about, ignoring the discomfort in her shoulders, and sucked in her gut and slowly slid past the bulge. She bumped harshly into the next protrusion but she confidently repeated the same manoeuver until she was beyond that one too. Once past the last obstacle, she went into a freefall and slipped down the smooth rock and landed in a heap at the bottom.

She was free! Nothing ever felt so good. She leaped to her feet and twirled about, enjoying the pleasure of moving her arms and legs again. What a gift! To be able to stretch! To be able to jump! Never would she take her freedom for granted again!

Taking in long breaths, she drank in the pleasure of her movement and savoured her sweet euphoria. But when she started to look around to see where she was, she stopped short and gasped with shock.

Lying in repose near a clear, underground pool, what she had seen all those months ago over the quarry near her Aunt's house, was the same Fire Tiger!

Chapter Twenty-Two

The Fire Tiger!

Struck dumb and frozen to the spot, Theo could only stare at it like the prey she was. Too afraid to move, she held her breath and waited.

The tiger was smaller in size this time and emitted a lambent glow while a swirling radiance rose from him like an eerie atmosphere. Although bright, it wasn't hard to look at, and it was unlike any light she had ever seen before.

The tiger remained resting on its belly, regal and composed, while gently panting and watching Theo, unhurriedly. The stripes on its hide resembled markings on other tigers she had seen, but the colours was replaced with muted shades of fire and light. Its head was massive and it dominated its frame. Large, golden eyes, stark against the intensity of its body, pieced through the brightness. When it looked at her, Theo felt as if it was peeling away every layer within her.

She stood still for a very long time. Again, she felt helpless in the face of this predicament. She didn't know what the Fire Tiger wanted, or why it was here, but she already knew the scope of its power. Although benign at this moment, she understood that it could shift into something far more unpredictable, far more dangerous, in a flash.

Theo stood motionless for a very long time, too afraid to take her eyes off the creature. Eventually, she realized that the tiger was happy where it was since it showed no signs of coming nearer. Before, Theo had been cramped in a hole for hours, and now she was trying to stand perfectly still, taxing her body in a new way.

Finally, with the discomfort too strong to bear, she bravely raised her head and stammered, "M-m-my legs are tired. I'm just going to sit down if that's okay."

The tiger just blinked peacefully at her and stretched out a wide, front paw.

Slowly Theo crouched down on a flat rock near her. Once seated, she began to feel a little more comfortable although she found it impossible to relax. Having no idea what kind of creature was before her or what its intentions were made her uneasy. But it seemed that staying put was the best way of not agitating it. For the moment, it didn't want to kill her, and that was the best she could hope for. She decided she could risk taking her eyes off of it to look about the cave and see where she had landed.

The narrow tunnel had taken her into a large chamber that was made up of the same granite and gneiss rock that was found everywhere on the mountain. However, in here there were also large pockets of crystals embedded all over the walls and floor. The light from the tiger affected the crystals in an unusual way, and they glowed as if they were on fire. They burned like mysterious, rock torches, strange as anything she had ever seen, but as beautiful as glowing flowers.

The tiger was lying on the rim of a large pool of water. Crystals encrusted its shore and bed, and they too shone like stars through a watery cloud. "How pretty," she thought, mesmerized briefly by the effect.

Theo scanned the cave and noticed that there was no passage in or out. She and the tiger were in a sealed space, and the tiny chute seemed to be the only entrance and exit. Stricken with the terrible thought that she would have to leave through same tunnel, she let out a sad sigh.

"I don't know what I would prefer," she said to the tiger, "to struggle back up through that hole or have you eat me."

The tiger just blinked languidly at her and offered no reaction to her voice. Still panting gently, it raised its snout upward to smell the air.

"Did you smell anything interesting?" asked Theo. "Or are you thinking about your next meal?" Watching the spiralling mass of lights effusing from it, she realized that was the wrong question to ask. This wasn't an animal as she understood them to be.

Its non-responsiveness was perplexing at first. But then it made her think.

"Are you really here, Tiger?" she asked. "Am I? Am I still passed out in the tunnel? Are you a dream?"

The tiger held its head still and stared unwaveringly at her.

"Or am I dead? Are you a ghost?"

Looking through her, the tiger slowed his breathing and went silent.

"Feels like I've been down here forever. Has it been days, or merely hours? I wonder where Eddie has gone. Has he forgotten about me so quickly?" Theo doubted whether she'd see the outside world ever again.

She looked into the vast depths of the tiger's eyes and said, "I'm having a really hard time with all of this right now. Things keep happening to me, and I don't seem to have a say in any of it. I really don't know how much more I can take."

The tiger twitched his ears a little but then reduced its radiance to a softer glow. Not that it changed its size but the subdued light made it seem less imposing. Noticing the shift, Theo relaxed a little more. "That is better," she said. "Thank you."

Looking at one of the flaming crystals, she marvelled, "That is an interesting trick. Did you do that? Will it last very long?"

The tiger shook its head as if something was tickling its ears. It turned and scanned about the cave a little before returning its attention back to Theo. It then surprised Theo by stretching its jaws into a long, wide yawn before rolling onto its side and resting its head against the ground. Deep breaths soon filled its belly, and from what Theo could see, it seemed as if it was asleep.

Theo shifted and stretched quietly, happy to be free of its scrutiny. She quickly and carefully got to her feet and crept back to the tunnel entrance. She looked up and could see the passage clearly, but except for the two protrusions, there was nothing to grip to help her climb back up. Even with the rope still tied to her waist, she would need someone at the top to pull. Crouching down, she crawled into the tunnel and called up as loudly as she dared, "Eddie! Eddie!" But there was only silence.

Dejected, she pulled backwards out of the hole and stood up. Beside her, as near as an arm's length, the Fire Tiger stood quietly, waiting for Theo to notice it. It had woken up in the seconds she was in the shaft and crossed the space between them without a sound. Theo was so frightened that she fell backwards and crashed into the rock wall behind her.

The tiger was incredibly large up close. The flames from its body did not throw heat which surprised her a great deal. If it wanted something from her, Theo had no idea what that might be. Shutting her eyes tight, hot tears of terror squeezed through her lids. She kept waiting for the impending strike as she assumed this would be her end, her last few moments. She braced herself for a long time until it became apparent that the tiger wasn't going to kill her.

Opening her eyes, Theo looked into the face of the impressive beast. Its head spanned the distance from Theo's waist to the top of her head. It filled her entire view. Its warm, salty breath huffed over her whole body.

Theo stared, wide-eyed, into its extraordinary disc-shaped eyes, and she became lost within the vastness of them. At some point, fear was replaced with astonishment. She was mesmerized by its powerful gaze. As she looked deeper into its eyes, she could feel a soft, enveloping sensation surround her much like being wrapped in cotton wool. There was no end to their depths, and Theo was drawn into a world of silence. She connected to it completely, and she drank in the profoundness which was softly yielding up to her. Unable to help herself, she raised her hand and slowly reached outward to touch the tiger on its forehead. To her surprise it felt like fur, and it was soft and warm, despite its electric appearance. The tiger stood quietly, happy to receive the touch. Theo softly patted its head, enjoying the texture of its coat, fascinated that she was able to touch it without being scorched or injured in any way. Then, without meaning to, she found herself saying, "Thank you, Tiger. Thank you for lighting the way out of the tunnel."

The tiger blinked contently for a few times as it accepted Theo's caress. Then, without warning, it abruptly broke away and rushed back into the middle of the cave. Theo followed to see what it would do. The tiger approached the far wall, and it climbed up to the crease at the ceiling and began to roar fiercely. The roar was so loud that Theo covered her ears with her hands. But this did little to block it out. The tiger roared, and the ground and walls began to shake. Theo lost her balance as the floor beneath her wobbled. She stumbled to the nearest ledge to help hold her balance while the tiger roared, and small pieces of the wall began to crumble and fall inward. It roared again, and larger rocks broke and rolled and bounced to the floor. The tiger roared until enough rock had fallen away and opened the gallery to another chamber. Theo's heart jumped to her throat when she saw it. The tiger had given her the way out!

Once done, the tiger stopped and bounded back to the centre of the cave. Theo was filled with excitement, and she wanted to rush forward to express her gratitude to the strange and awesome animal for freeing her. But, without warning, the tiger closed its eyes as its body expanded. The light in it grew until it filled the cave with a blinding and sudden explosion. Theo covered her eyes to shield herself from it, and when the light burned away and dimmed, she discovered that the tiger had gone and that she was left alone in the cave, with all the crystals burning twice as brightly as before.

Stunned, Theo stumbled forward to where the tiger had been. She spun about but the tiger was nowhere in sight. It had disappeared into thin air. Theo experienced its absence right away and, to her surprise, she felt the loss.

While she stood studying the space the tiger once occupied, Theo heard the sound of rocks falling over each other. Turning quickly to see what was making that noise, she looked up to saw Eddie and Kiryana climbing over the rubble as they crossed from the outer chamber into hers. Eddie was the first to enter the cave. When he noticed Theo standing there, his face lit up with joy as he ran over to her.

"Theo! Theo! Thank goodness, Theo! You are okay! I'm so relieved!" Eddie rushed to her and, in a burst of emotion, he threw his arms around her and lifted her off her feet.

With his face near her ear, he whispered with utter sincerity, "If anything had happened to you, I would have never forgiven myself."

When he finished, he put her back on her feet and looked into her face. "Theo, I'm so sorry I asked you to go down the tunnel. Can you ever forgive me?" Eddie looked so distraught that Theo feared that he would burst into tears.

Theo was happy to find out that he was concerned for her safety. "Aw Eddie, this whole thing is a big mess. But I'm okay so don't worry about it, alright?"

Not ready to let himself off the hook, he continued earnestly, "It was the worst thing I could have done to you. I was so intent on finding Kiryana that I wasn't thinking straight. I'm really sorry, Theo."

Theo looked into his brown eyes and felt his contrition. She didn't feel angry at him. Instead, she felt sorry for him because whatever hold her cousin had on him was tight. He wasn't making good decisions, and it was going to cause him problems down the line. She didn't need Clarity to see that.

Theo just nodded and smiled. Eddie looked down and saw the rope was still tied to her. Gently, he undid the knots and untwined the line. Theo was touched and felt affection for him well up inside.

Kiryana, who had been watching their exchange, approached quietly. When she caught Theo's eye, she smiled meekly and said, "I'm glad that you are okay too. I know we haven't been on the best of terms, Theo, but I wouldn't want anything awful to happen to you either. I'm glad that you are alright."

Theo nodded shyly. Not knowing how to respond to this she merely said, "So you've been here the whole time? Did you find what you were looking for?"

"No. I've been going over the crevices in the outer chamber and couldn't find a thing. Then we were looking for you. We were about to give up when the wall fell over," said Kiryana. She looked about, entranced by all the glowing crystals.

Eddie quickly interjected, "I needed to find the end of the tunnel, Theo. I was starting to feel desperate that we wouldn't be able to get you out. So how did you get out?"

Theo sucked in air and winced, "I'm not sure you would believe me if I told you."

Eddie, looking around at the cave and noticing the burning crystals, scratched his head as he replied, "Um, we just might actually. What is causing those crystals to light up like that? How did the wall fall down? What was that roar?"

"I've had an encounter," Theo replied softly, "an encounter with something extraordinary. It was in the shape of a tiger but I think it was something bigger, more immense. The tiger lit the way for me to climb down the tunnel then it opened up the cave so I could escape."

Eddie scrunched up his face as he tried to absorb what Theo had said. "A tiger? Lit the way? Opened up the cave?"

"Yes, and it wasn't the first time I've seen it. The first time was at my aunt's house, and it was the reason I was sent away."

Not sure what to make of what Theo was saying, Eddie widened his eyes with awe as he took in the colours emanating from all the shimmering crystals. "Something unnatural is going on here, that's for sure. A part of me thinks the sooner we get out of her, the sooner we will be back on firmer ground. I wonder if it's a power that we should be messing with."

Absolutely convinced by Eddie's thinking, Theo nodded vigorously, "Yes, I think you are right, Eddie. I don't think we can figure out what it wants. And if a way out has been given to us, I think we should be smart and take it and not wait for it to be taken away!"

Eddie, now ready to pack up and leave, turned to speak with Kiryana. However, during the course of their discussion, she had walked deeper into the chamber and was exploring it with rapt interest. By the time Theo and Eddie noticed her, she had climbed on a small, granite ledge that stretched above the glowing pool of water.

"Kiryana!" called Eddie, "what are you doing up there? Come down and let's get out before something else happens!"

If she heard him, she made no indication that she had. Kiryana's eyes were fixated on a crystal that glowed with an odd, green light.

Annoyed, Eddie called again, "Kiryana, we need to get a move on while we have the chance. Come on! Let's go!"

She ignored Eddie and continued to stare into the water.

Theo felt a sense of dread hit her like one of the rock walls that had just tumbled over. She knew immediately that their chance to escape had just passed.

As Kiryana continued to stare down into the water, her face broke into a wide, greedy grin. Finally, she looked up and beckoned for Eddie to come over. He jumped over the rocks with great strides and quickly arrived at her side. She smiled up at him then pointed to a crystal in the middle of the pool. When he saw what she was pointing at, his face fell and his body went rigid. He pulled back from the pool and looked helplessly at Theo.

Theo stepped to the pool's edge to see what it was. Even before she saw it, she knew. The air inside of her shrank as she wearily peered through the water's surface to search out the prize. Sadly, she realized that the wall the tiger had knocked down for her to escape also opened up the secret chamber for Kiryana to get in. And there was nothing Theo could do about it.

There in the bottom of the pool was a large crystalline object, hewn roughly into the shape of a dragon's head, glowing with an eerie, garish light. And there it was for all three of them to see: the Crystal Dragon found at last!

Chapter Twenty-Three

The three of them were rooted to the spot as they looked at the Crystal Dragon. Entombed in the water for an age, it almost appeared to wink from below and beckon them to release it from its liquid cell. Theo looked at Eddie with the same helpless expression he first gave her, and they both turned to Kiryana to see what she would do.

Kiryana couldn't take her eyes off of the Crystal Dragon. She drew in a deep breath and then held it for fear of scaring the moment away. After a shaky exhale, she began to feel safe enough to speak, ready to accept that the crystal wouldn't melt and disappear.

"There it is," she said with a reverent tone, "the Crystal Dragon! I found the Crystal Dragon!"

Finally, she looked up at Eddie, her iridescent eyes sparkling with elation. She was too thrilled to notice that he did not share her excitement.

"Oh Eddie! Eddie! This is it! This is it! This will change everything!" she gushed as she turned to him and threw her arms about his neck. "I can't believe we did it! I can't believe it!"

Eddie stood rigidly as he accepted Kiryana's embrace. He smiled weakly as she pulled away to look at him but said nothing.

"Eddie! It's unbelievable! All that work and suffering seems like nothing, now that we've found it! Can you imagine what people will say?" She paused for a second before continuing. "Can you imagine what Mother will say?"

Eddie shook his head as he drew his lips together in a tight line and deliberately said nothing.

"Oh my goodness," Kiryana continued animatedly, "finally after all these years of waiting, agonizing, thinking it will never happen, and it's here! I can't believe it's going to happen! I can't believe I'm going to get what I want!"

"What you want?" Eddie echoed coolly, now unable to stay quiet. "If you say so."

Kiryana, finally noticing that something was bothering Eddie, tilted her head and gazed seriously into his face.

"What's the matter Eddie?" she asked. "What's going on?"

Eddie took Kiryana's hands into his and squeezed them tightly. "So you find the Crystal Dragon. You finally get Clarity. You get what you want, Kiry, but what about us? What about me?"

Taken aback by Eddie's unexpected response, Kiryana searched for some sort of answer. Finally she stammered back to him, "Eddie, I –I-I thought you understood. I thought you knew this is what I wanted."

"So you don't love me then?" he asked, straight to the point. "Because I can't understand how you say you love me but won't choose me over that- that - rock."

Completely bowled over by his mutiny at this crucial point, Kiryana struggled to find the right thing to say to him. "You can't support me this whole time only to give it up at the end. It makes no sense. Why were you helping me find something you didn't want me to have?"

Eddie jerked his head back from her as he stepped away. "I don't know. I don't know! I suppose any time with you, no matter the excuse, was good enough for me. But I never thought you'd find it, Kiry. Honestly I didn't. So it didn't matter. When it was over, you'd come back to me, happily, with all that nonsense finally out of your system."

Kiryana stared at Eddie. She was now seeing him a little differently than before. "I don't know what to say. I always knew I was going to find it. I knew it! And I thought you understood this too."

Eddie shook his head to try and stop the truth from sinking in. "So you don't love me?" he repeated again.

Kiryana looked woefully into his soft, sad brown eyes and said, "Yes, I love you. I love you, Eddie. But what I feel isn't important. Well, it is not important enough. And I can't turn back now when I'm so close to finishing. This is my destiny, and I'm determined to see it through."

Crushed by her words, Eddie backed away from her, his eyes wildly searching her face. "So that's it then? You're going to do this? No matter how I feel? Or what will happen?"

Kiryana looked unhappy and scared. She took a deep breath and said, "I am going to do this, no matter what."

Eddie's head fell sideways to his shoulder as if she had struck him in the face. Gritting his teeth, he turned around and walked down to the centre of the cave, picked up his gear and hoisted it on his shoulders.

He turned to Kiryana and said, "Okay then, you made your choice. But if you don't mind, I'd rather not watch." He then looked to Theo and said sadly, "I'll wait for you at the cave's entrance when you are done."

Theo nodded and watched him as he clambered over the debris and through the newly opened passage. He didn't look back once.

Kiryana stood in shocked silence. She was deeply unsettled by Eddie's departure. Tears were rolling down her cheeks as she stared at the last space Eddie had occupied. After a while, she sniffled and wiped the moisture away with her sleeve. She then turned to Theo and bitterly said, "Are you going to have a go at me too?"

Theo looked at Kiryana and replied, "No one is having a go at you, Kiryana, least of all me. But I would much rather you didn't take the Crystal Dragon."

"Oh really?" she said snidely. "Well in that case..." Deliberately she started to unbutton her outdoor clothes in preparation to enter the water.

Theo wasn't going to be put off that easily. "Kiryana, look, I'm not trying to stand in the way of what you want. But I have reason to believe that this will end badly for you. I'm just trying to stop you from doing something you will regret. I've been having visions for months..." However, Theo couldn't finish her sentence because Kiryana had begun to scream when she heard the word "visions".

"Visions! Visions! Visions!" she shrieked as she looked up to the ceiling. "My life has been plagued by other people's visions! Lilith Crowe! My Mother! Now you! When does MY vision begin to matter?" She met Theo's eyes as she continued, "I may not be a prodigy Oracle, but believe it or not, I have a dream too. My own vision of how I want my life to be. Everybody thinks I want to have Clarity only because of what was predicted. But that isn't true. I want it because I have seen it in my own dreams. I may not have highfalutin visions like you or Lilith Crowe or grand ambitions like my mother, but I do have my own dreams, my own wishes, as they are."

Theo was shocked and couldn't think of what to say. She really hadn't thought about it that way before. Perhaps Kiryana was right to want to have her own say, but still, what about the danger? Wasn't it right that she understand this?

"Kiryana, I want you to find your own way but you need to know what will happen..."

Again, Kiryana didn't wait for her to finish. "Yes, I know Theo. There is a danger if I go through with it. I acknowledge that. You've done your part and now let it go. Because as I see it, your idea isn't more important to me than my own hope of what could happen. I know there is a risk; I am not blind to it. But in the end, it is my decision to make, only mine."

Kiryana pulled her shirt over her head and then wiggled out of her jeans. Theo looked on helplessly as her cousin stood in her underwear at the edge ready to jump in the pool.

Desperate to stop her, Theo searched for anything that might convince her otherwise. Finally she blurted out frantically, "I hardly have any family. I can't bear the thought of losing you too."

Kiryana paused and looked profoundly at Theo and said. "I know, Theo, I do. I am sorry about that. I am. I wish that things were different between you and me but here we are. I am sorry but you have to let me go too." And with that, Kiryana dived into the pool, causing a splash that rose high in the air before spilling over the edge to drizzle on Theo's shoes.

The pool wasn't very deep and it took no time for Kiryana to reach the bottom, with her long, chestnut hair spanning out behind her like a shell. The Crystal Dragon glowed stronger as she swam to it as if it were welcoming her. She wiggled the crystal and to her surprise it lifted easily, as if it jumped into her hands. A second later she was bursting through the surface with water droplets spilling down her face and hair. She swam easily to the edge until she had firm footing on the bedrock below. As she stood, she swung her hands forward, raising the Crystal Dragon, for the first time in many years, out of its watery grave and into the world above.

The crystal seemed perfectly clear at first glance. However, there were splotches of green veined throughout, and this gave the dragon its unusual spectral glow. The crystal had been sculpted to take on the features of a medieval dragon. It had a long, narrow snout with wide nostrils and spikey scales protruding from its skull. Its eyes had deliberately been shaped over green deposits making it seem disturbingly alive and watchful.

Kiryana carefully placed the crystal on the edge and lifted herself out of the pool. She jumped out shivering and scampered over to her pile of clothes and hurriedly threw them on again. She then rushed back to the crystal and picked it up to study it.

Theo, despite her misgivings, couldn't help but look on. She immediately felt the resting vibration of the Crystal Dragon and could sense its coiled power. She knew instinctively this crystal was not to be trifled with, and she prepared herself for what was to come. She was in a difficult position. She was distressed but she knew Kiryana would continue regardless of any further warnings from her. As tough as it was, there was nothing Theo could do but wait and see what would happen.

Kiryana found a large rock with a smooth surface and sat upon it. She placed the crystal on her lap and cupped her hands over the top of it. She closed her eyes and braced herself for the impact of sights and sounds the likes she had never seen before. She sat for minutes, holding her breath and squeezing her eyes shut, waiting to absorb the first shock. But nothing happened.

Kiryana opened her eyes and looked at the crystal with confusion. She turned it over but couldn't see anything that might kick it into action. She looked over at Theo with bewilderment, silently asking if Theo knew what to do to activate the dragon. Theo pretended not to understand. Perhaps this would turn out better than she had thought.

Frustrated and alarmed, Kiryana finally blurted out, "Is this some kind of cruel joke? What is going on? Why won't this work?"

Theo, starting to feel a little relieved, tried not to smile as she said, "I don't know. Who knows if it's even real? We are just going on information from a stranger."

Still unwilling to give up, Kiryana stood and started pacing with it. "Perhaps there is a command that is necessary, an incantation?"

If there was, Theo didn't see it in the letters or on the map. If she was of a mind to help her cousin, she might have suggested using her Clarity. But she wasn't. So she sat down and waited.

"We could always look at the map again," suggested Kiryana half-heartedly, knowing full well what the answer would be.

"We?" repeated Theo while raising an eyebrow.

"Fine," grumbled Kiryana. She accepted that nothing was going to happen at this time. "But I'll find a way eventually, even if I have to go to Ceres Theroux herself. I'm going to take it with me and figure this out on my own."

Kiryana threw on her coat, picked up her gear and carried the crystal in her hand, too afraid to let it out of her sight. Theo, happy to be leaving this place, didn't hesitate and followed.

They crossed the threshold and entered the outer chamber. It was a large, long cavern that opened up to a tall, craggy ceiling. Kiryana had pulled a flashlight out of her back pack and passed over the floor easily and swiftly. She had spent a lot of time searching for any signs of the hidden crystal and she knew the space well. Theo needed to rush to keep up with her.

They began climbing upwards on an easy slope until they arrived in the first chamber that Theo recognized. As they passed the opening of the chimney, Theo couldn't help shuddering with the recollection of being trapped in there.

Soon they exited the Old Man's Hall and stepped into daylight. The sun was beginning to sink low in the sky in front of them. Theo realized they had been in the cave for most of the day. Not until this point, however, had she felt the passage of time. Relieved to be released from this entire ordeal, she began to entertain thoughts of heading home.

Eddie, as promised, was waiting for them outside of the cave. He was leaning against a large rock eating a protein bar as they approached him. Still hurt from before, he tried to ignore Kiryana as best as he could. Too upset to notice, Kiryana came near and raised the Crystal Dragon with a disappointed look on her face. Eddie couldn't stop himself from asking, "So? Did it work?"

Kiryana shook her head balefully. Unlike Theo, Eddie didn't try to hide his smugness. "Ah well, I wish I could be more disappointed for you, Kiry."

Kiryana shook her head, "I'm not finished yet. I'm taking this back home with me to try and figure it out there."

Eddie looked over at Theo and gave her a knowing look. Then he said cheerfully, "You know, I like the sound of that – home! Home it is!"

Kiryana, annoyed that Eddie was so thrilled by her failure, decided to take issue with it. "You know, you don't have to sound so happy about it. At least you could try…"

But Kiryana was unable to finish her thought for at that moment the Crystal Dragon ignited with a blast of brilliant green light, as if it suddenly woke up. Surprised, Kiryana reeled backwards until she hit a ledge which supported her weight. She cupped her other hand around the Crystal Dragon and looked deep within to see what it would show her.

Eddie and Theo hurried to Kiryana's side but she yelled at them, "Stay back! Don't come near me!"

The light of the crystal increased and covered Kiryana in a bold, flickering glow. Theo's early sense about the crystal had been correct. She felt its power begin to unfold. Her heart sank into her stomach as she knew her fear soon would be realized. Eddie's face went white and he turned to Theo for help. She had none to offer.

Kiryana stared into the head of the Crystal Dragon as sharp lights beamed out all around. Her gaze was locked onto the crystal, and she stared open-mouthed into its verdant skull. Her eyes darted back and forth as she watched something invisible unfold in front of her. The Crystal Dragon was speaking to Kiryana and she was greedily taking it all in.

And then, without warning, it stopped. The light disappeared and the Crystal Dragon went quiet. Kiryana was released from its grip and she slowly slid down to the ground.

Eddie, too frightened to stay angry, rushed to her side, frantic with worry. When he tried to take the crystal from her, she pulled it back angrily.

"Kiry! Kiry!" he called loudly. "Are you okay? Are you hurt?"

Kiryana looked at him with bemusement before breaking into a long, hysterical laugh. "Am I hurt? Am I hurt? Oh yeah, I'm hurt. But I've been hurt for a long time."

She looked over at Theo and continued, her voice odd and strained, "Oh Theo, the things I've seen; so many things, so many more to come too!"

Theo was scared for her cousin. She reached out to Kiryana but recoiled as if her hand was on fire.

"I know who sent me the map. Can you guess? Even though she was warned that it might be dangerous. She said saving the family name was worth the risk. Saving her reputation was worth the danger. Even though there was a huge possibility that her only daughter might be hurt or even die in search of it, she sent the map to me."

Theo sighed sadly as she recognized the betrayal. "Oh Kiryana, I'm so sorry."

Kiryana continued, "I always knew Mother was hard, but I never believed she could be so heartless. I never would have believed it if I hadn't seen it myself."

Theo tried to find something to say that might make it better, "I'm sure it is not as terrible as that, maybe there is more…"

"No, it is," interrupted Kiryana. "It feels true. It has always been true. I have always been an accessory to her success, and my failure has reflected badly on her."

Eddie spoke softly so as not to alarm her, "Kiryana, my love, come away with me. Leave all this behind and come with me. It doesn't have to be this way anymore."

Kiryana slowly turned her head toward him and looked at him with faraway eyes, "That sounds really nice. I wish that was something I could do; I really do. But it is too late for me. I need to meet the Dragon face to face and finish what I started."

Eddie stiffened when he heard this, and Theo's blood ran cold. Before either of them could decide what to do, Kiryana was on her feet, leaping up and scrambling over rocks to climb higher up the side of the mountain. Running madly up the slope, she was intent on meeting the Dragon himself!

Chapter Twenty-Four

Kiryana flew over the side of the mountain with a preternatural knowledge of the nooks and footholds. She was unusually nimble and extraordinarily fast. Theo and Eddie struggled to keep up with her as she moved higher up. Quickly she rounded the side of the peak toward the inside face. Having reached the other side, Kiryana arrived at a long, wide plateau high above the ground below. She staggered to the edge and stood there waiting, searching for something to arrive, holding the Crystal Dragon above her head.

Eddie, a good athlete, struggled to keep up with her. He arrived at the same plateau and lifted himself to his feet and got his bearings. Seeing that Kiryana had stopped for the moment, he turned back to check on Theo's progress. Although it wasn't a difficult trail to climb, Theo was careful, fully aware of the drop below. It took her a few minutes to catch up to Eddie, and when she did, Eddie reached down to help pull her up to the hard surface.

When Theo saw Kiryana standing on the plateau, she fell to her knees. Unbearable, details of Theo's vision began unfolding before her and they were coming into full focus. She knew the rocky, sand-coloured ledge and the blurry green treeline in the far distance. She recognized the slant of the light hitting her eyes and the cold air rustling around her ears. She remembered the shape of Kiryana's outstretched body and the look on her face. But mostly, Theo knew the spot Kiryana was approaching as she moved closer to the edge - the spot Kiryana unknowingly would wait for her doom to rise from below. This was the moment Theo had feared for so long and now it was about to happen.

Unable to control herself, Theo screamed, "Kiryana!! Stop! Stop!"

Kiryana slowly turned her head over her shoulder in a reprise of what Theo had seen in her dream only a few nights earlier. Kiryana stood firm as she looked at her younger cousin but she just stared unseeingly through Theo. Kiryana turned back, uninterested in stopping what was already set in motion.

Desperate to save her cousin from what she knew was coming, Theo jumped to her feet and ran to Eddie. She grabbed his arm and forced him to look at her.

"I've seen this before!" she yelled. "This is what I saw in my vision! We have to help her!"

Eddie absorbed what she said. "What do you mean? How can we help her?"

Theo knew very well that something was about to kill Kiryana. They needed to pull her from the edge and get rid of the Crystal Dragon.

"We have to get her away from the edge! Something awful is coming! The Crystal Dragon will do something terrible!"

Eddie nodded and clenched his jaw. In an instant he was beside Kiryana. He tried to pull Kiryana's arms down to bring the crystal to the ground.

"What are you doing?" she screamed. "Stop it! The Dragon is almost here!"

Eddie ignored Kiryana and continued to struggle with her. To his surprise, she was stronger than he expected and he was having trouble subduing her.

"No, no!" she shrieked. "You WILL NOT stop me! No!"

Kiryana pushed hard against Eddie, and he was thrown off balance. She broke free of his hold and ran back to the same spot. She hissed a warning at Eddie not to try again, but before he could reach her, a large, green globe of light rose from beneath the ledge, like the kraken rising from a stormy sea.

Kiryana laughed with maniacal joy while Eddie and Theo stared at the glowing ball with horror. Neither one was able to move or speak. The sphere glowed with the same eerie light as the crystal but with much greater intensity. The Crystal Dragon increased its lumimosity in response to the mysterious ball, and bolts of visible energy shot back and forth between the objects.

"He is here! He is here!" shouted Kiryana with mad glee as she danced about. "The Dragon has arrived!"

Theo's skin crawled as she heard this. Kiryana had lost her mind. She was oblivious to the disaster that was about to descend upon her.

Theo tried pitifully one last time. "Kiryana, I beg you. Please, please stop. Please stop, before it's too late."

Kiryana looked past Theo and just laughed louder. "Oh, it's finally going to happen. I can't believe it's finally going to happen!"

She continued jumping about from one foot to the other, holding the Crystal Dragon high above her head as a greeting. She was inviting the Dragon to come to play, and it couldn't happen soon enough.

The ball of light rose high above the plateau and floated over their heads. It moved slightly from side to side then came to an abrupt halt. It hovered above them and aimed its green light onto Kiryana's head. Happy to receive what was coming, Kiryana stretched her arms back wide to welcome it in. A burst of silver and green washed over the plateau, and a low hum began to vibrate. Kiryana stood still and accepted the connection.

Kiryana's eyes widened as she stared into an invisible world. She gorged on all the sights that only she could see. She soaked it all in, smiling with wonder and amazement, while all the time the radiance from the globe and crystal grew at an alarming rate. And Kiryana trilled with delight. "It's so wonderful. Who knew? Who knew it could be so wonderful! Now I finally see! Now I can finally see!" But it was not to last.

Suddenly the bond between the Crystal Dragon and the sphere changed. Sharp fragments of lightning burst back and forth, like untended fireworks. Kiryana jerked forward then backwards, crying out as she did. Her face twisted with pain. That which had delighted her now tortured her. She closed her eyes to block it out but could not stop it. Her connection with the Dragon was set and she was unable to break free.

"No, no," she moaned, "too much! Too much! Too Awful! Enough! Enough!" Small, drops of blood began to ooze from her eyes.

The sphere and the Crystal Dragon were indifferent to her pleas and continued to ramp up the force. Theo looked on aghast as she watched her cousin writhe with agony. She hadn't seen this in her vision. But she didn't understand her visions enough to question it.

To her surprise, Theo was also feeling the energetic pull from the glowing ball, and she struggled to resist it. She looked into the centre of the sphere and began to see something form within the random swirls of pulsating energy. To her amazement she could make out the image of a man, like a shadow of light. This man was holding his arms high above him while a fury of beams shot from his hands. The head was focused on Kiryana as he pushed the ferocity of his power onto the helpless girl. Feeling Theo watching him, he raised his head and looked at her, setting his attention fully on her. Theo held her breath as she waited to see what he would do.

Then, clear as a bell, she heard his voice in her head, "You see, my dear? All this power is available to anyone who has the will to take it."

Shocked by his words, Theo was repulsed. She shook her head to block out his voice and covered her ears with her hands.

"That won't help, I'm afraid," the voice continued. It was a man's voice, dark and heavy.

Theo shook her head again and squeezed her eyes tight.

The voice went on, "Yes, all this power - so easy to harness, so easy to shape."

The effect of the voice was overpowering. Theo could not block him out, no matter how she tried. He wasn't using a corporal voice. He was speaking with an internal voice, driving his message directly into Theo's brain. It was unbearable. She could feel him inside her head, banging his horrible thoughts into the sides of her skull. Again he spoke and Theo cried out.

"Look at this feeble girl. She thought she could be as great as me?"

Theo tried hitting her head against the side of a boulder. The pain was instantaneous. Blood gushed from the wound but the voice did not stop.

"So many thought that this could be shared, be passed on. Only the truly great can have this power. Joke was on them."

His laughter filled her head, and Theo had to stop herself from jumping off the ledge. Too much, too awful!

"What do you want from me?!" Theo screamed.

"Want from you? To let you know I'm here. Here, waiting for everything. Waiting to be acknowledged," then he laughed, long and coarse. "Now that I have your attention, open your eyes and see this."

Just when she couldn't take it anymore, the voice suddenly quieted.

Theo was able to focus outside of her head once again. She blinked through the stinging tears and looked at the glowing ball. The figure had turned toward Kiryana again and was holding her in his view. He suddenly dropped his hands to his side. The fiery onslaught stopped and Kiryana was released from his grip. Her body slumped forward while she gasped for breath.

Looking up, she caught Theo's eyes. She was Kiryana again. She was still there. Looking forlornly at Theo, Kiryana silently begged her to make it stop. It was too unbearable. Theo looked helplessly at her cousin and shook her head. She didn't know how.

The respite was short-lived. The figure began to wave his arms wildly about. Like winding a motor, the energy within the sphere grew. Once he had achieved the amount he desired, he held it at the ready. Slowly he aimed the charge at Kiryana.

Again the ghastly voice was back in Theo's head, "Are you ready for this?"

Too aware of what was coming, Theo screamed. Months of dreams had prepared her for this moment, and she was too afraid to see it happen.

Eddie ran to Kiryana's side. He had been mesmerized by the strange apparition but Theo's scream woke him up. Unfamiliar with the non-mundane world, he had been overwhelmed by what he was seeing. It was the sound of

Theo's scream that jolted him back. Finally, he remembered himself. Quickly he realized that no matter what he had to pull his beloved Kiryana away from the monstrous thing. It was breaking her. In an instant, it was very clear what he needed to do.

Eddie grabbed Kiryana and placed himself between her and the globe. He threw himself over her like a shield and held her fast and firm. Unlike before, Kiryana leaned into the embrace and held him tightly. Eddie squeezed her hard and said clearly and strongly, "I love you."

Before Kiryana could reply, the ghostly figure released the blast and a large ball of light exploded into Eddie's back, pushing him forward onto Kiryana and knocking him backwards onto the ground.

Eddie hit the ground hard. His eyes widened as he stared helplessly into the sky above. His arm stretched toward Kiryana. His chest convulsed as the air rattled out of him. Then he crumpled and fell still.

"Eddie," Kiryana screamed. "Oh Eddie! What have you done! Eddie! Eddie!"

She dropped the Crystal Dragon to the ground and fell beside him, no longer caring about the monsterous thing near them.

Theo watched on as helplessly as before. She, too, felt a stabbing pain within her. She had not seen Eddie's death in her vision. How could that be? Still aware of the danger before them, Theo returned her focus to the malevolent spirit to see what it would do. The electric globe seemed to shine even brighter than before, growing with their pain and fear.

After a while Kiryana lifted her head, eyes stained with tears, mouth twisted with despair. She turned to find the Crystal Dragon lying lopsided on the ground beside her. She stared at its garish gleam and then looked up at the ball of light. In a fit of rage, she grabbed the crystal and ran with it to a pillar of stone. With a great swing she smashed it against the craggy rock. The crystal cracked opened like an egg, and a cloud of green smoke rose from it. Still not satisfied, Kiryana hit the crystal against the rock again, harder this time, and it shattered into hundreds of shards that scattered like ice over the surface of the plateau.

The effect on the glowing sphere was immediate. Without the Crystal Dragon to ground the spectre, the massive green ball began to flicker and dim. Theo could hear the heavy voice, neither upset nor hurried, say, "Until next time, my dear," as it crackled and faded away. Then the whole grisly thing dissolved into thin air and was gone.

Chapter Twenty-Five

Theo and Kiryana stood in disbelief as they looked at Eddie's lifeless body. They had watched him collapse, shake and release his last breathe of air. It was too cruel to be true. Eddie struck dead by the evil dragon.

"Eddie, Eddie!" cried Kiryana. "What did you do? Why did you have to do something so stupid?" She threw herself over him. Her shoulders shook hard with each sob.

She cried until she ran out of breath. She looked into Eddie's face as she ran her fingers over of his beautiful features.

"I'm so sorry, Eddie. I'm so sorry. I was wrong. How could I have been so wrong?"

Theo couldn't believe it either. Eddie was dead! And the terrible spectre was gone and Kiryana was still alive. What had happened? Who was the man in the sphere? Why did he speak to her? But there were no answers, only the sound of Kiryana's weeping.

Theo moved closer and looked into Eddie's silent face. Remembering all that he meant to her, it didn't take long for her tears to come too. In the short time she had gotten to know him, she learned very quickly to care about him.

Kiryana turned to Theo and asked, "Did you know this was going to happen?"

Theo shook her head vehemently. "No. I only saw your death."

"Then why aren't I dead, instead of him?"

Theo shrugged. "I don't know. I don't understand enough of what I see. I can't explain this."

"Oh Eddie, why, why, why you and not me?" Kiryana shook with heavy spasms as she tried to wrap her arms around him.

Theo waited patiently. All the pain and loss poured out of Kiryana in a deluge of tears. It took a long time for her to stop.

Kiryana picked up Eddie's warm hand and pressed it against her cheek. She looked at Theo with lost eyes and asked, "How am I going to be able to live without him?"

Theo just looked sadly at Kiryana.

Sniffling a little, Kiryana tenderly caressed Eddie's face.

"You know, Theo, this is all a stupid, huge mess. But it was supposed to be my mess. Why, oh why, did Eddie have to be so foolish? Beautiful, sweet Eddie, he deserved so much more than this. He deserved to be happy."

Struck by an impulse, Theo blurted out, "You deserve to be happy too, Kiryana."

Unable to hear this now, Kiryana just shook her head. "Happy? How could I be happy? From the beginning I was cursed. Some crazy woman decided to dump an impossible prophecy on me. Even now I can't be sure of what Lilith Crowe meant by it. I suppose I could say that my mother's success is worth more to her than I do. Perhaps that is what she meant by seeing a great truth. But I tell you, no word of a lie, it wasn't a surprise when I saw it. I saw Mother speaking to a stranger, telling him how necessary it was for her to have the map, so I could find the Crystal Dragon. I saw her do some awful things too to get her hands on it. I saw her place the package on my bedside table the night of my birthday party. When the stranger told her there was a great risk involved in finding the Crystal Dragon, she didn't falter for a second. She told him it didn't matter. One way or another, Mother was going to get what she wanted."

Kiryana paused for a moment to let the significance of what she was saying sink in deeper, "But here is the thing, Theo, that makes all of this so unnecessary, such a waste. When I saw the vision, when I saw the truth, I wasn't shocked. I already knew it. And without Clarity, too. I've always known that Mother's ambition was great. Much greater than her love for me."

Theo, again overcome by another wave of insight, interjected, "I'm sure you are wrong. I'm sure she loves you. She is just confused."

Kiryana tilted her head a little and she considered what Theo said. "I dunno. Maybe. Maybe we were all a little confused. All of us were, except Eddie. He seemed to know all along. And yet I wouldn't listen to him, wouldn't believe him. I already had everything I needed to be happy but I threw it all away to chase after something that never belonged to me in the first place. He asked me to let him be my destiny. And you know, I think he was right. But I was too stubborn to listen. And now it's too late. He has paid the price for my stupidity." She paused and hung her head. "Oh Theo, I love him so much! What am I going to do without him?"

Shuffling over, Theo embraced Kiryana. "I know you do. And he loves you very much too. I wish there was something I could do."

No sooner had she said the words when something in Kiryana twigged. She bolted upright, pushing away from Theo to look into her face. "Theo! Maybe you can! If you are a full-fledged Oracle then you should have all the abilities! Even if I didn't have the natural gift, I was a good student and learned my lessons well."

Not at all sure what Kiryana meant, Theo questioned, "All the abilities?"

"Yes, Theo! Medical energy! Oh my goodness! All higher-order Oracles are able to do all the functions! Which means you should be able to heal him!"

Theo was flummoxed and shook her head, "Kiryana, I don't know what you mean. I don't know how to do that."

"Oh, yes you can!" she shouted hopefully. "Yes, you can! But we have to hurry before his life force is all gone! Come on, we have to give it a try!"

Theo swallowed hard and stared helplessly at her cousin. She had no idea what to do. She was scared of fumbling about blindly, not knowing how to heal him and perhaps making things worse. "I'm sorry, Kiryana, I don't know how to do that."

"I'm sure we can figure it out as we go."

"I don't know if it's that simple. I've never done it before so I don't know what to look for."

"I'm sure you will know it when you see it!"

"I can't be sure about that. I'm sorry but I can't."

Desperate and determined, Kiryana finally lost her patience. "Enough excuses already!! Stop saying you can't when you are the only one here who can! And you know it! You have the gift and it's time to stop being afraid of it!"

Theo's jaw sagged open a little when she heard it. Theo had to accept that her cousin was right. How long had she been afraid of her gift? How long had she tried to hide it, to avoid it? The truth of what Kiryana said registered within Theo.

Theo finally stopped resisting and nodded. As frightened as she was of failing, it was her responsibility and hers alone. She moved in closer and looked over Eddie to see if she could see something that would guide her in. After a few moments of seeing nothing, she shrugged.

Not easily deterred, Kiryana suggested, "Try using your Clarity. You are looking to see what is happening to his life force."

Theo took a deep breath and slipped into that part of her. Flexing the strange muscle, her Clarity shifted her perception and changed the view of the world once again.

Everything appeared in a strange vortex of colour, and she could see how it all flowed together. Looking down at him, she could see blue and yellow eddies swirling about his head and extremities. But a cold, black mass was spreading through his chest where he had been hit by the blast. His life energy was seeping from this wound to mix with the air outside.

Unable to contain herself, Kiryana asked urgently, "So? Can you see anything? Does he still have a life force?"

"Yes, I can still see some of it. But it is bleeding out of him pretty badly. I don't know how to stop it. Do you remember anything from school that might help me?"

"Let me think. Can you try and push it back into him?"

"I can try."

Theo concentrated hard and placed her hands over his chest. With the power of her Clarity, she tried to push the branches of yellows and blues back into the black hole. But it was like trying to push water up a stream. The strings of life energy feathered about her fingers and mixed a little with her own before carrying on their way. She couldn't get them to change their course no matter how hard she tried.

"It's not working, Kiryana! There is something else I'm supposed to do but I don't know what it is!"

"Okay, Okay. Let me think." Kiryana wrung her hands together as she searched her memory for any information that might help. "We didn't study medical Clarity because they teach it at the academy. But we did study their history and structure. I'm trying to remember anything that might help but I can't think straight!"

Theo sighed. She was beginning to feel this was hopeless. More of the vibrant colours were passing out and the dead blackness was spreading further into Eddie's body. Even if Kiryana remembered anything, it might already be too late. Theo dropped her head and whispered to herself, "We need help."

No sooner had she said that than the image of the Fire Tiger popped into her head from out of nowhere. She recalled the memory of standing in front of his giant head and thanking him. Thank you for lighting the way out of the tunnel. *Thank you for lighting the way out of the tunnel.*

"Thank you for lighting the way out of the tunnel," she finally said softly as the image grew stronger in her mind.

Kiryana bolted upright when she heard it. "What did you say, Theo?"

"Thank you for lighting the way out of the tunnel," she replied without explanation.

"Lighting the way! Oh my goodness – that's it! Of course! It is the medical motto: Let your light show the way! Let your light show the way! Do you think that is it?"

Theo shook her head because she didn't know what light it meant. But she did recognize it as an important step. She decided it was more than a coincidence that she was reminded of this memory at this crucial moment. Fortified by this belief, she looked to her hands and tried to figure out how she could make her own light shine forth. If she couldn't get Eddie's energy to obey her, perhaps she could do so with her own.

She focused her whole attention on her hands and studied their whirlpools of colourful energy. She watched how they swished together, side by side, as they moved through her flesh. She suddenly was struck by the thought of blending all the colours together to make a larger, wider artery of flow. Not entirely sure on how to accomplish this, she focused her Clarity to visualize the energy streams merging.

At first the rivulets stopped rotating, which was encouraging, but soon they began to turn in the opposite direction. She looked at Eddie again and could see that the black hole was growing at an alarming rate. She didn't have much time for in a few minutes any chance of reviving him would be gone. As she thought of losing Eddie, her feelings for him filled her as she looked sadly at the recalcitrant rivers of his life slipping away.

But then something happened. His energy lines stopped moving and stilled. Theo's hands had begun to glow gently with a clear, white light. And to her relief, Eddie's life energy started moving toward it. His life energy was attracted to the clear light!

"Kiryana! Something is happening!" gasped Theo with astonishment. Kiryana clasped her hands and held them tightly with hope.

Theo moved her hands to the centre of the black hole but his energy steams didn't follow immediately. She knew she needed to increase the strength of her own illumination to get the life force to travel back. She tried to recall her feelings for Eddie and let them fill her up again. It worked to maintain the glow, but it wasn't enough to strengthen the luminosity. Frustrated by this, she decided she needed a stronger feeling. Then she remembered the Fire Tiger. It wasn't accidental that she should think of it at this time. She recalled standing in front of the awe-inspiring creature telling it how grateful she was that it showed her the way out of the tunnel: grateful for being shown the way out, *grateful for being shown the way out.* Grateful. Like how Finnegan was grateful too.

So she let her feelings of gratitude wash over her. And as they did, the light from her hands grew stronger. Their brightness shone purely. It was strong and clear. The direction of the draining colours changed immediately, and started flowing toward the bright light. Theo had managed to produce a beam strong enough to stop the life force from draining out. In no time, the blue and yellow streams were filling Eddie once again, moving toward the white brilliance emanating from her hands. The colourful runnels were returning to the black hole and pushing the darkness out.

"Thank you, thank you, thank you," Theo chanted as she kept her focus on her hands and their light. Although the colourful streams were moving in the right direction, they were not moving very quickly. But it did not matter as long as they were moving in the right way.

"Kiryana! It seems to be working!" laughed Theo incredulously. "I don't know how, but it is!"

Kiryana smiled brightly, ecstatic at the news. She was about to reply when something grabbed her attention. She squinted into the distance to make sure she wasn't seeing things.

"Theo, there is something strange coming from the horizon." Something in Kiryana's tone filled Theo with dread. And without even looking, Theo's instincts had already told her what it was.

She hadn't seen it since the night of the Equinox back at her Aunt Georgia's house many months ago. As much as she hated to do so, she lifted her head to look. Her heart sank when she recognized the jagged, blue line that was moving toward them at a breakneck speed. It was moving faster than the first time she saw it. It was the unholy Schism once again!

"What is that?" asked Kiryana, unaware of the full danger.

"I don't know what it is," replied Theo tersely. "But I do know what it can do! And we don't want to be near it when it gets here!"

"What?"

"I saw it the night of the Equinox. It demolished a two-hundred year old quarry!"

"What is it?" Kiryana gasped, her sense of alarm growing by the second.

"Something terrible," Theo replied. She remembered the moonlit landscape it ravaged.

"So what do we do?" asked Kiryana, eyes wide with fear.

"What do we do?" Theo echoed. "We get out of the way!"

189

Theo looked down at Eddie. The black hole had shrunk considerably. She hoped it was enough to save him. She pulled her hands off of him but to her dismay, the swirls of effervescent energy stopped pushing against the blackness and began to roll out of him again. It was clear that she needed to eradicate the dark mass for the procedure to work.

She sighed heavily and resigned herself to the task at hand. What else could she do? Slowly she put her hands on Eddie once again. But because of her apprehension, the light from her fingertips had dimmed. Fortunately, the life force was near enough to be pulled along, if at a slower pace than before.

"Oh Kiryana, I can't leave yet. I'm not done with Eddie. Until I fill the black hole within him, I don't think he is going to come back. And even then, I'm not sure what will happen."

Kiryana took Eddie's hand in hers and squeezed it tightly. She then said softly, "Do what you need to do then."

Kiryana watched as the horrible thing approached and dropped into the valley. Rocks and trees suddenly disappeared as if being wiped clean from a cosmic blackboard.

"Why is it doing that?" asked Kiryana, not entirely believing what she was seeing. Theo didn't know what to say.

The breeze picked up as air rushed from above to fill the vacuum that was left by the disappearing landscape. Both girls had to drop closer to the rock floor to secure themselves against the bracing wind. The black hole within Eddie's chest was getting smaller by the second, but Theo feared it would be too late. The Schism was moving towards them at an impressive speed.

Kiryana, fully aware now of the advancing danger, grabbed Theo's shoulder and nervously said, "Is there any way you can go faster?"

When Theo shook her head, Kiryana said, "Yeah, I didn't think so."

"Listen Kiryana," shouted Theo over the rising wind, "You can go, you know. No sense all of us getting tripped up over each other. I'm almost done here anyway. We will be right behind you once I've finished."

Although frightened by the approaching entity, Kiryana smiled bravely and said, "Nice try, cousin. Listen, we all go together or not at all."

Theo said, "You just really want to get yourself killed today, don't you?"

Kiryana gazed solemnly at Theo but then gave her a gallows smile.

Theo saw that the fissure was in the valley next to them and was near enough to hear its crackling and popping over the roaring wind.

"It won't be long now before it's here," Theo said with a strange calm. She looked down at Eddie. She saw that the black hole had been pushed to the

190

centre of his chest. "And it won't be long for you too. Too close to call this race."

Theo dropped her head and focused on the hole within Eddie. She watched it intently, willing each strand of energy to push out the darkness that lay in its path. She tried her very best to strengthen her intention in order to brighten her beam, but the oncoming Schism was too distracting. And yet, despite the approaching danger, she was not overwhelmed with fear, nor besotted with terror. This struck her as strange but she didn't question it. She was glad of it and let it be.

Kiryana huddled into her. Theo could see the reflection of the fissure's blue light against her smooth skin. Even if they had decided to flee, there was no way they could outrun this monstrosity now. Kiryana, too, had settled quietly into her new fate and waited patiently for it to arrive.

The gap in Eddie's chest was now only as big as an orange. Theo watched with relief as the hole was pushed from every side until it disappeared into a pin prick before fading all together, like an inverted star disappearing in a sky of swirling colour. And once the blackness was pushed out, Eddie suddenly gasped for air, brought back from the edge.

"Eddie!" Kiryana cried with bitter-sweet joy as she kissed him. Although now alive, he was still unconscious while his body grappled with its difficult adventure.

Theo scowled and looked to the fissure. Its proximity was now close enough to raise the hairs on her arms. How sad to have brought Eddie back only to lose him again so soon after. However, she didn't waver for a moment; she didn't lose her nerve. In the face of it, she took a deep breath and held it in anticipation.

The Schism rose from beneath the ledge, much like the the dragon globe had done before. Part of it touched an outcrop of rock and it simply disappeared. Tonnes of granite and gneiss rock vanished from the world as if merely unravelled, without violence, without sound.

Theo looked into to the centre of the thing. Still in her state of Clarity, she saw it like never before. While it appeared to be emitting a blue, eerie light, in fact, it had none - no energy, no movement of energy lines. The blue glow she saw was the light being destroyed at its entrance. Inside, there was nothing. There wasn't even the blackness she had seen in Eddie's chest. It was a nothingness that filled her with horror. This thing was not of this world. It was an unnatural thing. It was pulling everything into its void, its emptiness. It was draining the world away.

Kiryana screamed but her voice became lost in the whirl of air whipping about them. In seconds the fissure would touch them. Theo had no idea what it would mean to them to be erased like that. Would their life force be destroyed too? Theo was dumbfounded with the thought.

And then she heard it.

Whether she knew what would happen or simply remembered her last encounter, she couldn't say for sure. But when she heard the roar, she knew it was coming.

From atop the mountain behind her, the Fire Tiger appeared. It roared loudly again. It stormed forth, fully lit with fire and streams of blinding light. Five times as large as before, it pounced from its perch straight into the belly of the Schism. Like a flaming meteorite, it burned through the portal and disappeared into the void. Then everything went quiet.

At first, it seemed as if the Fire Tiger had been devoured by the gaping hole. The fissure continued pulsating but it had stopped advancing. Then, from within the emptiness rays of light, thin and delicate, slowly began to seep forth. The light became stronger and brighter, and soon, only light poured out, brilliant and brave.

From the centre of the illumination, the Fire Tiger returned. He crossed back over the threshold, and it all exploded in a burst of fire. Once the surge dimmed, only the Fire Tiger remained. The Schism was gone.

The Fire Tiger flew high into the air and landed on its coiled haunches on another plateau above them. It jumped again and soared higher, and then fell from the sky and landed near the girls. It sniffed the air for any further signs of the Schism, and when satisfied there were none, it walked towards them, shrinking in size and luminosity with each step. It stopped before them and stood majestically, silently. It looked at the girls with its huge, golden eyes.

Kiryana stared at the creature, frozen in its regard, too terrified to scream. But Theo boldly looked back at it and held the tiger's gaze for a time. Without warning, the Fire Tiger let out another great roar and flew to the mountain top behind them. And then it was gone.

When Kiryana was able to regain her ability to speak, she asked, "W-What on earth was that?"

Theo didn't have a good answer to give her cousin so she decided to say nothing. What could she say? She didn't know what it was or why it was here. All she knew was that the tiger was protecting her, and for that she was grateful. In any case, she was just happy to have made it to the other side of this ordeal.

192

Suddenly, the girls became aware of shouts coming from the valley. Theo got to her knees and crawled to the plateau's edge. From below, she could see a large group of police officers dressed in high visibility gear swarming about the newly demolished landscape. They were the search party tasked to find them, and no doubt, they had seen more than they had bargained for.

Theo jumped to her feet and began to flap her arms up and down. "Hey! Hey! We are up here! Up here!" she called.

A police officer quickly spotted her and yelled back, "Stay where you are! We will come to you!" He turned to the team around him and shouted orders. A rescue crew would arrive soon enough.

Theo smiled and waved back. Happy to know help was on the way, she went back to Kiryana and Eddie, both very much worse for wear.

"Won't be long now," said Theo matter-of-factly.

Kiryana smiled wearily and took Theo's hand and said, "Thank you, Theo. Thank you for everything."

Theo smiled softly. She replied, "I'm just glad that we're alright. And I'm looking forward to going home."

"Me too, Theo, me too!

Chapter Twenty-Six

Theo closed her case and sat beside it on the bed. She glanced around her funny, crooked room and knew for certain she was going to miss it. On the floor beside the bed were the rest of her bags and her few modest possessions. It had been a month since her return from the Appal Mountains, and she was finally prepared to leave and go to the Academy in Greenstone.

It seemed like ages since the police found them on the plateau after the strange events of that day. Of course there were many questions but there weren't many answers. Theo had described their trek to the Old Man's Hall and their search for the Crystal Dragon, but there wasn't much after that which she could explain. She deliberately omitted the kidnapping. She told the police that she went along with Kiryana and Eddie under her own volition. Theo considered it a white lie and felt with certainty that her journey with them had been fated regardless of how it had started. No need to include the authorities. When the police found them, Kiryana was weak from her ordeal with the Crystal Dragon, and Eddie was only just back from the dead and needed further medical attention. Both had to be carried out on stretchers to the waiting vehicles below. Only Theo was able to walk out on foot.

Despite the dubious nature of the journey, all three of them were received home with a hero's welcome. Some eyebrows were raised in reaction to Theo's white lie, but no one challenged it. Everything had turned out better than originally thought, and all were happy to have the three of them home safe and sound.

Eddie was moved immediately into the mansion to help with his convalescence. He slept like a hibernating bear for three days straight and then woke up refreshed and ate everything in sight. Mrs Henderson had quite the job keeping him full. He had no memory of being on the mountain or of what had happened to him there, and neither Kiryana nor Theo felt the need to remind him.

Kiryana left the Stokes mansion one kind of person and returned home another. The shift in her was dramatic. Talim and Chester felt it was a change for the better, but Mrs Henderson sensed a deeper burden in the girl and lamented her loss of innocence.

"She is only eighteen. It is too young to have the shine rubbed off the world," she said to anyone who would listen.

Kiryana never spoke of what she saw within the Crystal Dragon, but every now and then she would drift out of conversations and stare morosely into space. Without a doubt her obsession to acquire Clarity had been cured, and for the first time she began to make plans for a future that didn't include it. Soon she started to become excited about a different kind of life she could never have imagined before.

Kiryana was furious with her mother. From the time she was back, the normally serene house was filled with screaming and fits of temper. Chester worried that they would kill each other, but Mrs Henderson told him to stay out of it.

"That girl has a lot of anger to vent. Best to let her get on with it," she said looking at Theo, who nodded in agreement.

Kiryana didn't eat her meals with her mother anymore and came to the kitchen.

"Won't your mother be lonely?" asked Theo gently.

"Probably," scoffed Kiryana on the first day back, "at least, I certainly hope so."

Over time, she began to soften a little. She told Theo that she had invited her mother to eat with them in the kitchen. But Mrs Stokes never came.

"Too embarrassed to eat with us, I imagine," said Chester.

Even Talim, uninterested in drama, said, "Yeah, it was a pretty rotten thing to do to her own daughter, wasn't it?"

Everyone at the kitchen table agreed. And everyone else was going to know about it too as Kiryana had been complaining to her father, who had no interest in protecting his wife's reputation.

"Things are going to be different for Mrs Stokes now," said Chester bringing his eyebrows together. His words seemed prophetic when a message arrived from Greenstone suggesting that Mrs Stokes take an extended leave from the Greenstone Council to help her daughter recover from her ordeal. In practical terms, she had been suspended from her duties for an indefinite period of time. Mrs Stokes did not take the news well.

Initially, Wilhelmina was scheduled to travel with Theo to the Hill. When they returned home safely, it was decided that they all needed a good rest first so Wilhelmina went to Greenstone on her own. She told Theo that she would make arrangements to return for her when the time was right.

"There is nothing so important that it can't wait for you to be ready," said Wilhelmina to Theo before she left. "Besides I'm anxious to speak with the High Council regarding some of the things you have seen. Be prepared girl – there will be many questions."

Theo blanched at her comment. It was delivered with the usual blunt style but without any malice. Wilhelmina was doing her best to prepare Theo for her new life.

"I don't know if I can say anything that would be useful. I don't know what I saw or why it was there," Theo replied sincerely.

"What you say may be right. But it is the second time you've seen these, what, creatures, things? And that in itself is telling. These visitations are not accidental. Just prepare yourself for questions, that's all."

Theo nodded to show Wilhelmina that she understood. But did she really? What was the world like that she was about to enter? Truly, she had no idea what was waiting for her in Greenstone. Or what was expected of her now that she was pursuing the life of a high order Oracle. She could only wait and see when the time came.

Theo was given a chance to recuperate and spend time with her friends. She would meet Talim in the garden after breakfast and hang out with him while he busied himself with his work. Sometimes she rolled up her sleeves and helped, but mostly she sat on the warm stone bench enjoying all the lovely sights and sounds. By late morning, Kiryana and Eddie would come by and sit happily with them, soaking up the warm air within the double-sided walls. Then Chester would arrive after lunch when his jobs were done. There they would sit and chat about nothing in particular for hours. Theo felt grounded and connected to the people and the place; this was her home and it finally felt right. She was going to miss it desperately when she moved to Greenstone. She knew she was going to be sad to leave.

Early one morning near the time she was scheduled to go, she and Talim were in the garden alone. Talim was busy filling a bird feeder with food, and Theo was leaning with eyes closed against the stone fountain, letting the heat from the sun fill her up. Suddenly, Talim stopped pouring seeds and looked up to study Theo. Noticing that the rattling had stopped, she opened her eyes to find Talim staring at her, on the verge of saying something.

196

Sitting upright, she welcomed the question. "What? What is it Talim?"

After hemming and hawing for a bit, he shook it off and went back to pouring the bird seed.

Theo, now curious, wasn't letting him off that easy. "No, no you can't do that. What is it you want to say, Talim?"

Talim squatted back on his heels and scratched the back of his head. "Aw, it's kind of stupid. I'm sorry to even bring it up."

"Hey, if it's bothering you I'd just wish you'd spit it out - stupid or not."

Realizing that there was no way out, Talim took a deep breath and said, "Well, I am really bothered that you guys didn't ask me to go with you. I would have loved to go on an adventure! Especially hiking mountains! I can't believe you didn't ask me to go too!"

Theo would have laughed if he wasn't so sincere. Of course he thought that Theo had volunteered to go. Theo was unsure what to say. It would have been great to confide in Talim about what truly happened, but it also would jeopardize the harmony that had been achieved since her return. Looking into Talim's big, brown eyes she could see the injury of a rejected friend, and for the sake of everyone, she decided it was best to take the blame herself.

"Yeah, I'm sorry Talim. That was my fault. I didn't want Chester to worry too much so I asked them not to bring you along." What was another white lie in the service of protecting hurt feelings?

"Aw, Theo, why did you have to do that? There were timber wolves and a band of travellers and climbing through caves - not to mention a fire tiger and a weird flying thing. I would have loved to have been there." Talim's face crinkled with disappointment at the thought of what he'd missed. Like most things, the story of it sounded far more glamorous than what really had happened. It had been terrifying, and Theo was glad he hadn't been there.

"Talim, I'm sorry. I promise to include you the next time. Would that be alright with you?" she offered whole-heartedly.

It was enough to make Talim smile broadly. "Okay. I'm going to hold you to that."

She returned the smile and said, "It's a deal then."

Theo picked up two of her small bags and crossed the floor to her door. As she opened it, she could hear voices from the kitchen below. People had gathered to say good bye to her and just the sound of their voices caused a lump to form in her throat. She swallowed hard and tried to steady herself as she crossed over the threshold into the hall.

When she arrived in the kitchen, she was met by all who were near and dear to her - standing around and chatting casually. Chester came up to her and took her bags from her hands, and Eddie, now back to full form, winked at her as he sped past her to get the rest of her stuff from her room.

Mrs Henderson slipped her arm around Theo's shoulders and gave her a good squeeze. "It certainly won't be the same around her without you," she said with a good amount of emotion in her voice.

Theo nodded quickly, too afraid to speak else it burst the dam on her own rising feelings.

Chester smiled sadly and flanked her other side. "Yes, I, for one, will really miss you, my love. I hope they take good care of you in Greenstone."

Unable to help herself, she turned to Chester and wrapped her arms around his neck and hugged him for a long time.

Finally, he gently pulled her arms off of him and turned away blowing his nose into a tissue. He carried on to the sink and busied himself by getting a tall glass of water.

Talim chirped in with his usual cheerful manner, "Yeah, it's going to be really boring without you. Will you be able to come back in the summer for the holidays?" Then he paused and thought for a moment before asking, "Do Oracles have holidays?"

"As a postulate, you are in the Academy for a year or so. It's only when you are ordained that you are expected to be cloistered. I hope you'll be back at the end of term," said Kiryana. She then moved forward and took Theo's hands into hers before continuing, "I know we have had a shaky start, Theo, but you are family. I would like for you to think of here as your home."

Theo smiled widely into her cousin's bright, amber eyes and said sincerely, "Yeah, this is home now."

"Glad to hear it," replied Kiryana happily. "It's good to have a few people around that I can trust. By the way, Mother sends her good wishes. But she made an excuse not to come."

Theo looked thoughtfully at Kiryana before saying, "Tell her I said thank you for everything – and maybe I'll see her in the summer."

"Yeah, maybe by the summer, but we'll see," said Kiryana as she turned to Eddie who had arrived in the kitchen with the rest of Theo's things. He deftly dropped them by the door and looked out the window to watch a long, black car pull up in the driveway.

"Looks like your ride is here - and right on time too," he said as he turned back to the girls. "I'd better hurry if I want to get my goodbye in before you shoot off."

Eddie bounded back to Theo and stooped low to give her a strong embrace. Theo held him tightly as she said, "Now take care of yourself, Eddie. And don't let Kiryana boss you around too much."

He pulled back to look into her large, grey eyes and smiled. "Well, I can certainly try my best but I make no promises."

Theo chuckled knowingly and stepped back. She took a long look around the bright, sunny kitchen. She focused on the faces of Eddie, Kiryana, Chester, Mrs Henderson and Talim. She took a moment to commit them to memory to last her until the next time she would see them.

The black limousine parked just outside the kitchen. The driver immediately jumped out and scurried to the rear door to open it for his passenger. Wilhelmina Van Dorne gracefully climbed out, glanced back into the sedan and walked to the door with her usual purposeful strides. When she entered the house, she smiled and greeted the room. "Hello all. I trust everyone is well?" she said with her clear, clipped voice.

"Hello, Wilhelmina," replied Chester with great politeness. "I hope your journey was good. And that you are enjoying your time at Greenstone."

"Ah yes," she said, "the journey was pleasant enough. And Greenstone is as it should be. No point pretending you belong somewhere you don't."

Mrs Henderson agreed wholeheartedly, "Wilhelmina, never a truer word was said. So is everyone going to be where they belong?"

Wilhelmina looked down her nose at Mrs Henderson for a brief moment but then smiled warmly, "Well, that remains to be seen, doesn't it?"

"Indeed it does. Can I fetch you a cup of tea, Wilhelmina? Do you have time?" offered Mrs Henderson.

"No, thank you. I'm afraid we are on a tight schedule and we need to get back to Greenstone as soon as possible. It is kind of you to offer but goodbyes are still goodbyes, and there is no way around it."

She then turned to Theo and said, "So, are you ready?"

"I think so," Theo replied, letting her feelings of sadness and fear take roost within her.

Wilhelmina gestured to the driver who then came and collected Theo's bags and brought them to the car. Wilhelmina guided Theo out and waited patiently for the driver to finish loading the luggage in the trunk.

"Good luck, Theo!" called Chester, still blowing his nose into a soggy tissue.

The driver opened the door and Wilhelmina climbed in after a brief wave goodbye. Theo paused then took a deep breath and climbed in after her.

"Goodbye!" she called from inside the limo. "I'll miss you!"

Kiryana ran up beside the car and said without irony, "Hey Theo! Let the light show you the way!"

Theo just managed to reply, "You too, Kiryana, you too!" before the driver closed the door. She stared out of the tinted window with watery eyes as the car pulled away, watching her beloved friends disappear into the distance.

The limousine had a large, luxurious interior with two benches that faced each other. Wilhelmina had taken her place on the bench in front of her and Theo watched the older woman settle herself for the long journey into Greenstone. It wasn't until she felt a shift to her right that she noticed that someone else was in the back with them.

Startled by the presence of a third passenger, Theo drew in a quick breath and jerked back for a better look. Sheathed in a black hood, the stranger pulled it back to reveal her face. And there, sitting beside her, was the High Oracle herself, Ceres Theroux!

Stunned, Theo's jaw dropped open. The last time she had seen Ceres Theroux was at the Equinox celebration when Theo was certain the High Oracle had spoken to her.

"I'm afraid I just couldn't wait for you to arrive at Greenstone before meeting you, my dear," Ceres said with her rich, lilting voice. "I hope you don't mind if I tag along for the ride."

With her hood off, Theo was able to have a good look at Ceres Theroux. Obviously older than Wilhelmina, Ceres still had the posture and complexion of a younger woman. Her white hair was softly upswept in a style that framed her face perfectly. Her makeup was subtle yet effective, drawing Theo's attention to her startling clear, blue eyes. She wore a simply cut grey dress that flattered her slim figure. For a woman rumoured to be a hundred years old, she didn't look anywhere near that age.

Theo was too overwhelmed to speak, but Ceres carried on as if she had. "I am glad to see you too. Let me see: the last time I saw you was at the Equinox Celebration, was it not?"

Too amazed to be afraid, Theo stammered incredulously, "You remember seeing me?"

"Why of course! I remember everything. So, I thought I'd come along for the ride to get to know you better."

"And to make sure nothing unsavoury happens on our journey," interjected Wilhelmina curtly.

Ceres frowned at Wilhelmina a little before continuing as pleasantly as before, "Oh I'm sure the trip will be fine, don't you worry, Theo. Sometimes I think Wilhelmina likes to say things to shock people."

Wilhelmina scoffed and turned to look out of the window.

"I have heard what happened from Wilhelmina but I would also like to hear it from you too. She tells me you are experiencing prophetic visions. Is this true?"

Theo nodded vigorously. The idea of unloading her experience to Cerex Theroux, the High Oracle, made Theo smile with hope. Perhaps Ceres would have the answers that had eluded her.

"Yes, I've been having these dreams for months. And it wasn't until the night I was kidnapped by Kiryana and Eddie that I knew the dreams were about Kiryana."

"Kidnapped?" Ceres raised an eyebrow but didn't say any more.

"So in the dreams, I could see Kiryana standing on the edge of a mountain with a large, spherical object rising up to kill her."

"Was there something in the sphere?" Ceres asked intently, staring at Theo.

Feeling that she already knew the answer, Theo nodded. "Yes, there was a man inside. And he spoke to me. But I didn't know this until it happened. I didn't see him in my dream."

Alarmed by this fact, Ceres demanded urgently, "What did he say, this man?"

"He said the Crystal Dragon was a joke, his joke. He said that all that power could be available to anyone who wanted to take it. He said he wanted everything," she replied, glad to share the experience with someone who would know how to deal with it. "It was horrible to have his voice inside my head."

Ceres' face pinched tight but she didn't say anything. She glanced at Wilhelmina and gave her a serious look.

"Do you know what it means? Do you know who the man was?" asked Theo, feeling lighter after unburdening herself.

Ceres took a moment and then replied, "I'm afraid I do. We believe it was Orfeo Cotswold. We, everyone on the Hill, had hoped he had died quietly some years ago. We haven't felt his presence in years. Not until your encounter with him a month ago had we reason to believe he was alive."

Theo only knew the few stories about him, and with the little she had heard, she felt her stomach tighten with fear at the mention of his name.

Ceres leaned in closer to Theo until she could see the dark rims around the Oracle's ice blue eyes. Ceres continued, "So we have questions and worries about him: where has he been, what has he been up to, and why has he come back?"

"And then of course there is the Fire Tiger, and the Schisms, which have started to appear at various times over the last year. But only to you have they both appeared twice. You see, Theo, things are rarely as accidental as people pretend they are. We are wondering why all these things are happening to you."

Theo shifted uncomfortably. Her anxiety was deepening even though she couldn't begin to understand what was going on. And of course, there was the private meeting in the cave with the Fire Tiger. She wasn't sure if she should tell them. But Ceres was as sharp as they come and could see the thought flash across Theo's features.

"What is it, girl? Spit it out."

"Erm, well, I saw the Fire Tiger another time."

Both women were surprised by her announcement and leaned in to hear more.

"Um, it was in the cave where we found the Crystal Dragon. No one but me saw it."

"Interesting," said Ceres. "What did they want?"

"They?" queried Theo.

"They," repeated Ceres, "I would guess gender does not feature into this creature."

Theo nodded. Although it had the shape of a tiger, it did not embody the qualities of a regular animal. What "they" wanted, she did not know.

"I don't know," said Theo. "But it, um, they helped me out of a tunnel and broke down a wall so I could leave the cave."

"So no Schisms at that time?"

"No, no schisms. And it was quiet most of the time. I was really grateful they released me."

Ceres and Wilhelmina exchanged meaningful looks but did not share their thoughts. Then Ceres turned to Theo and lightened her tone, "We are not blaming you for these things, Theo. We know they are not your fault. But you are the intersection point at which many things are converging. Until we understand why they are being drawn to you, we think it's best to keep you with us in Greenstone. At least there, you'll be safe."

Theo looked over at Wilhelmina for reassurance. At this moment, she was the closest thing Theo had to a friend. "You can trust Ceres. She is the best one to protect you," Wilhemina affirmed.

Theo looked back at Ceres and saw the glint in her eyes. "We want to make sure we understand how you fit into all of this and help you do whatever is necessary."

Theo let this wash over her as she sat quietly for a while. Nothing that Ceres said felt untrue. As frightening as it was, Theo took comfort in the fact that she was going to the best place in the world to help her figure it all out. She was going to the place where she truly belonged.

After a long stretch of silence, Theo finally piped up, "I do have a question though. I'm hoping you can answer it."

Ceres nodded her approval allowing Theo to continue, "I'm confused about my visions. For months I kept seeing Kiryana being killed by this ball of light. But when it happened, it didn't happen that way at all."

Ceres smiled knowingly. "Ah yes, visions are tricky things. You will soon learn this. A thing can be fated but free will is always at play at the same time too. Didn't Eddie step in the way of the beam? To sacrifice himself for the girl he loved? Free will is a powerful thing, Theo, but nothing is more powerful than an act of true love. As long as I've lived, I have never known a force greater than love."

"I suppose," Theo responded politely, not entirely sure what Ceres meant. Thinking for a moment, she asked, "What about Lilith Crowe's prediction? I'm sure Mrs Stokes didn't act out of love."

"No, she did not," replied Ceres crisply. "It is a dangerous thing to build your life on someone else's destiny. Each person's fate is her own. Mrs Stokes is now learning the truth of this the hard way."

Still not satisfied, Theo continued, "But why did Lilith Crowe predict Clarity for Kiryana? It's obvious she was never going to develop it. Why put her through that ordeal?"

"Predicting the future is an art, not a science. You will grow to appreciate this in time. And for the record, Kiryana did have Clarity, if only for a moment. Why Lilith was able to see this, and only this, will remain a mystery. I cannot say why the forces developed this way. You see, my dear, even with extra sight, there are still things we Oracles do not understand."

Theo listened carefully to Ceres but she wasn't happy with her answers. She realized very quickly, however, this was the only response she was going to get. She let the matter drop.

"So are you ready to begin your studies at the Greenstone Academy?" Ceres asked pleasantly, moving Theo along to brighter things.

"I think so," replied Theo. But she wasn't confident about what it would be like, having only her experience at Wilhelmina's school to compare it with. Theo looked back at Wilhelmina and even she looked pensive.

"Well, prepare yourself, Theo. Not many girls get the privilege of entering our world."

Ceres turned her attention to some papers she had brought with her, signalling that their conversation was over. Theo sank back into her seat and began to look out of her window at the scenery streaming by.

So much had happened in her young life and so much more was about to happen. She was both excited and anxious about it all. But for the moment, she was held in a brief respite between her past and future. Theo deliberately pushed all thoughts out of her head and slid into the silence of sitting still. She stared mindlessly out the window, absorbing the hum of the car moving beneath her, heading into an unknown world that had not yet come into view.

Follow Theodora Yates' journey in the next book
The Haunted Corridor

Coming Soon!

Printed in Great Britain
by Amazon

72992720R00128